"I kn

There was a long silence from the other end of the phone. "Mother, did you hear me?"

"What kind of nonsense is this, Meg?" Lydia Haycock's voice finally came on the line. "What's going on?"

"At first, I only caught his profile," Meg said softly. "Then the camera swung back to him as he was turning. It was him, Mother. I know it. He looks exactly the same, except his hair is longer and ... and ... snow-white." Meg's voice broke as she felt herself coming apart. She fought it, knowing how her mother hated any display of emotion.

"Margaret, you listen to me! Your father's dead. He died nineteen years ago!"

"No, Mother. He's alive and he's somewhere in Thailand."

Dear Reader,

We're offering you a different sort of April shower this month—a shower of new authors! And, to help us celebrate our new stars, we're offering you a chance to enter our Superromantic Sweepstakes! See the back pages for details. Meanwhile, enjoy the debut novels of these fresh Superromance talents....

Georgia author Patricia Keelyn's heroine, Maura Anderson, will do anything it takes if it means *Keeping Katie*. As soon as Sheriff Alan Parks meets Maura and her young daughter, he knows he's in over his head, but he can hardly help her when he represents the very thing she's fleeing...the law.

Twilight Whispers by Canadian author Morgan Hayes is set in a magnificent New England mansion with a dark secret—somewhere on the premises a murder has been committed. Claire Madden's new house comes complete with its own handyman, but for someone who claims to know nothing about the crime, Michael Dalton is maddeningly resistant to her efforts to solve it.

Brenda Hiatt, an established Regency romance author, has written her first contemporary Superromance novel, a time-travel tale set in South Carolina. In *Bridge Over Time*, Kathryn Monroe finds she's switched places with her ancestress, Catherine Prescott. While the modern heroine mysteriously finds herself preaching women's lib, freeing slaves, and falling for renegade farmer Ryan James in 1825, Catherine Prescott lands in a whole new world, equipped with airplanes, race cars...and a man who makes her want to forget the past.

And Janice Carter takes her readers to exotic Thailand in *Ghost Tiger*. Meg Devlin is convinced that the brief newsclip she witnessed pictured her father, whom she'd believed missing in action for nineteen years. Her best hope of learning the truth lies with Conor Tremayne, the reporter who'd shot the footage she'd seen. But despite her attraction, her doubts magnify about trusting Tremayne—a man who'd sell his soul for a story.

Marsha Zinberg
Senior Editor, Superromance

Janice Carter

Ghost Tiger

Harlequin Books

TORONTO • NEW YORK • LONDON
AMSTERDAM • PARIS • SYDNEY • HAMBURG
STOCKHOLM • ATHENS • TOKYO • MILAN
MADRID • WARSAW • BUDAPEST • AUCKLAND

ISBN 0-373-70593-X

GHOST TIGER

Copyright © 1994 by Janice Hess.

This edition published by arrangement with Harlequin Enterprises B. V.

® and TM are trademarks of the publisher. Trademarks indicated with ® are registered in the United States Patent and Trademark Office, the Canadian Trade Marks Office and in other countries.

Printed in U.S.A.

ABOUT THE AUTHOR

Ghost Tiger is Janice Carter's first Superromance novel. She has always loved writing and sold her first romance novel, a Harlequin Intrigue, on her fortieth birthday—confirming, she says, the adage about life beginning at that age. Janice is a schoolteacher and lives in Toronto, Canada, with her husband and two teenage daughters.

"Memories of a past trip through Southeast Asia inspired the setting for this book," says Janice. "And recent controversy over the fate of MIAs from the war in Viet Nam led to a 'what if' game, that led finally to *Ghost Tiger*."

For my parents,
Gene and Bill Carter,
who believed in me
and helped me to
believe in myself

A big thank-you to
Dawn Stewardson who advised,
edited and encouraged—nonstop.

CHAPTER ONE

"HEY, GET OUT of my dinner!"

Meg almost laughed at the cat's expression—guilt and surprise dilating the pupils of his amber eyes—but really, this was too much.

"Move it!"

Bomber leaped off the coffee table and skulked into the bedroom. Meg tightened the sash of her robe and opened the pizza box. At least he hadn't figured out how to pry loose the lid. She lifted out a slice dripping with every item but pineapple. Pineapple on pizza was a concept she'd never understood. Meg sank onto the couch and groaned. Friday night—pizza night. And only one more week of teaching before spring break. What more could a person want?

Well, she could think of one or two things, but David had moved out almost six months ago and desperation hadn't yet driven her to the local singles' clubs. Besides, thus far she was enjoying her new solitude; ordering pizza beat the hell out of meal planning and the place didn't need as much tidying since David had traded their cosy row-house apartment for a lofty condo penthouse. David was a real slob, though his television fans would never guess it from his perfectly-groomed good looks.

Knock it off, Meg admonished herself. Don't spoil your Friday night by getting maudlin. She took another bite of pizza, reached for the cold beer on the end table and thought about the coming holiday. So far, she hadn't decided what to do with her two-week semester break. Her mother had invited Meg to Cape Cod, but Lydia and Jeffrey would be busy opening up their antique shop for the coming tourist season. And who was she kidding, anyway? She'd have no problem spending a month or more with her stepfather, but two weeks with her mother would be more than either one of them could take. No, scratch Cape Cod.

Equally unpalatable was the thought of trekking to Atlantic City to cruise the casinos with Julie. Lots of men, she'd promised, without knowing how that casual remark had sealed Meg's decision not to go.

Meg set her empty plate on the coffee table. A gray-and-white striped face peered out from underneath. "Well, Bomber, back for another try, are you? Dream on."

The cat dashed across the room into the kitchen. "Okay, go ahead and sulk. See if I care." Meg picked up the television guide and flipped through it. Absolutely zero TV tonight. She should have picked up a video.

Flicking the remote control and taking another swallow of beer, Meg tuned in to the local station. It was just after six o'clock and habit still prompted her to watch the Boston news. Or was she prompted by the thought of anchorman David Houston? Maybe I *am* perverse, Meg reflected as the face she'd awakened to for almost two years sharpened into focus on the screen.

She raised her beer in a mock salute. Looking good, Dave. Sounding good, too. But is that the beginning of a Southern drawl? Must be taking voice lessons from your Texan belle. You know the one—her daddy was a major sponsor—and she came to KLRT to learn the ropes. And did she ever. Had you all tied up in knots in no time.

David's affable face disappeared from the screen to be replaced by footage of a crowd standing in front of what looked like a camp of some kind. Intrigued, Meg turned up the volume. The baritone of an off-camera announcer filled the room.

"For many refugees, this crude, makeshift camp is the first home they've had in years. And it may prove to be the only home many of them will ever know. Funding for the camps here in northern Thailand dribbles in from various foreign agencies but is never enough.

"The staple diet is rice and fish and, were it not for basic medical supplies provided by an anonymous donor, the plight of these people would be hopeless indeed."

The camera panned the chicken-wire perimeter of the camp, searching forlorn brown faces peering out at the mob of journalists. Suddenly the camera shifted to a group of safari-suited Westerners and a face, strikingly familiar, loomed in the background.

No. Impossible. Meg's heart lurched mid-beat. She crouched toward the television, getting as close as vision permitted. Go back, she implored the camera. Back to the people standing in front of the building. Telepathically it seemed, the camera did. There, facing her straight-on, beaming across countless miles of

electrical pulses and airwaves, was an image she hadn't
seen since she was twelve years old: her father's face.

Meg couldn't move; she could scarcely breathe.
David Houston's sparkling smile reappeared and his
television-school voice chatted on while Meg sat,
mesmerized by a vision from the past. A vision of the
dead.

She shook her head in disbelief. She had to be mistaken. Seeing things. Too much stress from this past
term. Maybe even some kind of psychological fallout
from David's leaving. That was it. Rejected by the two
important men in her life. Daddy, then David. God,
she'd better phone Mother. Tell her. Lydia and Jeffrey always watched the news at eleven o'clock instead of six, but just in case...

Willing herself to the wall phone in the kitchen, Meg
pushed out the sequence of numbers to Cape Cod,
then stood, drumming her fingers along the coiled
telephone cord. She breathed a sigh of relief when
Lydia answered in a normal voice.

"Hi, Mother, are you alone?"

"Alone? Why, not exactly, dear. I mean, Jeffrey's
in the den and I'm in the kitchen. What is it? Is something wrong?"

"No, not really. You didn't see the news on KLRT
tonight, did you?"

Lydia Haycock laughed. "You're not calling to ask
me just that, surely."

"Well, uh, actually I am. There was a short feature
on one of those refugee camps in Thailand and...and
I caught a glimpse of someone in the crowd who
looked very much like...Daddy."

There was a long silence in Cape Cod. "What kind of nonsense is this, Meg?" Lydia finally asked. "What's going on?"

The documentary played again in Meg's mind as she recounted it scene by scene—for herself as much as for her mother—half hoping that replaying it in her head would convince her she had not been mistaken.

"At first I only caught his profile. Then the camera swung back to him as he was turning. It was *him*, Mother. I know it. He looks exactly the same, except his hair is longer and...and snow-white." Her voice broke. She felt herself coming apart and fought it, knowing how emotion distressed her mother.

"Meg, I don't understand what's happening. I know you've been feeling down ever since David left—"

"Mother...Mother, listen to me, this has nothing to do with David. And *he* didn't leave—I asked him to go. There *is* a difference." She took a calming breath. "Look, I didn't call to talk about David. I called to talk about seeing Daddy."

"Margaret, you listen to me. Your father has been dead for nineteen years." Lydia's steely interruption brooked no argument. She'd long ago closed the book on any discussion about Joe Devlin and Meg knew there was no point arguing.

She consciously unclenched her fist. "Do me a favor, Mother. Please watch the late news. Would you do that much for me? I'll talk to you later." She hung up, resisting a desire to slam the receiver into its bracket.

So much for motherly advice. It had always been like this whenever the subject of Joe Devlin came up.

From the moment her mother had crumpled the telegram reporting her father missing in action in Vietnam, all discussion of him had ceased. Any reference
to him, any attempt at reminiscence, had drawn nothing more than a tight, end-of-conversation look.

Meg had tried to understand. Surely the pain of a
daughter was nothing compared to that of a young,
attractive widow. And when her mother had remar-
ried three years later, she became even more determined not to talk about Meg's father.

Meg wandered aimlessly back into the living room,
recalling the summer day she and her mother had met
Jeffrey Haycock. They'd stepped into his antique shop
and bingo! An impulsive week's vacation in Cape Cod
had changed Lydia's life. She'd learned to loosen up,
had even acquired a sense of humor in response to
Jeffrey's dry wit. And Meg, herself, grudgingly came
to love Jeffrey, too. Now, after almost sixteen years of
marriage to Jeffrey, it was no wonder that Lydia didn't
want to believe what Meg had witnessed.

But her father might be alive! Meg puttered around
the apartment, unable to shake the thought from her
mind. There were end-of-semester reports to grade and
a new mystery to read but nothing could divert her attention from the clock. Its hands crawled to ten minutes to eleven. She set up the video recorder, switched
on the television and sat down on the carpet to wait.
Bomber prowled restlessly amid the discarded pizza
remains.

At least she didn't have to endure David's plastic
smile again. A perky brunette anchored the late news.
The broadcast went on forever and for a panicked
moment Meg thought the Thailand feature might not

be repeated. Then suddenly it was there—the tanned, creased face, strong and handsome, as Meg remembered. The VCR whirred softly in the quiet flat.

Meg sat, fighting tears, aware only of the roaring in her ears and the painful thudding in her chest. When the footage was over, she uncramped her legs to switch off the machine. She had just pushed the rewind button when the telephone rang.

"Margaret?" Lydia's voice sounded distant and bewildered.

"Did you see him, Mother?"

A long pause. "Yes."

Caution edged the reply, almost daring Meg to insist the face was Joe Devlin's.

"And?" Meg wanted Lydia to be the first to say it.

"Well, it did look like him . . ." Lydia faltered, then seemed to gain momentum from the slight admission. "But it must be a coincidence, dear. If your father were alive, why wouldn't he have contacted us?"

Meg closed her eyes. Why, indeed? She'd been asking herself that same question all evening. But trust her mother to voice it right away, rather than rejoice at the possibility Joe might be alive.

"Of course, I haven't said anything to Jeffrey," her mother was saying, "because we really don't know for certain at all. Do we?"

"Of course not," Meg whispered. "But I think we ought to contact someone. Perhaps father's former commanding officer. What was his name?"

"Braith-something. Colonel Braith-whatever. Why don't you look it up in your father's old papers and call me back in the morning? All right, dear?"

"And then what?"

"I don't understand."

"Then what are we going to do about Daddy?"

"We?"

Lydia's question was whisper soft but it reverberated around Meg's living room.

"Yes, we. Or aren't you interested in finding your husband?"

"Don't take that tone with me, Margaret. You've no right—"

"Mother, I'm sorry, but whether you want to be part of this or not, you are. And I definitely intend to call the Pentagon or whoever I have to in order to get to the bottom of this."

"Do what you like, Margaret. You always have."

Meg heard the resignation in her mother's voice. She knew Lydia would rather pretend the whole thing was a dreadful mistake. But she'd make her mother part of the investigation if she had to drag her kicking and screaming into it. There was no way she was going to let Lydia passively allow Joe Devlin to slip out of their lives again.

She replaced the receiver and watched Bomber slink into the bedroom with a crust of pizza in his mouth.

"So when I called the Pentagon," Meg said, "it was like talking to a stone wall. Apparently Braithwaite died more than five years ago." Meg watched her mother set her teacup back in its saucer.

Lydia's hand shook slightly. The sandwiches she'd brought from Cape Cod were beginning to curl at the edges, still untouched an hour after her arrival. There was seldom anything edible in Meg's refrigerator. Habit had driven Lydia to bring lunch.

"And?" Lydia finally asked, her long fingers massaging the crease between her eyebrows.

Meg stared at her mother's pale face, wishing she could ease the worry and strain she saw there, wishing she'd feel comfortable about wrapping her arms around her mother and telling her everything would turn out all right. But no doubt Lydia would resist such a show of emotion.

Instead of moving toward her, Meg sank back in her own chair. "Mother, I think you should tell Jeffrey what's happened, but I realize that's your affair. What's my affair—I mean, *our* affair—is finding out if that was Daddy in the film or not."

"It wasn't." The denial was hoarse but insistent.

"Well, the officer I spoke to said he'd call back, but probably not until next week. I didn't know what phone number to give him while I was at work, so—"

"You didn't give him mine! Margaret, I can't have people calling me at home about this."

"No, Mother. I didn't give him your number, only mine. I'll borrow Julie's answering machine. There's probably no rush, anyway. Waiting for a prompt call-back from a government department is like expecting to win the lottery this weekend."

"How did you get so cynical, I wonder?" Lydia bent to retrieve her handbag from the floor. "I'm going now, dear. It's been a long day. If someone does call you back about all of this, I do hope you'll be discreet when you phone me at home."

Meg said her goodbyes, then collapsed against the closed door. It's amazing, she thought, how quickly a thirty-year-old woman can be reduced to a child by her mother.

She was sitting down to try some of the now-quite-dry sandwiches when the telephone rang.

"Miss Devlin, please."

The voice was deep and masculine with the even, neutral tones of bureaucracy. Meg pegged him for a military man immediately. "Yes, this is Meg Devlin."

"This is Sergeant Colborne calling from the Pentagon. I understand you were making an inquiry about a Lieutenant Joseph Devlin."

"Yes, you see, I—"

"Our records show that Lieutenant Devlin was reported missing in action, presumed dead in April 1972."

"Yes, he was, but the reason I called is that I think he may be alive."

There was a pause. A click sounded across the connection, as if the phone was placed on hold. Meg was about to speak when the baritone returned.

"I'm sorry, Miss Devlin, but I've only received a note that you had made an inquiry. Perhaps you'd fill me in on the details?"

Meg took a deep breath to calm her nerves. "I was watching a news special last night about refugee camps in northern Thailand. There were some shots of the camp and a man who looked like my father was in them."

"I see. So...even though we're looking at a time gap of almost twenty years, you think a face you saw on TV could have been your father?"

The question was obviously intended to make her feel foolish, and it did. She could almost picture herself on the other end, hearing someone else make a similar claim.

"Look, I know it sounds crazy, but you see, his body was never found. My mother and I never had a chance to bury him. Do you understand?" Meg stopped. She was beginning to sound hysterical, and hysteria wasn't going to open any doors at the Pentagon.

She bit hard on her lower lip. "The man I saw last night," she finally managed, "was my father."

"What station was this report broadcast on?"

"KLRT here in Boston."

"And has your father made any previous attempt at communication?"

She took a deep breath. Either she wasn't making any sense at all or the man was being deliberately obtuse. "This wasn't an attempt at communication. I simply saw him on the six o'clock news."

"Has he ever made *any* attempt at communication?"

"Well, of course not. He was supposed to be dead."

The man cleared his throat. "Precisely. You've had no contact from your father in twenty years because he was reported missing, presumed dead, and I think it's safe to say that he must indeed *be* dead. Otherwise, you'd have had some communication from him."

"Isn't it possible that he was held prisoner for all those years?"

"Possibly, but not likely." The voice softened to a patient condescension. "Anyhow, if you actually saw him, presumably he's no longer a prisoner. And if that's the case, why hasn't he contacted you?"

Meg wanted to laugh, but there was nothing funny about the conversation. "We seem to wind up at the same dead end every time, don't we?"

"I beg your pardon?"

"Look, Sergeant—"

"Colborne."

"Yes. I want you to consider this a formal request to do whatever it takes to begin an inquiry into the possibility that my father, Lieutenant Devlin, is still alive."

There was a pause. "I can't promise any kind of formal inquiry, Miss Devlin. I can only promise to pass the matter on to my superior officer. He'll determine what steps should be taken from there."

"That isn't good enough," Meg objected.

"I'll call you back next week, if I have anything new to report."

The tone of his voice suggested that wasn't damn likely. Meg decided to toss the ball back into his court. "I'll be waiting for your call, Sergeant, and if it doesn't come, I'll contact my congressman. I'm prepared to take this as far and as high as I have to—"

"That's your right, Miss Devlin. Good day."

Meg stared at the telephone long after the connection had been severed, wishing all kinds of ignominious physical discomforts on Sergeant Colborne.

And her mother wondered why she was so cynical.

WHEN MEG ROUNDED the corner and saw The Meeting Place bistro she could feel nervousness balling up in her stomach. She wished she could take back her impulsive telephone call to David; wished even more that she'd chosen any other eatery than their old haunt.

She spotted him at once, sitting on the windowed side of the restaurant with his back to the door. There'd been a time, she couldn't help recalling, when he'd have been facing the other way.

"I like the breezy way you come into a room," he used to say.

All so much cow manure, of course, along with everything else he whispered so endearingly.

Meg tacked around the closely-packed chairs and tables, resisted the impulse to tap him on the shoulder and sidled into the chair opposite him.

"Hello, David."

He glanced up quickly from the menu, caught off guard.

"Meg! You look absolutely marvelous!"

"Been holidaying in the South, David?"

"I don't get your drift."

"The accent—mah-velous," she mimicked, exaggerating the intonation.

David's frown delighted her. She could almost hear the warning bells going off in his mind. Oh, no, this is going to be one of *those* kinds of lunches.

"Just teasing," she added, letting him off the hook. After all, she had information to get.

The familiar TV smile eased across his face, making her wish she hadn't let him off quite so easily.

"Seriously, Meg, you do look stunning. Different somehow. Have you changed your hairstyle?"

"Nope, same old unmanageable tresses. You look different, though. What is it? Something with the hair. It's parted on the opposite side."

The smile became sheepish. "That was Charlene's idea. She thought it improved my camera profile."

It was Meg's turn to smile. "David," she teased, "how can perfect be improved on?"

He had the grace to flush, ever so slightly. "So," he said, putting an end to that line of conversation, "what can I do for you?"

She hesitated, saved for the moment by the waiter arriving with a carafe of wine and two glasses. She had to frame her request in just the right way or he'd interpret it as a ploy for attention.

David cleared his throat. "Meg, whatever the problem is . . . I'm happy to help out in any way I can. I have some news of my own. There's a possibility I may be moving out of the anchor position to something a bit bigger." He leaned across the table, his voice hushed in secrecy.

Meg could tell he was dying to spill the beans but she kept her face indifferent. No way was she going to be sidetracked from her purpose in arranging this meeting.

"Another time, David, I—"

"Oh, well, then . . ." Uncertainty always left him speechless. "Uh, Charlene and I have announced our engagement. I don't know if you've heard."

Forcing herself to keep her eyes focused on his face, Meg shook her head. "No, I hadn't heard. Congratulations." She waited a moment before going on, startled more by her lack of feeling at the news than by the announcement itself. "Actually, I asked to see you about something quite personal and . . . and unsettling."

David ran a manicured hand through his styled, blond hair and began to look distinctly like a cornered rabbit. Meg curbed an impulse to smile. She guessed what he was thinking—that she was trying to make a last pitch for him.

"Oh?" He assumed an indifference that didn't fool her at all.

"I was watching your news broadcast last Friday." She gritted her teeth at the preening pleasure that appeared in his face. "There was a short feature on one of those refugee camps in Thailand."

"Yes. Rather moving, wasn't it?"

"For me, yes, but not for the reasons you think. I caught sight of a man in the background who I think was my father."

The smile slipped. "But your father's dead."

"He's supposed to be."

"Meg, after all this time, surely you can't believe the man actually was your father."

Meg sighed. She seemed destined to repeat the same answers to the same questions over and over again. "My mother watched the broadcast later that evening. She was shocked by the resemblance." Meg paused to sip some wine. She had to slow herself down, keep control.

"So what did you do?" The reporter in David was now alerted.

"I tried to contact his former commanding officer but he's dead now. Then I spoke to someone who called from the Pentagon and... Well, he wasn't very helpful."

"How do you mean?"

"He just gave me the usual bureaucratic line. You know the kind of doublespeak they use. Said he'd call me back this week, but so far I haven't heard a word."

"It's only Wednesday."

Meg shrugged. "There was just that tone in his voice. The standard 'Don't call me, I'll call you.'" She waited for David to pick up his cue.

"Well, uh, what can I do?"

"I want to find out who the journalist was who did the feature."

David looked at his watch, peered out the window beside him and then took a long sip of wine.

It took Meg only seconds to realize he was keeping something from her. She recognized all the signs. Too bad she hadn't been this good at interpreting them when they were still living together.

"What is it, David? Something you want to tell me?" She purposely made the question flippant.

"I had a phone call just this morning. Some military type calling from Washington. He was inquiring about the same news clip. Quite a coincidence."

Meg frowned. She'd bet there was no coincidence at all. The why of it was another matter. "I have to know the journalist's name, David. Then I'll be able to find out where exactly the refugee camp is located."

"And then?"

She ran an index finger around the rim of her wineglass. "I haven't worked that part out yet."

His shrug told her she might be wasting her time. "I'll see what I can find out. Those clips are usually done by free-lancers. And I'll have to call New York because we picked up the feature from the national broadcast. Are you still at the old place?"

"Yes." Think I'd give up a good apartment because my man walked out? she wanted to say.

"I'll call you. Really." David flashed his famous smile.

"Thanks, David. I appreciate it." Meg reached for her purse.

"You're not going?"

There was surprise in his voice. Meg smiled. He was usually the one who rushed off.

"Sorry, I have to. Talk to you later." She waved her fingers and headed for the door, sensing his eyes following her. When she stepped out onto the pavement, she leaned against the brick facade to catch her breath. It wasn't often she one-upped David. The experience was exhilarating, but not enough to stop her from realizing she didn't know the answer to his question, "And then?"

CHAPTER TWO

THE UNEXPECTED knock made Meg spill the coffee she was pouring. Leaving the chain in place, she cautiously opened the door. Her friends didn't normally drop by at ten on a Saturday morning.

Bomber's pink nose wedged itself into the gap at chest height.

"Your cat?" asked a partially visible man.

"Yes." Now, what did she do? Open her door to a stranger because he was holding her cat hostage?

"He's wet," the man said, stating the obvious. "It's pouring out there."

"Yes . . . well, he doesn't mind the rain. And he just goes in and out as he likes—uses my kitchen window and the fire escape. Thanks for bringing him upstairs, but if you just leave him there, I'll let him in when he's dry."

The man bent to put Bomber down and Meg caught a glimpse of part of a hawklike nose, dark brown eyes, the sleeve of a damp, tan windbreaker and a very long section of denim leg.

"Perhaps I should start over again," the man said, straightening and positioning one eye in the chained space. "I came here to see you. You are Margaret Devlin?"

The heel of Meg's hand pressed against the door. The name outside the front entrance still read D. Houston; she hadn't gotten around to changing it.

"The name's on your cat's ID tag," he continued. "And this is the address I got from David Houston. He contacted me through NBC in New York. Said you wanted to see me about a feature I did on refugee camps. Name's Conor Tremayne."

So David had come through, after all. Meg quickly pulled back the chain and opened the door. Bomber raced in and curled his wet body around her ankles. She ignored him, focusing on the man in the hallway. He was at least six-two, lean and somewhat haggard. Bordering on disreputable, in fact. That might have prompted her to rebolt the door if not for who he said he was.

She stepped back and gestured him inside. "I've just made some coffee. Would you like a cup?"

"Please. Black." He sank onto the sofa, making himself comfortable.

Meg fumbled with the coffee in the kitchen, spilling the hot brew all over the counter. The thought that she might be on the verge of getting information about her father spun circles in her mind. She forced herself to slow down, automatically wiping up the mess while taking deep, calming breaths. Then she picked up the two mugs and headed for the living room.

"I expected David to phone me with the information I wanted," she said, handing him one of the mugs. "I certainly didn't expect you to show up in person."

He flashed a polite smile that altered her original judgment. Perhaps "disreputable" was a bit harsh. Maybe "tired" was more accurate.

"I was already on my way from Bangkok to New York when Houston called NBC and I had to come to Boston on business, anyway." Tremayne took a long swallow of coffee. "Ah, that's good. Sorry for my appearance, but I took the first available flight and still haven't had a chance to get over my jet lag."

"I'm sorry if David led you to believe this was an emergency. It isn't, exactly."

Tremayne shrugged. "That's okay. As I said, I had to get to Boston as soon as possible, anyway." His hand rubbed at the creases in his face.

Meg amended her mental description of him again. He looked exhausted.

He withdrew a pack of cigarettes and tapped it against the coffee table until a cigarette fell out.

"Oh . . ." Meg began.

A question appeared in his face.

"I prefer people don't smoke here," she explained, wishing the "oh" hadn't slipped out. He *had* come to help her.

He gave an indifferent shrug and tucked the pack into his shirt pocket. "I figure a cup of strong coffee and a cigarette make a good start on the day. I like to end it with a shot of good bourbon."

The grin on his face suggested other, unnamed pleasures. Conor Tremayne, Meg decided, was as far from her type of man as anyone could possibly be. But what did she care about that? All that mattered was that he'd come to help her. "Shall we get to the point of why I wanted to talk to you?"

"Guess so. But first, I'm curious to know what your relationship is with this Houston guy."

Meg drew herself up in the armchair. She had the uncomfortable feeling she looked just like her mother. "I don't have a relationship with David Houston."

"His name is on the box downstairs."

So far she was batting zero in her efforts to appear logical and businesslike. "Look, this really has nothing to do with why I wanted to talk to you."

"Just curious."

He reached for his coffee again, dismissing the subject in a manner that made her feel even more foolish. "I meant that I don't have a relationship with David *now*," she said, emphasizing the last word.

"Ah. Well, then, let's get back to that film you were asking about."

"Where was it shot and when? Did you meet any of the people in the film? Talk to any of them?"

Conor raised a hand. "Whoa! Do you always charge headlong into a conversation?"

"Sorry, but it's important to me."

He must have heard the urgency in her voice. "All right," he said. "Let's take those questions one at a time. First, I shot the clip in northern Thailand. About fifty miles from a town called Chiang Rai. It's right on the Mekong River and a lot of refugees cross over there. And when? For that, I'll have to check." He dug into the black leather bag he'd been carrying, retrieved a well-thumbed steno pad and flipped through it. "Hmm, here it is. I went up to the camp—it's about fifty miles from Chiang Rai—on February 17th. Was there another question?"

"Yes. Did you talk to anyone in the film? I mean, any of the Westerners?"

"Sure, I talked to a lot of them. Why?"

Meg took a deep breath, trying not to let her excitement show. "There was a man in the background who looked very much like my father. Too much to simply pass off as coincidence. I...I wonder if you might have talked to him."

"Did you happen to tape the clip?"

"Yes."

Conor watched her rush to set up the machine. He'd already made a quick assessment of her, taking in everything from the smear of jam on her right cheek to the dark circles beneath those eyes that were an impossible shade of blue. Contacts, he wondered? Though she didn't seem like the type to go for vanity things like that. Certainly not if she hadn't bothered to tame all that red hair or remove the jam while she was in the kitchen. She was forthright and he liked that. Hadn't backed down from his nosy question about Houston.

He also liked the way her narrow hips stretched against the gray cords she was wearing and when she bent to search for the cassette in the rack beside the television, he caught an inviting glimpse of lacy undergarment in the swaying vee of her man-size shirt. He felt a twinge of regret that he'd come on business. Must be getting old, Tremayne; there was a time when you wouldn't let a little thing like business interfere with pleasure.

Meg looked around at him. "All set?" When he nodded, she pressed the play button and sat back on her haunches to watch, her anxiety level sky-high. As the image of her father appeared on the screen, she pushed another button to freeze the picture.

"There!" She pointed to the screen. "See that man? The one in the background behind that group of people? The tall one with the snow-white hair?"

Tremayne nodded at the screen. "Yeah, I see him. In the safari shirt."

"That's him. I know that's my father."

"Uh-huh. Okay, keep going. Let's see the rest of it."

The tape played on. When the mystery man reappeared, Meg stilled the action. "There he is again. Now wait, I'll zoom in. He's looking right into the camera in the next shot."

The face that had been haunting her for a week peered out of the television at them. Meg turned to say something to Tremayne, but something in his expression made her hesitate. He was staring intently at the screen, as if memorizing each detail of the blurry face. His stillness was animal-like, alert and waiting. Then he blinked once, awakening to her own study of him, and turned his gaze on her. Trapped by the same quiet scrutiny he'd given the face on the screen, Meg felt self-conscious.

She got up from the floor and walked back to the sofa, uncomfortably aware of Tremayne's eyes tracking each movement. "I *know* that man's my father," she murmured.

"When did you last see him?" The question was gently put.

"I was twelve when he . . . when he disappeared."

"Remember him well?"

She nodded, but Tremayne merely continued to watch her, as if expecting her to go on. "He was a wonderful father. Funny and always up for adventure. As different from my mother as night from day. They quarreled a lot.''

This time, Tremayne raised a questioning eyebrow.

''Daddy had a real Irish personality. He was very...emotional and my mother was...is always calm and cool. Of course, he wasn't around a lot because he was a career officer. Then there was the war.'' She paused for a long moment. ''It's so unbelievable that he might be alive, and yet I desperately want to believe it.''

Tucking her legs up beneath her on the couch, Meg closed her eyes. When she opened them, Tremayne still hadn't spoken a word or made even a murmur of sympathy. She was grateful for that.

''So,'' she announced briskly, ''I really have no option but to pursue this as far as I can.''

Conor got up and switched off the VCR.

''Miss Devlin—''

''Meg.''

The name fit, Conor thought. Slightly old-fashioned in an age of creative names, but simple, straight and unequivocal. Like her.

''All right, Meg. I'm sorry, I don't want to dash your hopes, but to be perfectly honest I didn't meet that man on the screen. I'm certain if he had anything to do with organizing the event, I'd have been introduced to him.

''That's what it was,'' he explained at the question in her eyes. ''The agency operating that particular camp had just received a grant from the Thai government and was hoping the U.S. would match it. They staged the media show to capture the hearts of people over here.''

''It all sounds so contrived,'' she murmured.

''Desperation forces people to do a lot of questionable things.''

She watched him finish his coffee. The wistfulness in his remark jarred with the image of the burned-out journalist he'd initially presented. A complicated man, she decided, and so very different from David. The comparison her mind was making startled her. She had a sudden flash of waking up with this black-haired man's lined face next to hers on the pillow. But why on earth was she imagining that?

God, her hormones must be out of whack. What was she going to be imagining by the time she hit the ''Seven Months After David'' mark?

''More coffee?'' she asked, off the sofa and almost in the kitchen before he answered.

''Uh, no more for me, thanks. I just realized the time. I've an appointment downtown in twenty minutes so I gotta run. Look, I realize I haven't been much help to you, but perhaps I can find out something more. One of the crew might know this guy.''

Something in the tone of his voice told her it wasn't likely.

Then he added, ''Can't make any promises. And you know— Well, maybe the guy's not really your father. Perhaps you're better off accepting the fact that—''

''He's dead?'' she finished. ''I've been hearing that for twenty years.''

"But have you been listening?" He shrugged at her and headed for the door, stopping by the couch to pick up his leather satchel.

Meg reached the doorway a step ahead of him. "Thank you for coming, Mr. Tremayne. I appreciate the trouble you took." She knew she sounded stiff and unappreciative, but the last thing she needed to hear was a question that could have been posed by her mother.

"I'll call you tomorrow, then." And, with a curt nod, he was gone.

But Meg scarcely heard his promise. Northern Thailand. Near a town called Chiang Rai. On the Mekong River. As she closed the door behind him, her mind was already filled with plans.

SPIRALS OF MIST rose from the damp pavement. The sun was just poking through the clouds, warming the aftermath of a chilly April shower. Conor stood outside the Victorian row house he'd just left and stared at Meg's second-floor window.

Then he turned, strode briskly down the street and rounded the corner to the pay phone he'd spotted earlier. He slid the door closed against the traffic and deposited a quarter.

"Yeah," he said when the operator came on the line. "I want to make a collect call to Langley, Virginia." He gave her the sequence of numbers, drumming his fingers on the metal telephone shelf as the operator asked the person at the other end of the line to receive the call.

"Are you crazy?" shouted the voice after consenting.

"Rough day, Gallagher?"

"Where are you calling from? Is that a safe line?"

"It's a pay phone or are you worried about your own people at that end?"

"Cut the smartass remarks, Tremayne. Did you see her?"

"Yep, just came from her place."

"And?"

"She doesn't know anything. I'd stake all I've got that she's had no contact with the subject at all."

"All you've got," muttered Gallagher. "That's a joke. Okay. I've just seen a copy of the film myself. Subject's identification confirmed."

"Yeah, it *is* Devlin. Now what do I do?"

There was a sharp intake of breath. Tremayne grinned, knowing his mentioning Devlin's name over the phone annoyed Gallagher.

"Uh, look," the voice, degrees cooler now, went on. "I'm working on something here. Call me back tomorrow, 'round noon. Meanwhile, stay away from the woman. We may have to use her and I don't want it to look like she's being rushed into something."

Conor smiled at the suggestion. From what he'd already picked up about Meg Devlin, he doubted anyone could rush her into anything unless she wanted to go along. He agreed and hung up, knowing there was no way he was going to let Gallagher tell him how to run the show as far as the Devlin woman was concerned. He'd see her again tomorrow. Screw Gallagher.

LYDIA HAYCOCK'S black pumps tapped across the ceramic-tiled foyer to the front door.

"Margaret!" she exclaimed. "How... how nice of you to surprise us."

Meg forced herself to keep a straight face. She knew her mother hated unexpected visitors. Still, she couldn't help but admire Lydia's self-control. She wished she'd managed some herself earlier, when Tremayne had dropped in.

"Sorry for the lack of notice, Mother, but I left in a bit of a hurry. Is... is, uh, Jeffrey here?"

Lydia paused as she was hanging up Meg's jacket. "Why are you asking?"

"Because I have to talk to you about something."

Lydia lowered her voice. "He's just closing up the shop. He ought to be back any moment." She shut the closet door and led Meg by the arm along the hall toward the family room. "I asked you to warn me if you planned to come here and discuss this... this business."

"Mother, it isn't *business* we're talking about."

Lydia closed the French doors between the family room and the living room beyond, then turned back to Meg.

"Margaret, I can't have you coming into my home and... and upsetting me when Jeffrey will be back so soon."

"Mother, please." Meg reached out a hand to her mother's arm. "Relax. I came because I had a visit today from the journalist who filmed that news story. About the refugee camps."

Lydia's face paled. "How could that be?"

"I asked David to find out who had filmed the story—"

"You told David about the film?"

"Yes. It's okay, Mother, you don't have to look at me like that. David will be discreet."

"And you don't have to take that tone with me, Margaret. I have every right to expect privacy and discretion from you."

"Mother, I'm sorry. Look, let's start over. I talked to David because he has a lot of contacts in the media and I knew if anyone could help us get information, he could."

"But I thought you were going to wait until you'd heard from that man you were speaking to at the Pentagon."

"I don't ever expect to hear from him. He gave me the standard brush-off, Mother. If we want to prove that man was Daddy—"

"We?" her mother interrupted sharply. "You keep going on about 'we' as if I were a partner in all of this . . . this nonsense."

The accusation reverberated around the room. A familiar hurt washed over Meg but she persisted. "The man who came to see me was a photojournalist named Tremayne. He said the film was shot in a place in northern Thailand in February. He . . . he said he didn't know the man we saw in the background but he was certain the man wasn't one of the people running the camp."

"And?"

"Well, he offered to try to find out if any of the crew knew the man."

"Meg." Lydia's tone had softened.

A sign of pity, Meg decided. Her mother seldom used her childhood nickname.

"Meg, if that's all he could tell you . . ."

She didn't need to finish the sentence to spell out the word futility. It mocked Meg from every corner of the room.

"At least I have the location of the camp, Mother, and Daddy—or the man in the film—was there for a purpose. Whatever that reason was, it may draw him to the camp again."

"What are you saying?"

"I'm going there to have a look at the place myself."

"Oh, Margaret, that's the most ridiculous thing I've heard since you first called me with this story! I don't understand what's happening to you. You're usually so much more . . . sensible. Is it the breakup with David?"

"For God's sake, Mother, none of this has anything to do with David. I wish I could make you understand that my life doesn't revolve around David Houston. It might have, months ago, but not now. David and I are finished. And please don't sidetrack me from this. I intend to find my father."

Lydia opened her mouth but the sound of the front door clicking shut silenced her. Footsteps echoed across the hallway floor and paused outside the French doors. There was a gentle tap before they opened.

"Hello, Jeffrey," Meg greeted the stocky, gray-haired man in the doorway.

"Meg. What a pleasant surprise!" Jeffrey's broad face shone as he came into the room to give her a hug.

"I hope you're staying for dinner," he said.

She forced herself not to look at her mother's face. "Sorry, Jeffrey, but this is a flying visit. I just came to tell you both that I'll be away for a couple of weeks and not to worry if you couldn't reach me at home."

"Good heavens, this is unexpected, isn't it? I thought you'd decided to spend the break spring-cleaning."

He was teasing, of course. Meg's aversion to housework was a family joke.

She managed a faint laugh. In spite of his informal joviality, Jeffrey Haycock was no fool. He could spot anxiety in a meditating monk. "I guess it was the thought of it that forced me to make plans to go away."

"Wonderful. Where are you off to?"

Meg risked a quick glance across at her mother. She was staring at some fixed point on the nearest wall. Her mouth was set in a thin, red line. "Thailand," Meg replied.

TREMAYNE CLUTCHED the bunch of irises, feeling decidedly foolish. It had been a long time since he'd bought flowers for a woman. Not since Mi Mi, and even then, he'd done it merely as a formality. There was something about this Devlin woman.... He'd be sorry to leave. Perhaps the next time he was in the States he'd look her up, though as soon as he thought it, he knew he never would.

He paid the cabbie and took the steps up to the front door of the house two at a time. He pushed the buzzer, but the door was ajar and he didn't bother waiting for an answer. Tremayne climbed the narrow staircase to the second floor, wondering why he was feeling such anticipation.

This time tomorrow he'd be on his way back to Bangkok and Meg would be simply a memory. The thought rankled. Still, his plane didn't leave until six in the morning. Tremayne tapped eagerly at the door on the second landing.

No response. Maybe she was sleeping in. He knocked more insistently.

A door swung open behind him, on the opposite side of the landing. "She's gone."

Conor spun round. The old man standing in the doorway peered out at him through wire-rimmed spectacles.

"Gone?" Conor parroted.

"Yup. Left at daybreak."

"Where? Did something happen?" Conor's mind raced with alarming possibilities.

"Don't worry. Said she was going east—not in the States, but way east. Thailand, I believe. Left her cat with me. Said she'd be gone a couple weeks at least."

"Uh, thanks." He had reached the ground floor before a question wafted down to him.

"Who should I say was calling?"

Conor smirked. Who indeed? "Don't worry. I'll tell her myself." He pushed through the front door, tossed the flowers into the gutter and marched briskly toward the phone booth around the corner. Gallagher wasn't going to like this development one bit.

But Gallagher surprised him.

"Uh-huh," he said, pausing to take in the information. "Okay, Tremayne, this may fit into our plans even better."

"What plans? My job is finished, Gallagher. You said to make contact, find out what she knew and report back. End of assignment."

"You're finished when I say you are, Tremayne. Now listen closely, because I'm not repeating this and I won't be talking to you for a few days."

Conor squeezed the receiver until his knuckles whitened. What he wanted to do was to substitute the telephone for Gallagher's neck. *One day I'll make the bastard pay.*

"Are you ready?"

"Yeah, go ahead."

"Find her. It shouldn't be hard. She'll inevitably end up at the American Embassy in Bangkok, looking for help. I'll wire someone there to be ready for her. Then I want you to do whatever you can to help her find her father."

"Are you crazy? Her father's supposed to be dead." Conor's voice thundered out the cracks in the phone-booth door, catching the attention of a couple passing by. He slammed the folding door into its frame and turned his back on their curious stares.

"Where have you been, Tremayne? I told you yesterday I was working on something from this end. I want Devlin more than I want anything in the world. And you're going to help that woman—and me—find him. Understand?"

Conor knew better than to protest. He'd heard that tone in Gallagher's voice before.

"So when do you want me to contact you again?" he asked, hating himself for yielding; at the same time, already looking forward to seeing her again.

"I don't know. I'll call you next week sometime. Will you be at your place in Bangkok?"

"Initially, I guess."

"Okay. And, Tremayne, you're to use only the contact at the embassy that I've told you about. Not a whisper to anyone else there. Understand?"

"Sure, anything you say, boss." He emphasized the last word as unpleasantly as he could. He hung up and stepped out onto the pavement, trying to shake the sense that this assignment was headed for disaster.

CHAPTER THREE

NOTHING IN MEG'S thirty years could have prepared her for the East.

She staggered into Don Muang Airport in Bangkok, dazed from lack of sleep, and was bumped toward Customs by throngs of tourists, businessmen and porters. The looped handle on her suitcase had broken in transit and she was forced to stoop, pushing the case along on its wobbly wheels while clutching shoulder bag, purse and a trench coat. By the time she passed through Customs, she was ready to move up her departure date by two weeks and leave immediately.

Outside on the steaming pavement, the suitcase toppled over in defeat. Meg leaned forward, letting the shoulder bag and coat slip off her arm onto the suitcase. Then she dug into her purse for a tissue, blew her nose twice and decided she was as ready as she'd ever be to tackle the world. Or at least, Bangkok.

"You need taxi?" A round, smiling Asian face positioned itself in front of hers.

"Please."

"You have hotel? If not, I know good place—Western-style."

Meg hesitated. She'd traveled enough to know she was doing everything wrong. There hadn't been time to purchase a guidebook, much less reserve a hotel room. And heading into a strange city with a cabbie who promised a good hotel—they *all* promised good hotels and received a commission for doing so—was breaking a cardinal rule of travel.

But the temperature outside the terminal must have been at least eighty-five degrees, her feet were swelling over the ridiculous pumps she was wearing and at that moment, she'd go anywhere with anyone if there was a cool shower at the end of the road.

"Is it in the center of the city? I don't want a hotel in the suburbs. Downtown Bangkok?" she repeated at the quizzical look on his face.

His smile widened. "Okay, you bet. Downtown." He stowed her luggage in the trunk of his beat-up Fiat sedan and ushered her into its dingy interior. The air inside was thick with cigarette smoke.

Meg rolled down the rear window and studied the faded identification card hanging on the back of the driver's seat. The crumpled photograph of the driver smiled crookedly through the stained plastic. The text was all in Thai.

Terrific. It could be a wanted poster, for all she knew.

The taxi pulled an abrupt U-turn in front of the logjammed traffic, leaving hundreds of upraised fists in a billow of black exhaust. Meg leaned back against the seat and closed her eyes. If it was her destiny to die in Bangkok's rush hour, she didn't want to see it happen.

Half an hour later the cab squealed up to a two-story white stucco hotel that Meg figured must have been new somewhere around the turn of the century. Which century was another question.

The driver insisted on following her inside—to collect his commission from Reception, Meg figured. A motley group of people stared listlessly at her as she headed for the check-in desk.

"With bathroom or without?" the clerk asked at her request for a room.

"With."

"Anything else you'd like?"

Meg frowned. "What do you mean?"

The diminutive man shrugged ambiguously. "We can supply you with any request."

"Well, I think a hot bath, a meal and twenty-four hours' sleep will do just fine, thanks." Meg swept up the key and gestured to her luggage. "You have a porter?"

"One moment, please." The clerk shouted in Thai to the office behind the counter. Seconds later, a wiry, blue-jeaned young man slouched out the door.

"Mr. Nit, please take these luggages up to room 212." The clerk smiled at Meg. "Should you be having a change of mind about anything, please call the desk."

Meg followed Mr. Nit toward an elevator. He poked the button several times, muttering what sounded like obscenities while the elevator chugged down from the second floor.

Moments later, after a desperate attempt to calculate an appropriate tip in the Thai *bhat* currency followed by a cursory inspection of the room's facilities, Meg collapsed onto the double bed, closed her eyes for a catnap and woke up several hours later.

Her body insisted it was dinnertime, but a glance at the digital clock radio by the bed confirmed the city of Bangkok and its residents were in the middle of a night's sleep. At least, some of them were. There was a loud argument taking place outside in the corridor.

Meg stretched an arm to the telephone on the night table. A call down to the front desk assured her that yes, a toasted cheese sandwich could be brought to her room at once and was there anything else? Of course. Imported beer or local? And something more?

She stifled her irritation. It was, after all, three in the morning and no doubt the clerk had been dozing pleasantly. But what more would she want at that godforsaken hour?

By the time the order arrived, Meg was just about ready to turn down the covers and slip back into bed. She downed half the beer, ate most of the surprisingly tasty sandwich and switched off the light. Flashes from headlights in the street below swept through the curtains and every once in a while, voices rang out. The last thought Meg had before losing consciousness was to wonder if there were any creepie-crawlies in the bathroom that would squeeze out under the bottom of the door into the bedroom.

MEG TRUDGED down the long, paved drive that wound out of the parkland estate of the American Embassy. It was past noon, the sun beat down mercilessly and she was beginning to wish she'd eaten lunch in the popular commissary that drew many tourists to the embassy. At least a good American-style meal might have compensated for what had turned out to be a futile inquiry.

The clerk had been polite to a fault and she had been quickly advanced to the head of a long line of visa applicants. Embarrassed, yet grateful not to have to wait, Meg had found out how and where to purchase bus tickets to Chiang Rai.

"Most tourists just go to Chiang Mai," the woman had proclaimed. She was Thai but spoke with a faint American accent. "You can see just as many antiquities in Chiang Mai and the trip is not so long. Better you go to Chiang Mai."

The impassive courtesy in the receptionist's face altered slightly when Meg asked about the refugee camp outside Chiang Rai. "So sorry," she'd murmured, her eyes already shifting to the person next in line. "I know nothing about this place."

"Perhaps you can tell me if anyone by the name of Joseph Devlin has registered here at the embassy. Maybe he's collecting mail here or something."

The receptionist deftly handed Meg over to an American who'd suddenly appeared in the office.

"May I help you?" the young man had asked.

"I'm looking for a man called Joseph Devlin. I was wondering if you have a list of Americans living in Thailand."

The man motioned Meg to an adjacent cubicle. He hovered over her while she sat down, giving an impression of wanting to be through with her as quickly as possible. "And is this man a relative? Has he been reported missing?"

She smirked at that. Sure, missing for twenty years and this is the first time anyone's gone looking for him. She took a deep breath and plunged in.

"The man is my father and he was reported missing in action in Vietnam."

The man remained silent, but raised an eyebrow.

"But I have reason to believe he may be alive. He...he was seen in the vicinity of a refugee camp near Chiang Rai." It was a small white lie, but she was prepared to spin even bigger ones if necessary.

He whistled a long sigh through his pursed lips. "Well, Miss...uh, what's the name again?"

"Devlin."

"Right. Well, Miss Devlin, I can check our list of American citizens living in Thailand, but I have to warn you that the list is composed only of people who have taken the trouble to register with us. And that isn't necessary, you know. You should also know that the camp you speak of is off-limits to tourists and can't be visited without permission from the Thai police. I strongly advise against going there. If you're arrested—for it's not likely the police will issue you a permit—there's little the embassy can do for you." He excused himself and disappeared through the No Entry door leading to the interior of the embassy.

Meg decided bureaucrats worldwide must take special training in how to accentuate the negative. All of their petty rules and regulations appeared to be designed only to hurl obstacles at unsuspecting citizens. She tapped her fingertips on the top of the small desk while she waited for the anonymous man—was he afraid to identify himself?—to return.

He did so while she was looking out the barred window at the beautifully manicured grounds. When she turned toward him, she knew by his face that he wasn't going to be helpful.

"Sorry, Miss Devlin, it appears that your father's name is not on our list. We've no record of him at all. As I said, it's doubtful that Thai police will permit you to visit the camp. However, I'll be happy to contact them on your behalf. If you can let me know where exactly you're staying here in Bangkok, I'll call you when I get the information."

The concession was more than she'd hoped for, although the pessimism in his young face had told her he didn't expect to be successful. She gathered up her canvas handbag and, just before leaving the reception area, lowered her head to peer through the glass partition separating the office behind.

"Thanks again for your help," she called out. But the man had his back to her and was speaking animatedly into a telephone.

"RICKSHAW?" A teenage boy straddled the seat of a bicycle rickshaw in the line of taxis that waited on the main road outside the grounds of the embassy.

"Uh, no, thank you," she replied, uncomfortable at the idea of a young boy bicycling her all the way into town. Instead, she squeezed into one of the three-wheeled, engine-powered taxis known as tuk-tuks, that were everywhere in Thailand's capital. The tiny and windowless vehicle swung about, spewing out a blast of noxious exhaust that left Meg coughing all the way into the center of the city. She motioned for the driver to let her out a few blocks before her hotel.

Five seconds on a sidewalk steaming with heat and the decay of litter, shouldered from all sides by people, Meg wished she'd stayed with the taxi. Everywhere was the reek of car fumes and the stench of garbage.

But she knew the walk would be good for her. She'd always walked to brainstorm solutions to problems. And right now she had a big problem. She had to find a man who'd been missing for most of her life.

One step at a time, she thought, and headed in what she hoped was the right direction to her hotel. The canals snaking throughout the busy streets would have been picturesque except for the oil slicks and debris floating on their black surfaces. Meg looked away from them but the flow of pedestrian traffic impeded her efforts to enjoy the fairy-tale temples on the opposite side of the boulevard.

She held a tissue to her face and pushed on. The allure of the "mysterious" East had degenerated into the reality of a polluted, hustling landscape that combined all the worst elements of the West.

Meg waited at an intersection for the light to change, gazing at the crumbling brick entrance to her hotel—the Malaya—down a side street. The air-conditioned darkness of her room beckoned, even with the cockroaches. Outside the hotel, a stout Thai matron had set up a cart, sun umbrella and blender. A handmade sign advertising Es Jus perched against a huge basket of various tropical fruits. Meg's mouth began to water.

She waited patiently in line while the woman scooped up a handful of ice cubes, threw them into the blender, added chunks of fresh pineapple and a cup of water and switched the machine to top speed. Then she poured the drink into a tall glass that had been sitting n a bucket of gray water. The man ahead of Meg drank slowly, smacking his lips appreciatively.

The woman held up three fingers and beamed a hearty smile. Three *baht*—less than a dollar. Meg couldn't decide between mango or a strange round fruit with dark green bumps.

"Might just as well swallow a glass of strychnine," advised a voice behind her.

She spun around to face Conor Tremayne. His face was flushed from the heat and the pale yellow cotton shirt he wore stuck in damp patches to his chest. A khaki backpack was slung casually over one shoulder.

"What are you doing here?" She hoped she didn't look as foolishly surprised as she felt.

"I live here, remember?"

"How did you find me?"

He grinned then. "Got your address from the embassy and thought I'd look you up."

"I just came from the embassy. How—"

"Followed hard on your heels. Except I had the sense to stay in my cab until it reached the hotel."

The woman at the juice stand spoke up, gesturing to Meg.

"I wouldn't if I were you," Conor put in.

"*He* drank it," Meg replied lamely, nodding at the Thai who was just finishing his drink.

"He lives here. His guts are coated with the stuff. Unless you want to spend the next couple of weeks crawling to the toilet, you'll avoid the water, ice cubes and raw vegetables."

"It's so damn hot here," she protested, half aware of the underlying whine in the remark.

"Come on," said Conor, taking her by the arm. "We'll have a cold beer in the bar. By the way, how did you happen to chance on the Malaya?"

Meg felt her spine stiffen. There was something damn maddening about the man. He was as pushy as her mother. But a cold beer did sound wonderful. She slipped her arm out of his. "It came highly recommended," she announced, walking primly ahead, and stepped into the lobby.

A chilling blast of air vaporized the beads of perspiration on Meg's forehead. She stumbled, blinded by the sudden move from brightness to dark. Conor's arm shot out to steady her. The instant pressure of his hand on her elbow was oddly reassuring. And it felt good to enter the lobby of the hotel in the company of a man. A definite challenge to all those listless stares! But when she was seated opposite Conor in the small, American-style bar, Meg's self-assurance began to fizzle.

Her problem, absurdly enough, was that he was darn good-looking. He'd certainly changed from their last meeting. It was amazing what a shave could do. Thick black hair, fashionably long, fell in a sleek curve to the nape of his neck. He had a strong nose, sharp jaw and eyebrows that almost joined together in a pronounced, brooding line.

That was the key word. *Brooding.* There's something a little too experienced about this one, she decided. He's seen a lot of the world and it's all reflecting back out from those dark eyes.

Meg shivered in the air-conditioned chill. She had a feeling Conor wasn't the type of man one could easily shrug off.

"Cold?" Conor asked, signaling for a waiter.

"I'm surprised that tourists don't get pneumonia or something, going from one extreme temperature to another."

"I'm sure they're felled by dysentery long before pneumonia can step in. What'll you have? Beer? A shot of Mekong whiskey?"

"Beer, please. I can imagine what Mekong whiskey must be like."

"Well, it does grow hair on your chest." His eyes flickered almost imperceptibly. "And that would be a pity."

Meg turned to watch the waiter bring their drinks from the bar. She'd never been one for such adolescent banter and was disappointed that Conor Tremayne would stoop to it. There was a long silence while the waiter poured beer into tall glasses.

"Cheers," he said, holding up his frosted glass.

She raised her glass slightly in acknowledgement and took a small mouthful. The beer's mild yeastiness was crisp and refreshing and she swallowed half of it in one long gulp.

"That's quite a thirst. Shall I order another?"

Meg shook her head. "No, thanks, I haven't eaten much yet today. I'll be flat on my face if I drink anymore. So," she continued, assuming a businesslike tone, "how did you happen to be at the embassy inquiring about me? And how did you even know I was in Thailand?"

Conor was relieved he could drop the coy act. He admired a woman who could get to the point without playing games, even if it meant more trouble for him. Besides, with someone like Meg, he'd be better off being as honest as he could—not that he could be all *that* honest.

"I dropped by your place in Boston and your neighbor told me you'd flown off to Thailand. I figured you'd decided to come looking for your father without waiting for me to get you the information you wanted."

Meg studied his face for a moment. The answer seemed legitimate enough and the frankness in his eyes was persuasive. But why had he gone to such trouble?

"You still haven't answered my question. Why bother to track me down through the embassy?"

"Is it so hard to believe that a man would take some trouble to look for you?"

Meg felt a rush of warmth in her face and couldn't think of a thing to say.

Conor let the question hover between them for another long second before he added, "Besides, I know a good story when I hear one. I don't have an assignment at the moment and frankly, I could use some cold hard cash. I thought you might be interested in exchanging the services of a trustworthy tour guide for the exclusive rights to your story. There's a great deal of interest right now in the fate of all those hundreds of veterans missing in action and—"

"Look, Conor, let's get something straight, right off. I've no intention of selling 'my story' as you call it to you or any other journalist. I'd never consider revealing such a...a...personal and tragic event in my life to entertain millions of people. So if that's all you wanted, thanks for the beer—I'll leave the tip." Meg pushed back her chair, rummaged in her pocket for some coins, which she threw on the table, and headed for the door.

Conor watched her push her way around the crowd at the bar and sighed.

Well, you blew that one, old fellow.

He swept the handful of American coins—useless in Thailand—off the table, exchanged them for a *baht* note and left the hotel. He'd catch her later—perhaps when she ventured out of the hotel to eat dinner. Of course, she might decide to eat in but he knew enough about hotels like the Malaya, to bet that she'd prefer to risk the local restaurants.

His hunch proved correct a mere hour later when Meg stood hesitantly in the front entrance of the hotel. Watching her from a kiosk across the road, Conor saw the usual bevy of taxi and rickshaw drivers descend and the determined shake of her head. When she turned to saunter along the sidewalk, he followed. A block farther on, she stopped outside a café whose specialty was fresh crab.

Quickly he crossed the street to where she was standing. "They're delicious and cheap, too. You can get a crab, bowl of soup and a beer for well under five dollars."

Meg turned from the plate-glass window and the tank of live crabs sprawling inside. She wasn't surprised by the comment because she'd seen Conor's reflection behind her own in the window. She supposed he'd been following her from the hotel but, rather than being annoyed, she felt almost pleased. It was probably nothing more than a sudden attack of homesickness, yet the chance to talk to another American in the sea of incomprehensible Thai around

her was welcome. Even if that American was somewhat tactless and crass.

"Have you eaten here, then?"

"Many times. The place is almost a legend, even in
Bangkok. The food's good and inexpensive, as I said.
Would you like company? I was about to get a bite to
eat myself."

Her hesitation came purely from principle. She
didn't want him to think she'd already forgotten his
tacky business proposal. "All right," she finally said.
"Judging by the number of Thai people inside, the
food must be good."

Inside the small restaurant the cement floor was littered with bits of crab shells, paper and cigarette butts.
Long tables were covered with sheets of white paper
that served as disposable tablecloths. A busy waiter
brought glasses of water as soon as Conor and Meg sat
down.

"Don't—"

"I won't," she interjected and smiled. "I'll have a
beer, though."

The youth spoke rapidly to Conor who nodded,
then answered back. Although his Thai lacked the
high-pitched tonal quality of the boy's, it was just as
quick and fluent.

"How many crabs can you eat?" he turned back to
Meg. "They're small, so I recommend at least two or
three. And would you like soup or noodles with it?"

"Two crabs will be fine, thanks. And noodles sound
good. Do they have sauce or what?"

"The most common dish is called phad Thai. Rice
noodles stir-fried with bits of vegetable and meat.
They're spicy but quite good here."

Meg agreed and Conor placed their order. "Perhaps I should explain what I said earlier," he offered after the waiter left. "My proposal was tactless. I'm sorry." Conor paused to drink from one of the beers their waiter had deposited on the table.

Meg waited for him to go on.

"I understand," he continued, "how sensitive the whole topic is for you. I could see when you were talking about your father back in Boston how deeply hurt you must have been at his disappearance. And I can understand how easy it must be to grab onto any bit of information that gives you hope of finding him. How old did you say you were when he went missing?"

She was tempted to slough off the question, switching to safer talk, but the sincerity in his voice was soothing and invited confession.

"Almost twelve. Just before he disappeared, he'd written that he was up for another rest-and-recreation period and asked if I'd mind celebrating my birthday with him and Mother in Hawaii. I was ecstatic at the thought. Needless to say, there was no celebration at all."

Conor waited a moment, then asked, "Did you learn anything at the embassy?"

"No, nothing. The man I spoke to said people don't have to register with the embassy if they don't want to, and they've no way of finding out about Americans living here."

Conor made a cynical sound. "Well, they can if they want to. The Thai police keep pretty close tabs on foreigners. This country isn't a democracy as we know it. The king is revered but hasn't a lot of power. The military runs the show. The embassy wants to keep a political arm's distance from appearing to interfere. Thais are really big on appearances.''

''The man did say he'd find out about the chances of my getting a permit to travel up to the camp from Chiang Rai and he gave me the name of a bus company where I can get a ticket.''

''You could travel by plane. It's quicker and more comfortable.''

''I thought I'd like to see some of the country. I have two weeks and apparently it's only an eighteen-hour bus trip.'' Meg paused. ''At least if I have no success, I'll get a holiday out of my visit here.''

''You could also travel by car.''

Meg shook her head emphatically. ''From what I've seen here in Bangkok, the people drive like maniacs.''

''I meant by *my* car,'' he replied. ''Wait, hear me out. First of all, I've a better chance of getting a permit to go up there than you do. Secondly, I have a car and I know the roads. I speak the language and have already been to the camp. What more could you want in a guide?''

His sudden grin took her aback, but she wanted to be certain he wasn't still after a story. ''This is the second time I've heard your 'guide' proposition,'' she finally said.

The grin turned sheepish. ''At the risk of sounding tactless the second time around, too, maybe we can talk it over again later.''

''No. No way. That's not going to be part of any deal we might make.''

''Okay, you win. No story.''

Meg eyed him suspiciously. "Then what's in it for you? Why bother?"

"As I said before, the appeal of your company, no work at the moment and, to be honest, just plain old curiosity. Besides, you'll be paying for the trip. What do you say?"

She stared at him, intrigued by the earnestness in his face. It made him look ten years younger. And his pitch was irresistible. As compelling, she realized, as the fervor in his dark eyes and the boyish flash of his smile. If she declined, would she merely be doing so out of perverse pride? After all, everything he said made perfect sense; and the unavoidable truth was, she desperately wanted someone to go with her.

"I'll think about it," she promised.

He nodded and smiled. "Good, and now that business has been dealt with, let's crack into our crabs."

LYDIA FROWNED when the doorbell rang. Jeffrey was on a buying trip near Martha's Vineyard and she'd hoped to finish the painting while he was gone. The Closed sign was up in the shop adjoining the house, so maybe whoever... The bell rang again, followed at once by a persistent knocking.

"What a nuisance," she muttered, wiping paint-streaked hands on the cleaning rag. Obviously whoever it was wasn't going to simply take the hint and go away. She headed for the front door in annoyance.

"We're closed today!" she announced immediately, intending to send the intruder packing.

The gray-haired man in a hunter-green trench coat smiled. "Mrs. Devlin?"

It had been sixteen years since anyone had addressed Lydia by that name. She could feel the adrenaline working its reverse action inside her—slowing everything down to a dead calm.

"I'm Mrs. Haycock now. Is there something I can do for you?"

"I hope so. My name is Gallagher—Noel Gallagher. I knew your husband years ago in 'Nam." He cleared his throat and paused. "You probably wonder why I'm here—"

"Mr. Gallagher, I'm wondering a lot of things and why you are here is certainly at the top of the list." Lydia gripped the edge of the door. She hoped her voice concealed the apprehension she felt. If only Jeffrey were home.

The man scratched his head and looked uncomfortable. "Well, it's simply that what I have to say may be hard to believe. Have you been watching the news lately?"

Lydia could only stare at him, her anxiety now turned to dread. Thank God, she thought, that Jeffrey's not home.

"Of course. What—"

"I happened to be watching the news last week and I swear I saw Joe in one of those specials about the refugee camps in Thailand. I could hardly believe my eyes and spent the next couple of days trying to find your address. Would . . . would you mind if I came inside for a few moments?"

She hesitated. The man's name did sound familiar. Maybe Joe had mentioned him in one of his letters.

"Not at all." She managed a smile. "Forgive my poor manners. It's just that I'm rather shocked . . . as you can imagine. My husband should be back any moment," Lydia added, hoping the lie would keep the visit brief. She opened the door and stood aside to let Gallagher in.

He was a slight man, no taller than she, with thinning hair and the look of a businessman or salesman. When she took his coat, she noticed that his suit was well cut and expensive. He sat down in one of the chintz armchairs in the solarium, seeming ill at ease.

"Would you like a cup of tea?" Lydia asked, regretting her brusque manner at the door.

"No, thank you, Mrs. Dev—uh—"

"Haycock."

He smiled, obviously embarrassed. "Mrs. Haycock, it's...it's all been so long. The reason I came is to find out if you'd heard from Joe. Last news I had, he'd gone down somewhere in the eastern region of Vietnam. Then there was that television report. I swear the man was Joe. Had to have been. Or his twin, anyway, and Joe never mentioned anything about a twin. Did you see the special, too?"

Lydia nodded. "The man certainly looked like Joe but...but I can't believe it was."

"Maybe not, but the odd thing is he looked just like Joe would have looked today if he'd...that is...if he were here. He didn't look like the Joe I chummed around with. Do you know what I mean?"

"Yes, I understand what you're saying, but the man couldn't possibly have been Joe. If Joe has been alive all these years, why hasn't he contacted me?"

Gallagher shook his head. "It's a puzzle, all right. And you say you've heard nothing in all these years?"

"Not a thing, Mr. Gallagher, and now—"

"And your daughter? Has she had any contact with him to your knowledge?" He leaned forward in his chair, his face intent and serious.

Lydia felt a twinge of impatience. "Mr. Gallagher, neither of us has heard from Joe since he was reported missing. We've accepted the fact that he's dead, and the coincidence of seeing another man who looks like him hasn't changed that belief. Now, unless there's anything else I can do for you..." She rose from her chair and went to the hall closet.

He seemed reluctant to leave but finally stood, still shaking his head at the mystery of it all.

"Mrs. Haycock," he said, taking his coat from her, "if you should happen to hear from Joe—oh, I know it's a long shot—but just in case...here's my card and I'd appreciate a call."

Lydia scanned the plain white card embossed with his name and its title, Investment Counseling, and frowned. "Mr. Gallagher, I don't see—"

He stopped buttoning his coat to explain. "Well, I owe Joe a favor. He went out of his way once to risk his life for me. I never expected to have the chance to repay him after he went missing, but now...whatever I can do to find out if he's still alive..."

He let the remainder of the sentence drop. Implying, Lydia thought, that he seemed to be the only person interested in doing so. The gibe offended her. What did he know about her or her efforts to find her missing husband? Really, it was enough that her own daughter should make the same accusation. But a complete stranger!

"My husband is dead, Mr. Gallagher," she repeated emphatically. "And by the way, how did you manage to find my address without knowing my married name?''

Gallagher paused in the doorway. After a long moment, he said, ''I thought I mentioned it. A buddy of mine works at the Pentagon. He tracked down your address. My apologies that he neglected to tell me you'd changed your name, as well. I hope to hear from you, Mrs. Haycock. Goodbye.'' He turned and walked down the sidewalk to a navy blue car.

Lydia waited in the doorway until the car drove off. She didn't believe his explanation about the address. But what bothered her more was the expression on his face when she'd asked. The amiability had been replaced by a coolness that pierced right through her. As if he were already planning his next step and she'd become no more than an anonymous face in a crowd.

She locked the door and headed at once for the second-floor stairway leading to the attic. Half an hour later, she found what she'd been looking for in a carton of letters. God only knew why she'd bothered saving them. For Meg, originally, but later she found herself unable to hand them over. Getting rid of them was too obvious a denial of thirteen years with a man she'd once considered a hero.

Joseph Devlin. Summa cum laude graduate of West Point. The catch every girl dreamed about. Except the reality turned out to be so very different. Lydia sighed and leaned against the trunk that had been shipped home in lieu of Joe's body. So many years...so many wasted years. She felt the blur of tears and picked up the thin blue piece of stationery that had slipped into her lap. Here it was.

Noel Gallagher. She squinted in the gloomy attic, deciphering Joe's backhand scrawl. "It's taken me some time to figure out this new guy, Noel Gallagher, and it's a damn good thing I finally did because I just found out today he's going to team up with me on a couple of missions. He's got to be the sneakiest, most ruthless son of a B I've ever met. And you can imagine I've encountered a few in the service." The letter was blacked out then by the censors and there was no further reference to Gallagher.

Lydia folded up the paper and tucked it into her shirt pocket. She had a bad feeling about the visit from Gallagher. He'd appeared so frank, almost bumbling in his sincerity. Certainly he didn't match the description of the man Joe wrote about. But doubt nagged. Why come all this way for information he could have obtained through his friend in the Pentagon? Hadn't an officer there told Meg their records still showed Devlin as missing, presumed dead?

She packed up the rest of the letters and decided to look up the name of the hotel in Bangkok that Meg had called from on arrival. Of course, there was nothing Meg could do about the incident all the way from Thailand. But Lydia had to discuss Gallagher with someone. And she wasn't yet ready to confide in Jeffrey.

MEG'S EYES blinked open. Her heart's thudding echoed the pounding on her door. The glow of the clock radio told her it was almost daybreak.

"Open!" a muffled voice commanded from the hall.

The doorknob jiggled, then a key turned in the lock. Meg bolted upright in bed and just had time to clutch the sheet to her when the door burst open, spewing half a dozen policemen into the center of her room.

Meg gasped. "What on earth . . . !" came out high-pitched and terrified.

One of the men, in a tan uniform decked with stripes, strode over to Meg's bed. His face was pugnacious and he thrust out an arm, barking, "Passport!"

"All right, all right." Meg tried not to look at the guns in their hands. She was more frightened than she'd ever been in her life, but there was no way she'd get out of bed in front of a bunch of leering soldiers.

The one who exuded authority merely by twitching his face glared down at Meg. For a frightening moment she thought he was going to fling her out of bed.

"Passport!" he shouted.

"There, over there in my bag." Meg pointed to the chair by the window.

The officer grabbed the purse and flung it onto the bed. "Passport!"

While Meg fumbled in her bag, the other men nosed around the room, opening drawers, lifting up the assorted toiletries on the chest and poking through her open suitcase.

Meg located the passport, dropped it from her trembling hands, then picked it up again, opening it to the identification page, and thrust it at the officer.

He peered at it for some time, grunted and tossed it back onto the bed. Then he walked over to the men rummaging through the suitcase and spoke rapidly to them.

"Excuse me, but I hope you people have a search warrant." She forced the words out but her voice was an indignant squeak. The police glanced up, then turned back to their examination of her belongings. "I said," she repeated, gathering her courage "do you have a search warrant?"

"They don't need one—unfortunately."

All eyes in the room shifted toward the door where Conor stood, framed by the dim light from the hall. Meg couldn't recall ever being so grateful to see someone.

The head officer marched over to Conor and demanded his passport. Meg began to think that word was the only English one the man knew. After the officer examined Conor's identification, he nodded at Meg and jerked his head toward the door, signaling the others. When they'd left, Conor bolted the door behind them.

"What—what was all that about? They just burst into my room when I was sleeping. They even had a key." The words poured out in a gush of fright and relief. Meg felt tears well up and her throat close.

Conor sat on the edge of her bed. She was a pretty sorry sight and he was almost tempted to smile. Her reddish-gold hair exploded around her face, making her look about twelve years old.

But he'd been standing in the doorway long enough to know she'd handled the whole business with aplomb.

"Are you all right, Meg?" His hands instinctively came up to her shoulders, bare except for the narrow straps of a silken nightgown peeking above the sheet.

She nodded, still too choked up to speak.

"You've just had your first encounter with Thailand's drug squad. Not a very pleasant bunch."

"But why me? I don't have any drugs with me. I don't use anything stronger than aspirin."

This time he did smile. "This hotel has a reputation for hosting drug dealers, users, hookers, transvestites—you name it. Whatever vice your heart desires can be delivered right to your room, day or night."

She returned his smile with a faint one of her own. "So that's why they kept asking me if I wanted anything else. I thought they just had an overachiever on the room-service desk."

The room filled with Conor's laughter. "You've got a lot of spunk, Meg Devlin." But he swore under his breath. He had an ugly feeling Gallagher was behind the raid. When he'd reported to Gallagher after returning Meg to the hotel last night, Conor had casually mentioned that she'd checked into a local fleabag. At his further remark that he'd had trouble convincing her to go north with him, Gallagher had paused, then simply ordered him to arrive at the hotel at daybreak. The permit was on its way and the Devlin woman would be ready. Bastard!

Meg gave a nervous laugh. "The spunk was all show, believe me. They had a key, Conor." The statement was pitched as a question.

"Probably got it from Reception. You have to be careful here. Sometimes the cops run a scam with the hotel people. They plant some dope in your belongings and extort American currency from the victim as a favor instead of an arrest."

"That's awful!"

Conor shrugged. "It happens everywhere, Meg, not just in this part of the world. Now, I'll wait outside your door while you get dressed. I have some good news for you."

"What?"

"I got a permit to travel up to the camp. For me and my assistant. So—" he stood and grinned down at her "—you just got a new job."

CHAPTER FOUR

LYDIA REPLACED THE telephone in its cradle and gently rubbed the furrowed ridge above her eyes. Suddenly, life was getting very complicated. She had a sense of being swept up in a flood of events completely beyond her control. The recent collision of past and present would not turn out well. She was certain of that now. Meg had vanished into thin air.

"Checked out! Checked out!" The hotel clerk's high-pitched voice had repeated. "No forward," he'd insisted when Lydia, fighting a surge of panic, had pressed further.

So, now what? she wondered. She hated this helplessness—the lack of control that seemed now to dominate her life.

"Lydia?" Jeffrey called from the front door. "Ready to go?"

"Hmm?" she murmured absently. "Yes, dear, I'll be right there. Just checking my lipstick." Lydia automatically patted the smooth chignon at the nape of her neck, ran a finger along the edge of her lower lip and, picking up her purse, headed along the hallway to her husband.

She hadn't yet found the right time to tell Jeffrey why Meg had gone to Thailand. She only hoped that her daughter would be sensible enough to contact her with a new address as soon as possible. The thought brought a quick, cynical smile. Sensible and Meg—a paradox indeed!

MEG'S HEAD rolled against the back of the passenger seat in the Toyota as it took a sharp curve, awakening her.

"So," she began, running her tongue along the inside of her mouth to loosen the sleep, "I'm curious. I know you said you'd see me today, but at five-thirty in the morning in the middle of a police raid?"

Conor smiled. "Do you always come out of a deep sleep with an instant question?"

She straightened in her seat, pulling down the T-shirt that had crept up above the waistband of her cotton jeans. "I wasn't *that* asleep."

"Enough to snore."

"I don't snore."

His grin widened. "That's what everyone says who snores."

Meg held a hand against her eyes, shielding them from the flash of sunlight as the car rounded another curve. She leaned down to get her sunglasses out of the pack at her feet.

"I'm not everyone and when I say I don't do something," she announced, "I don't. Now, please answer the question."

The whimsical puff of hair that stuck out from the back of her head was at odds with the pose she was attempting to strike. Conor smiled. He had the feeling she consisted of layers of personae. He wondered when he'd get to the real Meg Devlin. Even more, he wondered if he'd still like what he found.

"There's no mystery to it, believe me. It's a long drive to Chiang Rai. When I got the clearance, I knew you'd want to leave right away. I'm sorry I didn't call last night, but it was late when I got home and found the permit had been hand-delivered."

"How come such VIP treatment?"

"Why so suspicious?" he countered. "I've established a few contacts with Bangkok police since I've lived here."

"How long have you lived in Bangkok?"

There was a slight pause. "About ten years."

"Don't you ever miss home?" she asked.

"Home?" Conor turned from the windshield.

He made the word sound foreign.

"The States—America."

Conor continued staring at her, then went back to his driving. He had a sudden flash of his brother, Eric, slumped in his wheelchair. After a long silence, he muttered, "I left home when I was eighteen."

The curt response eliminated the next question she'd had poised. No point in going into family if the concept of home drew a blank. *And I thought I had family problems!*

"Can we go straight on to Chiang Rai today?" Meg steered the talk in another direction.

"Too far. We'll stay the night in Chiang Mai and head north early in the morning." He braked, allowing a bus jammed with people to overtake him on the two-lane paved highway.

Meg shivered. "I'm glad I decided not to rent a car and drive myself. They tackle the road like lunatics."

"Just be grateful you're not a passenger sharing a seat with three or four other women, their kids and their chickens."

"You're speaking from experience?"

"I've done my share of local transport. It can be damned uncomfortable, especially when someone decides to bring a goat on board."

"You're joking."

"Yeah, kind of. Actually, the biggest animal I traveled with was a pig. On its way to market and not too happy about it. Wouldn't get off my foot the whole trip. I'd gladly have butchered the thing myself."

Her laughter filled the car, easing out the wrinkles of tension between them. Meg leaned back into the seat. The picture of Conor wedged in a row of diminutive Thais and one large hog stayed with her a long time. His low-key, easy humor pleased her. Perhaps, she thought, this trip won't be so difficult, after all.

The miles of crops and green plantations gradually gave way to hills studded with patches of jungle as the populous regions of central Thailand disappeared. Letting the fallout from her early wake-up call by Thai police catch up with her, Meg dozed off again.

Occasionally, Conor glanced over at her. He knew the road well enough to be bored with the drive and found himself drawn to his passenger. Tiny puffs of exhaled air billowed the strands of hair that fell across her forehead and cheek. She was as attractive in sleep as she was awake. A patch of red crept up along the cheek pressed against the headrest and she clung to the side of the seat like a youngster clutching a teddy bear. But there was nothing childlike in the sleeping form that curved against the door.

Full breasts strained against the dipping neckline of her T-shirt, and taut thighs filled the jeans she wore. Conor clenched his jaw and forced his eyes back to the road. He had a long day ahead of him!

He suddenly recalled the scene at the Malaya Hotel that morning. Bloody vice cops and bloody Gallagher, too. Of course, she'd agreed to leave Bangkok after being rescued from such a nasty situation. He sneaked another look at her, sleeping innocently at his side. There was a quality about the woman that begged for loving and protection—two things he hadn't given a woman in a long time.

When he pulled off the road almost two hours later, Meg was still sleeping. Conor patted her gently on the shoulder.

"Meg? I'm stopping here for a break."

"Hmm?" She raised her head and looked about in confusion.

"Where are we? Are we in Chiang Mai?"

"Not yet. At least another three hours. Are you hungry?"

"A bit, but I'm dying for an ice-cold cola. I don't understand why I'm so tired. I don't usually sleep like this."

"You're not used to the heat and you're probably still suffering from jet lag. It takes a few days to acclimatize. Come on, I'll treat you to that drink and a bite to eat."

Conor opened his door, climbed out and stretched. He waited while Meg brushed her hair and straightened out her clothes. "Lock up," he reminded her. "Otherwise the radio might go missing while we're eating lunch."

"Sounds like home," she muttered, stepping out into the glaring sun. "O-o-oh, that's bright. And sticky. Is it always like this?"

"It'll be cooler up-country."

"Up-country?" she asked, puzzled.

"In the hills."

"Is that where Chiang Rai is?"

"Not exactly. It's on the Mekong River at the foot of the hill-tribe territory."

Meg considered this for some time. "So you're saying we may have to go beyond Chiang Rai to find my father?"

She was quick, he had to give her that. He nodded. "It's a possibility."

"I never really thought. I guess I ought to have been prepared for something like that. It makes sense, of course. That might explain how my father's managed to escape publicity or notice for so long."

Conor realized that the news had upset her. He also noticed that she never once mentioned the other possibility—that the man might not be her father at all.

"Let's eat," he said, taking her by an elbow. They walked across the paved road to the tables and chairs outside the highway café he always stopped at on visits north. "A good meal, a cold drink and a rest-room break will help get rid of some of that jet lag."

They sat down at a table in the shade of a sprawling banyan tree and Conor ordered lunch. He smiled when she downed her soft drink in one gulp. "More?" he asked.

She wiped the edge of her mouth with the back of her hand. "I might burst. But I'm still thirsty."

"Water?"

"Dare I?"

"It's okay. They've got Evian water here."

She was amazed. "Here? In this dinky place in the middle of nowhere?"

"A lot of foreigners travel this road to Chiang Mai and, believe it or not, this is one of the best restaurants in the north."

When the waiter had brought plates of wide rice noodles flecked with bits of vegetables, greens and shreds of chicken, Meg wasted no time testing the accuracy of Conor's claim. "Delicious!" she announced around a mouthful of noodles. "Though it's a bit difficult keeping these things around my chopsticks."

"Watch how the locals eat. Tuck your head down to the plate and scoop the noodles toward you."

After a few unsuccessful attempts, Meg decided to use the large spoon next to her plate. It was either that or take all day to eat lunch.

"Glad to see you can be resourceful," Conor remarked.

He was teasing, but she felt a girlish thrill at the implied compliment. She watched his expert use of the chopsticks and envied his relaxed, casual manner in the midst of a culture and people that were completely foreign to her. Of course, he'd said he'd lived in Thailand for ten years. But she had a feeling he'd probably fit in as easily anywhere else.

She had to admit he seemed very different from the solemn, haggard man who'd knocked at her door on Saturday. Less than three days ago, though it felt like years. And yesterday, when she'd met him in the street outside her hotel, he'd been testy and more than a bit pushy. An aggressive journalist who'd say and do anything to get a story.

But since their departure from Bangkok early that morning, he'd been almost solicitous toward her. Meg wondered if he'd really accepted the fact that there'd be no story for him in the trip to Chiang Rai. She hoped so, because he was all she had for the moment. She had no choice but to trust him.

"You're quiet all of a sudden," Conor remarked from across the table. "Anxious about getting to Chiang Rai?"

Meg nodded. His habit of getting to the crux of the matter took her aback. She wasn't sure she liked having her mind read so easily.

"I suppose I don't need to remind you about getting your hopes up and all that nonsense? Guess you've heard lines like that a lot in the past."

The sudden appearance of a saffron-robed man holding a metal bowl and wandering from table to table provided escape from his questions. The man, thin with a shaved head, smiled shyly at them but bypassed their table.

"A beggar?" she asked as the man headed away from the restaurant.

"No, a Buddhist monk. They receive food and drink from the local shopkeepers and take back to the monastery whatever leftovers people here don't want."

"Sounds like a hard life."

"It is, but learning humility is part of their training. It helps when they go into the army."

"The army?"

"At the age of eighteen, most young men here are encouraged to spend a year in a monastery and a year in the army."

"What a strange combination. It must be very confusing for them—to adjust to two such different philosophies, I mean."

"Not as difficult as you think. Oddly enough, the disciplines involved in both types of training are very similar. And these youngsters have the benefit of learning some of the moral issues of both army and Buddhism. Like the yin and yang of Chinese philosophy—two sides of a coin." Conor got to his feet to pay the waiter. "We'd better leave. We've a long drive ahead of us."

Meg followed him across the road to the car. "I can't imagine our soldiers back home having to put in a year in a monastery and beg for their food."

Conor, reaching in front of her to unlock her door, paused to say, "No, neither can I. Most Westerners are only interested in one side of the coin."

Meg didn't miss the sarcasm in his voice. Conor Tremayne, she concluded, was not going to be an easy man to get to know. Why that realization daunted her, she couldn't say. Except that the voice inside that kept reminding her he was a stranger and a journalist in need of a story was weakening. Alongside it, she heard another, smaller voice whispering, "Trust." The other side of the coin? she wondered.

"TELL ME something about your father."

Conor's unexpected question threw Meg. Not that she hadn't expected the question to pop up at some time during the trip. They'd just stopped for a break at another roadside café and she was still feeling dazed from the monotony of sitting long hours in a car. She stared incomprehensibly at Conor, trying to put together an answer.

"Tea?" he asked when the waitress appeared.

"It must be ninety degrees in the shade," she grumbled. "Don't they have cold drinks?"

"Tea's better in the heat than soda. Makes you sweat and the evaporation cools you off."

"An interesting theory, but I'll take a cola thanks."

Conor shrugged, gave the order and got back to his question. "What kind of man was your father?"

She hesitated, searching for the right words. "A man's man, I believe the expression is. He was a sportsman and a hunter. Very attractive, too." Meg paused. "I . . . I think he enjoyed the company of women. There were quarrels when I was growing up about flirtations at parties and so on. Nothing serious. I mean, I'm certain he was never unfaithful. He adored my mother. It was just that he was very charming." Meg took a swallow of the soft drink in front of her and pulled a face. "Yuck! Lukewarm Cola."

"There's more tea in the pot," Conor teased. "What kind of relationship did your parents have? I mean," he hastened to elaborate at her frown, "you referred to their arguments that day I came to your place in Boston."

"They argued about silly little things, but I always had a sense of something deeper and more serious in their quarrels. As if they both had made a decision not to fight about what was really bugging them. It used to frighten me when I was a kid. There was a time when I thought they'd actually split up. My mother took me to my grandparents' for a whole summer. At the end of it, we were all together again and everything seemed okay. He went missing less than six months later." Meg stared down at her drink, toying with the plastic straw.

Conor waited before continuing. "The only reason I asked is that I'm trying to piece together some explanation for his disappearing act all these years. There has to be a good reason why he's never contacted you."

"Don't think that same question hasn't been plaguing me since I saw that film. Perhaps he's tried to get in touch with me and hasn't been able to."

"Perhaps." Conor's voice indicated doubt.

"Some people never experience close family ties. My father disappeared and left a huge gap in our lives. Just because you obviously had no strong family unit—" She stopped, shamed not so much by the childishness of the gibe as by the wince of pain she caught in his face.

"Finished?" he asked.

She nodded. He tossed some money on the table and headed out to the car. Chastened, Meg followed. After all, she reasoned, he was the one who'd brought up the whole issue of relationships.

An hour of uncomfortable silence later, the car slowed at the outskirts of a large city. Throngs of people rode bicycles or walked along the shoulders of the highway.

"Chiang Mai?" she asked.

"Yes." He bit the answer off without bothering to look her way.

Wonderful conversation this trip, Meg thought. Stimulating and quite pleasant, really. She smiled, stifling a desire to toss back a flip comment. She'd gotten used to sulking silences with David. Though sneaking a glance at the way Conor changed gears and braked impatiently for traffic, Meg doubted the word *sulk* could apply. Repressed fury might seem a touch melodramatic. Ice-cold anger would do. Bottled.

The image of Conor exploding fascinated her. Meg knew she had a perverse streak in her. She'd secretly enjoyed needling David the last few weeks of their relationship. But Conor. How far she could push him would be a challenge.

She stared out the car window as they drove into the heart of the city, passing blocks of tin shanties followed by modest, stucco bungalows and sweeping pagoda-style buildings. A long way from good old Boston, Massachusetts. No, best not to push at all. He was her only ticket into the refugee camp.

"Is this rush hour or something? Where are all these people going?" Meg jerked her head toward the window. "Some kind of holiday?"

A spray of water shot across the windshield. Conor braked sharply, lurching forward to the bumper of the taxi ahead of him.

"Jeez," he muttered. "Of course, I should've remembered."

"What?"

"Close your window quickly," he shouted, cranking up the handle at his side.

A drizzle of water trickled down the outside of her window the moment she'd finished rolling it up. She peered out to see a small boy holding a water pistol in his hand. He flashed an enormous, toothless grin.

"What's going on?"

"Songkran," Conor explained. "Thailand's celebration of New Year."

"In the middle of April?"

"It's based on their astrological calendar. It spans four days. There are prayers, visits to temple with food to be blessed and offerings to monks to gain merit for the next life. The last day is a bang-up water party. Everyone is fair game. They use water pistols, hoses, buckets—anything that'll hold water. Fortunately it all ends at dusk, but I have to warn you, we might get wet when we get out of the car."

"Sounds like fun."

"Our hotel is just down this road across the street from the hotel. I booked a couple of rooms for us before we left Bangkok."

"You were lucky to get rooms if there's a big holiday."

"Well, April isn't exactly the height of the tourist season here. Too hot. This is mainly a Thai celebration. Here we are. I suggest we make a dash for the door and get our luggage out of the trunk later."

The car swung into the drive of a cream-colored two-story hotel. Meg saw a line of uniformed staff waiting, armed with buckets and hoses.

"Surely they wouldn't—"

But Conor was already out of the car, sprinting past the lineup toward the carved wooden doors of the hotel.

"What happened to chivalry?" Meg wondered aloud. "Well, I wanted to cool off. Here's my chance."

She scrambled out, ducked her head and ran. A torrent of water crashed over her shoulders before she'd cleared the front of the car. She raised her head, gasping, to the laughing face of a young girl in a white uniform. The girl was even wetter than Meg. But not for long. A man in chef's whites took aim with a plastic hose and soaked the rest of Meg.

The shock of the icy-cold water took her breath away. Then she laughed—a loud, hearty peal that encouraged the others to take aim. Meg grabbed for the hose and turned it on the line of hotel employees. They split ranks, screaming encouragement and giggling at the horrified expressions on the occupants of a tour bus that had just pulled into the drive.

The sudden diversion allowed Meg a chance to dash through the open doors into a cool, tiled lobby. The only signs of water battle inside were several puddles leading up to a teak reception counter.

Conor was leaning against it, wearing a grin on his wet face. His black hair glistened under the dim glow of the overhead lights. There were just a few large dark patches on his shirt and pants. Meg guessed he'd run the gauntlet faster than she had.

Conor watched her trail a wake of waterdrops behind her as she made her way across the lobby. Her legs swung out stiffly in half circles, weighted down by her sodden jeans. The T-shirt clinging to her torso left no doubt about the way she'd look in a bikini—or less. Conor politely forced his gaze up away from the dark areolas poking against the wet, pink fabric.

"Everyone man for himself at Songkran," he quipped. He held aloft a shiny key. "Let's get out of these clothes. I've bribed the clerk to collect our luggage."

Conor noticed the man behind the desk ogling Meg and swiftly ushered her by the elbow to the elevators. "I've been here before. We're on the second floor, with a view of the canal."

When the elevator door closed, the dampness from their clothing filled the interior with vapor.

"It's like a sauna in here," Meg murmured. Conor stood close to her, his arm brushing hers as the car began to ascend. The enclosed space made Meg's heady swim. She needed a huge gulp of fresh air. As the car reached the second floor, she literally jumped out.

Conor led the way down a hallway richly carpeted in an Oriental floral design. The place was obviously a big step up from the Malaya Hotel.

"You're in here," he announced, stopping to unlock a door and, stepping inside, motioned to another closed door in the wall opposite the double bed. "I'm in there."

He turned abruptly to retreat but Meg was right on his heels. The tip of his chin banged against her forehead.

"Sorry! Are you all right?" His hands automatically went to her shoulders and rested there.

"Just wet." She smiled up at him. "It was fun, wasn't it?"

He returned the smile. "You handled your first Songkran with adequate dignity."

She laughed. "I don't think my charge into the hotel could be described quite that way."

"Well, perhaps a slight exaggeration." Conor's mouth hovered at her hairline, his breath stirring a curling tendril of hair. His fingers made a languid sweep up the sides of her neck and settled into the twisted mass of wet curls. "You're soaked," his lips whispered against her forehead.

Meg shivered. She was certain steam was wafting from her body. When his mouth trailed a line of light kisses across her brow, she instinctively raised her face to his.

Conor let his lips brush down to the tip of her nose. Then he cupped her chin in his palm, tilting her mouth to his.

It started out as a getting-to-know-you kind of kiss. Lips tracing lips—tasting the salty-sweet mix of heat and water evaporating off skin; parting the fullness of her mouth to find more sweetness inside. Conor lost himself then. Urgency overtook him, demanding more.

He moved his fingers down her neck and along the ribbed neckline of her T-shirt. He felt the intake of air from her mouth on his and knew it was as good for her as it was for him. So good. So damn wonderfully good. Quickly now, brushing past the round swelling of her breasts, his hands reached for the bottom edge of her shirt and began to pull it up.

Meg arched into the curve of his body, lost her balance and stumbled back. His hands stopped, resting casually on her hips. Their lips moved apart. She seized the moment, knowing at once she had to end this. Immediately.

With a toss of her hair, she leaned against the wall and forced a cheerful smile.

"Happy New Year," she said.

The hotel clerk appeared in the doorway with their luggage as if on cue. He grinned at their soggy appearance. "No need shower now. Right?"

Conor passed a hand across his face and swore silently. "Wrong, my friend. A cold shower. That's what I need right now." With that, he waved a finger at Meg and strolled through the door connecting his room to hers.

CHAPTER FIVE

GALLAGHER ROLLED his chair up to the computer terminal and switched it on. When the demand for the password flashed on the monitor, he quickly typed in "Oz."

Ironically, he'd gotten the idea for the code word from Devlin himself. They'd been paired as a team for little more than a month when Devlin had made a remark about the surrealism of Laos.

"This joint is weirder than the Land of Oz," he'd said. "Even the locals are munchkins compared to you and me."

Devlin had been struck by the comparison, going on to point out that Gallagher himself resembled the Scarecrow in search of a brain. Devlin had been like that. Always looking for a way to put him down or get a rise out of him. It was one of the reasons why Gallagher had come to hate him, even before it all fell apart that day almost twenty years ago.

From the beginning, everything had gone wrong....

They were supposed to take a truck down the stretch of road between Ban Houie Sai and Luang Prabang. The territory in between was unofficially held by the Communist Pathet Lao, but bands of ragtag royalist soldiers roamed the area engaging in sniping contests with the insurgents.

The war in Vietnam was winding down, while the struggle for control in neighboring Laos was just in high gear. Yet the country was still open to tourism, and "hippie" backpackers looking for the ultimate "trip" unknowingly risked their lives to visit the opium dens in the countryside.

Traveling as backpackers had been Devlin's idea. Getting the truck was Gallagher's job and when the deal fell through, Devlin razzed him unmercifully. They couldn't fly, not with the type of cargo they were carrying, and so they settled on a local bus. Two days before they were to leave, one of the buses was stopped along the same route by a bunch of Pathet Lao and the driver had been executed.

So Gallagher's nerves were already on edge by the time they boarded their bus. It was packed with locals fleeing one war zone and heading into another. They brought with them families, huge baskets of clothing, food, and any animals they could carry. The bus sounded like Noah's Ark. Gallagher felt the stirrings of a migraine before they'd gone ten miles.

None of it seemed to faze Devlin. He sprawled back in his seat and dozed. Gallagher was wedged between a window and a Laotian who sat cross-legged on the wooden seat with a black rooster on his lap. That was why, when the bus unexpectedly fishtailed to a stop, Gallagher had so much trouble getting out.

Devlin was already kicking open the emergency door at the rear of the bus by the time Gallagher identified the soldiers blocking the road as Pathet Lao.

"Devlin!" he shouted, scrambling over the man next to him.

Devlin stood at the door. Everyone in the bus was screaming and trying to squeeze past him or crawl out through the windows. "Head toward the river. Good luck!" Devlin called out before jumping onto the road.

Gallagher pushed through the melee. Chickens flapped in panic and youngsters wailed. Outside, he heard the staccato sound of semiautomatic rifles. He knocked aside a woman standing in the doorway and leaped to the ground. His right foot came down on the edge of an overturned basket and twisted. A knife of pain seared up his leg. Damn! All he needed. And where the hell was Devlin, that son of a bitch?

The hysterical confusion in and around the bus gave him the chance to cut across the paved road into the trees. There was a shout behind him and the deafening rat-a-tat of an AK-47. Not daring a glance behind, Gallagher ran, pounding his injured right foot into the forest floor. It would only be a matter of time before they came looking for him. Someone on the bus would report that two *farangs* had disappeared into the jungle.

He had no idea where he was heading. He knew the river was west of the road because they'd followed it for part of the trip. How far was another problem. A big one, given the pain in his foot. The pack, weighted down with its precious cargo, thumped against his back. Sweat rolled down his face, filling his mouth with salt and the dry, iron taste of adrenaline. He ran and ran until his chest threatened to burst. The pain in his foot and leg was becoming unbearable. But he shut out the thought that he might not make it. He would make it. He *had* to. If only to get Devlin.

A branch struck his face. His right forearm shot up to protect his eyes, blinding him. He stepped forward into space, a gasping freefall, instinctively curling his body into a fetal ball ready for the landing.

He never knew how or exactly where he ended up, only that when he regained consciousness he was staring into the cold black tubular muzzle of an AK-47....

Gallagher flicked off the computer switch. As the machine whirred softly to a stop, he thought again about Devlin's ridiculous nickname for him—the Scarecrow. The memory elicited a quirk of a smile. Devlin had him pegged wrong from the beginning. If there was any character from Oz he resembled, it was the Tin Man. Except that Gallagher wasn't looking for a heart. He wanted that cold void inside to stay just as it was. It was what he needed to ensure that finally, Devlin would be his.

TREMAYNE CAUGHT a glimpse of her out of the corner of his eye. She was wearing sunglasses—understandable, considering they were driving northeast at midmorning—but he'd seen the rim of shadow at breakfast. Apparently she hadn't slept any better than he had. He cursed himself for the hundredth time since last night.

You'd think, at the ripe age of thirty-eight, that hormones would be more controllable. He'd behaved like an adolescent jerk scoring his first real kiss. And even though the whole thing had been no big deal, it had definitely occurred at the wrong point in time. He'd have been better off keeping his lips on her forehead in a brotherly gesture. The problem was he didn't feel brotherly toward her at all. Not a bit.

Anyway, she'd liked it, too. Her response had suggested she could handle herself in the big world of sexuality. Still, his timing was all off and because he couldn't keep his lustful thoughts to himself, he'd drawn an invisible line between them. Now he had to make sure that line didn't widen into a gap. He had a job to do and he'd hoped to gain enough leverage with Gallagher to buy himself out of this moonlighting career.

He watched her roll a square of scarf into a headband and then, arms raised, flip the wild mane of hair into a ponytail. The sleeveless shirt she was wearing gaped, revealing a flash of underarm and a white bra. Conor shifted his gaze back to the windshield of the car.

"Is it always this hot here?"

The unexpected question—the first thing she'd said since they'd driven away from the hotel—startled him enough to make the car swerve slightly.

"I'll turn up the air-conditioning," he offered, fiddling with the knobs on the dashboard. "It should be a bit cooler up-country but this is the hottest time of the year. The monsoons are approaching. I should warn you, too, that the place we'll be staying at in Chiang Rai won't be as comfortable as the hotel yesterday."

"That's okay. I've done enough camping in my life to know about 'roughing it.'"

She sounded offended, as if she wanted to clarify that she was no sissy. Conor didn't reply. He doubted that camping back in the U.S.A. would be sufficient initiation for what might lie ahead.

Then she showed him that he shouldn't underestimate her.

"About last night," she began. "I think we should clear up what happened right now before... well, before we get to Chiang Rai. I can't afford to be sidetracked by... by any superficial display of hormones—if you get my drift. You've kindly offered to take me to this camp and there's nothing in this trip for you as far as a story is concerned, so..."

"You're telling me you want to keep our 'relationship' on a strictly business level," he finished for her.

There was a slight pause. "Yes, that's it exactly."

"Fine," he said. Another layer peeled away, he thought. It was ironic, really. She'd beaten him to the draw and specified the terms right away. No, he had certainly better not underestimate her. Though he felt a small disappointment that she obviously didn't want emotional involvement any more than he did.

THEY ARRIVED in Chiang Rai in the late afternoon. In spite of the heat and her fatigue, Meg felt her pulse quicken at the thought that she was now that much closer to her destination. She stared out at the dusty street lined with a blend of old and new; concrete boxes adjoining wooden pagoda-style buildings trimmed with elaborate carvings and framed with bursts of frangipani and hibiscus trees.

"When will we go to the camp?" she asked.

"The camp's at least thirty kilometres upriver. We'll have to hire a boat and get some supplies for the trip. I'm aiming for tomorrow morning."

As if sensing what she was feeling, he added, "I've a friend here who can arrange everything. We'll stay at his place and leave at daybreak. Okay?"

Meg failed to hide the disappointment in her voice. "I guess. Will I be able to make a telephone call from here?"

"A phone call? Where to?"

"I didn't leave a forwarding address for my mother."

"There's no phone where we'll be staying, but I know you can make long-distance calls from the local post office."

Tremayne took a side street, then steered his battered green Toyota along a graveled drive into a compound of buildings nestled behind a high fence. Half a dozen chickens flew across the dirt courtyard.

"This is my friend's place. He sometimes rents out rooms to *farangs*. As I said before, it'll be a bit rough but it's authentic."

"Farangs?"

"Foreigners."

He pulled the car up in front of a wooden structure that looked like a fancy tree house on stilts. The engine had scarcely been turned off when a man in a brightly-colored sarong tripped down the stairs from another similar tree house across the compound.

Forming his hands prayer-fashion, he bowed slightly to Conor and then to Meg. Then his face creased in a warm smile. "Welcome to my humble house, Mr. Conor. What an honor! I am sorry we have not prepared something special for your arrival."

Conor returned the man's greeting and introduced Meg. "My friend, Mr. Pran, and this is my friend

'rom America, Miss Meg Devlin. Please forgive me for
ot giving you adequate notice of our arrival. We are
ere on business, Mr. Pran, but we will need your as-
istance.''

Pran beamed and gave a quick nod. "It is an honor.
Come, I will show you and Miss Meg to your bunga-
ows and then we will talk over some refreshment.
Okay?''

His warm hospitality was engaging and, in spite of
er earlier glumness, Meg found herself warming to
im. ''Very pleased to meet you, Mr. Pran.''

He nodded politely and, clapping his hands, gave
nstructions in Thai to the young woman and older
man standing a few yards behind him.

''Everyone is so formal,'' Meg murmured. ''I hope
you'll tell him to call me Meg.''

''Thais are keen on formality, especially where
names are concerned. I've known Pran for almost five
years and I've only just begun to address him without
the Mister. Because you're a woman, he'll only address you formally.'' Conor reached into the trunk of
the car and handed Meg's suitcase to the girl. He
grabbed his own backpack and indicated that Meg
should follow the girl.

''Pran's wife?'' Meg asked.

''No, his daughter.''

''He doesn't look old enough. She must be at least
eighteen.''

''She is. Pran was only that age when he got married. You may or may not meet his wife. She's very
shy. Usually stays inside the family's house when there
are visitors.''

Meg slung her backpack and purse over her shoulder and walked to the foot of the stairs of one of the tree houses. "These are amazing." She looked up at the small cottage on stilts. The roofline swept upward in replica of a pagoda and the roof itself was thatched with layers of dried palm branches.

Conor smiled. He remembered the first time he'd come to Pran's home years ago and had also stood in awe of its simple beauty.

Meg scanned the courtyard area. It was apparent that there were no plumbing facilities inside the bungalows. "Where's the washroom?"

"Oh, sorry. Forgot about that. See that concrete shed over there? The bathroom part is in one half and the washing room is in the other."

"The washing room?"

"Well, it's not exactly a shower as we know it. There's a cistern of water and a plastic bucket affair. Whatever you do, don't get into the cistern. You scoop out the water and pour it over you. Soap up and, uh, rinse off the same way."

"Sounds like camp. Okay, a good drenching in cold water is just what I need." Meg headed up the stairs to her bungalow. At the top, she called down. "Where will you be if . . . well, if I need you?"

"My bungalow's over there—next to Pran's house. Settle in and relax. I'm going to be arranging things with Pran."

"I'd like to be in on that, too."

He shook his head. "Sorry, Meg. Pran's a very traditional guy. He wouldn't feel comfortable discussing business with you there."

"But I'm the reason why we're here in the first place. Couldn't you..." She saw something immovable in his face and decided not to push. Muttering about how ridiculous the whole thing was, she stepped inside the bungalow where the young girl was meticulously folding sheets around a mattress lying on a bamboo mat on the floor.

"I'm Meg and really, I can do that myself."

There was a light giggle. The girl covered her mouth with her hand and seemed embarrassed. Then she said something that sounded like, "No ingrish."

Meg pointed to herself and repeated, "Meg."

More giggling followed by, "Lek."

Introductions over, the lack of language brought all talk to an end. They smiled at one another and then Lek backed out of the doorway, giggling all the while.

Meg slid her backpack and purse onto the floor. "Well, at least someone finds me interesting and amusing."

The bungalow's design was almost elegant in its simplicity: paneled teak walls and a polished floor spotted with bamboo mats. A window set in each of three walls provided some cross ventilation and the bungalow itself, shaded by the trees, was remarkably cool.

Meg slumped onto a squat wooden chair in the center of the room. She had a sudden craving for a thick, chocolate milk shake. Or a soft cozy bed, she thought, eyeing the thin mattress on the floor. Or a deep dive into a clear, cold swimming pool. Or—she shook her head at the unexpected image of Conor's smiling face. A cold shower, she decided, then thought immediately of last night and Conor's parting remark. Silly how something as insignificant as a kiss could cause such tension.

She forced herself out of the chair and began to unpack her suitcase. A good dousing in a Thai shower would do the trick. She closed the wooden shutters at the windows and slipped out of her clothes. Wrapping the sash of her silk kimono around her waist, Meg gathered soap, shampoo and towel and headed outside for the shower stall. Although there was no one in sight, she felt ridiculous crossing the dirt courtyard in a flowing, peacock-blue robe. The clothes she'd hastily thrown into her suitcase in Boston had fit right in with cosmopolitan Bangkok. But Chiang Rai was another matter.

When she opened the corrugated tin door of the shed, she realized how much of another matter it was.

A large concrete cistern filled up most of the interior. Dead insects and bits of leaves floated on the brackish water. An orange plastic bucket perched on the ledge of the cistern. A slatted wooden frame covered part of the cement floor that sloped toward a drain in one corner. There were no windows, but light entered through the six-inch gap around the perimeter of the shed between the roof and the walls.

"Well—" Meg sighed "—it sure ain't the Hilton." She hung her robe on a nail on the back of the tin door, positioned her toiletries along the ledge and scooped up a bucket of water. Taking a deep breath, she emptied the bucket over her head and gasped. By the time she was finished, though, her skin had a healthy ruddy glow and she felt terrific.

As she headed back to her bungalow, she heard a soft giggle. Lek stood at the base of the tree house that

Conor had said was used by the family. She motioned
for Meg to wait and ran up the stairs into the house.
When she returned seconds later, she was carrying a
folded cloth that she unfurled into a splash of bright
red and yellow. Then she pulled Meg by the arm toward the guest bungalow.

Inside, Lek helped Meg out of the kimono and
showed her how to wrap the cloth sarong-fashion,
tucking the ends into the hollow between Meg's
breasts.

Standing back, Lek grinned and nodded in satisfaction. "Good. You." She pointed at Meg.

Meg was touched by the gift. She held out the kimono to Lek, but the girl shook her head.

"Please," Meg insisted.

Lek giggled again, but refused to take the kimono.

"I know it's absolutely useless, but it would look
lovely on you," Meg went on, knowing the girl didn't
understand a word she was saying.

"She'd probably rather have something from your
cosmetic bag," said Conor from the open door of the
bungalow.

"Oh, of course." Meg negotiated an awkward bend
in the sarong and plucked her cosmetic bag from the
inner pocket of her suitcase. The immediate delight in
Lek's face confirmed Conor's guess.

Lek pointed to a bottle of pale pink nail polish. Meg
nodded and handed the girl a new tube of red lipstick
and a small plastic jar of hand cream to go with it. Lek
clutched the treasures to her chest and bowed her
head, speaking a stream of Thai as she left.

"You've made a conquest," Conor said after Lek
had gone.

"I hope her father doesn't mind. I mean, Lek certainly doesn't need the makeup. What did she say as she was leaving?"

"Profuse thanks. It would make a flowery translation."

Meg tried to be casual as she walked over to the table where Lek had earlier placed a thermos of tea. She wished she was still wearing the kimono, which wasn't nearly as revealing as the sarong.

"Tea?" she inquired without looking up.

"No, thanks. I've been drinking homemade beer with Pran."

He paused. Meg glanced up from pouring the tea to catch him staring. She felt the telltale heat of a blush creep up her neck and face. "So," she said, "what's on the agenda?"

"We head out to the camp first thing in the morning. Pran's arranged a boat for us. As soon as you're, uh, dressed, we'll make that phone call and get supplies."

"Supplies?" Meg knew she was beginning to sound either senile or hard-of-hearing but none of what he was saying matched what she'd had in mind when they left Bangkok. She'd thought the camp was just a short car trip beyond Chiang Rai.

Conor smiled patiently. "I'll explain everything in full detail when you're ready. Finish your tea and meet me outside in, say, ten minutes?" He paused in the doorway and cleared his throat. "By the way, your, uh, knot's slipping. But it looks terrific. Really."

Meg forced herself to wait until he'd left before checking the front of the sarong. It had indeed slipped, exposing an almost-indecent stretch of bosom.

Damn him and his smirking grin anyway, she thought.

Dressing took less than the time allotted. She decided on a cotton print sundress, grabbed her purse, camera and sunglasses and met Conor as he was getting into the car. Pran stopped talking when Meg approached and bowed courteously to her.

"Miss Meg, you and Mr. Conor will honor us with a meal this evening?"

"Thank you, Pran, that would be lovely." Meg waved to Lek, standing nearby, and joined Conor in the front seat. The car pulled out of the compound and onto the main street.

Once outside, Meg could more fully appreciate the tranquil beauty of Pran's home. Outside the walls, the town was a noisy confusion. Uniformed schoolchildren on their way home waved to their car and, at one stop, ran up to Meg's opened window to ask for candy.

"Candy?" she repeated once the car continued on through the intersection. "Well, at least they weren't demanding money."

"They associate tourists with sweets. I don't know where or when the whole thing started, but you'll have to be firm with them or they'll pester you nonstop. In the hills, the kids ask for American cigarettes, too."

"I draw the line at cigarettes. Speaking of which, I've noticed you haven't had one since the bar in Bangkok. Have you quit?"

"Didn't think you'd enjoy the trip with a smoker."

"You mean you just quit—like that?" She snapped her fingers.

He flashed a grin. "Takes a bit of self-control, that's all."

"Hmm," she murmured. She recalled that last night his self-control hadn't been much in evidence.

"I can summon it when I have to—or want to," he added, reading her mind.

"You said you'd explain about tomorrow," she prompted, not liking where the talk was heading.

She was good at getting back on track, he noted. He parked the car on a side street and switched off the engine. "Okay, this is how it'll go tomorrow. Pran's asked a friend of his to take us by boat up the Mekong to Chiang Saen. That's a small town on the Thai side of the Golden Triangle. The camp's just five kilometres outside of town."

Meg's head was swimming with words hauntingly familiar. Mekong. Golden Triangle. Words she'd read about all those years of trying to forge a link with her missing father. Words that had been written in his letters. Words from his world. She averted her face to the window.

"Everything okay?"

His question was gentle and gave her time to take control. She nodded.

"All right. I told you in Boston that the camp was about fifty miles from here. But the road isn't very good so the best way to travel is by boat. Once we're at the camp, we may have to go farther into the hills."

"Do we go into the hills right from there or return here first?"

"It'll be quicker just to keep on going. That's why we need supplies and if you need any particular clothing—not to say that the kimono wouldn't cause a sensation in the hills, but—"

Meg laughed. "I've got jeans and shorts. Will I need rain gear?"

"No. The monsoons don't start for another month or so. Got good walking shoes?" His eyes followed the long stretch of bare leg to her sandals.

"Jogging shoes."

"They'll do. We're in business, then. Let's do some shopping." Conor opened the car door and started to get out.

"What about my telephone call?"

"Oh, right. We'll hit the post office first. I'm not sure what time they close up for the day."

Meg followed him down a maze of streets and into a white stucco building resplendent with flag and life-size portrait of the king of Thailand. Conor spoke to a clerk at one end of the main room.

"See that telephone over there?" Conor pointed to the wall opposite the office counter. "When the call has been put through, the operator will ring the phone. Just pick it up and you should be connected right away. Don't forget the time difference. You'll probably be getting your mother up in the middle of the night."

Meg hesitated. She didn't want to alarm her mother, but on the other hand, she might not get another chance to call. "It'll be okay. Thanks. How do I pay for this?"

"When you've finished, just go up and ask the rate. Have you got enough *bhats*?"

"I don't know. How much will it cost? "

He frowned, then said, "I think I paid about thirty dollars the last time I called New York from here."

"Will they take American dollars?"

"Are you kidding? They love them. Want me to stay with you?"

"No, I'll be fine." She wasn't sure she wanted him breathing down her neck while she talked to Lydia.

"Okay, then. Maybe I'll take a minute or so and check my answering machine in Bangkok."

She waited by the phone while he walked toward the row of telephones on the opposite wall. The phone she was standing beside rang.

Meg picked up the telephone, mentally stringing together the right words to convince her mother that she knew exactly what she was doing in a remote corner of Thailand with a man she barely knew.

CHAPTER SIX

"YES, DEAR, I can hear you. It's just that..." Lydia turned to look over at Jeffrey, lying next to her in bed. His eyes were closed but she was certain the phone had awakened him. She lowered her voice. "I think you're being very foolish. Yes, yes, I know. All right, what's the name of the hotel there? No hotel? Well, how do I get in touch with you? Isn't there any number at all? What's the name again? Pran... You'll have to spell the last name for me. Okay, I've got it. Now, when are you flying home? When? You'll have to speak up. That's about ten days. Please phone again in a couple of days when you...after you..." Lydia looked at her husband once more. He'd awakened and was propped up on one elbow.

"All right, dear, thanks for calling. Keep in touch. Bye."

Lydia hung up the phone and sank back onto the bed. She reached up to switch off the table lamp and relaxed with a slow, calming exhale.

"Meg?" Jeffrey asked, stretching out beside her.

"Hmm. Calling to say she'd left Bangkok to visit some place in the north."

"Is everything okay? You sounded a bit anxious."

Lydia rolled onto her side. She could barely make out his features in the dark but she knew there'd be an expression of concern in his handsome face.

"Well, apparently she's met a man and she's traveling with him. They're staying with a friend of his. In a place called Chiang something. I've written it down."

"I think you can trust Meg's judgment. Don't worry, she's a big girl." He reached out his arms and wrapped them around her.

Lydia closed her eyes. She hoped she'd get to the bottom of this mystery without having to tell Jeffrey. Not that she was afraid to; she knew him too well for that. More that resurrecting Joe meant dealing with all the unresolved feelings she'd buried the day she received the telegram—something she wasn't prepared to do at this point in her life. Just as she dropped off to sleep, she recalled how Meg had accused her all those years ago of burying her emotions.

So be it, she decided. Let the feelings and Joe stay well buried.

MEG REPLACED the receiver and walked over to the counter. After she paid the clerk, she scanned the room to see if Conor had finished.

"Two calls to America in one day," said the clerk, handing Meg her change and jerking her head toward another line of telephones on the opposite side of the large room.

It was easy to pick out Conor's tall back in the lineup across from her.

Why was Conor telephoning the States? she wondered. And who was he calling?

She saw him hang up the phone and head for the counter to pay for the call.

He flashed a two-hundred watt smile as he walked toward her and Meg felt her pulse quicken.

"All set?" he asked. "How did your call go?"

"Fine. I woke up my mother, of course, but she was relieved to hear from me. I gave her Pran's name but didn't know his address or if he even had a phone."

"He doesn't. Sorry, I should have given you the address, too. At any rate, you'll be able to call your mother back after we've been to the camp."

"What if we don't find out anything?"

His smile disappeared. "We'll have to discuss our options then. Come on, let's go back to Pran's. He's planning a special dinner for us."

She started to follow him out of the post office but hesitated. "Did you make your own call?"

Conor stopped, turning back to look at her. "Yes."

Meg waited for him to mention his call to the States. Instead, he turned around and walked out to the street.

"Coming?" he asked. "We've shopping to do for tomorrow."

An hour later, Meg was still mulling over Conor's obvious lie. Perhaps, she reminded herself, he really had made a call to Bangkok. Perhaps the girl in the post office had been mistaken.

"MORE BEER?" Conor asked.

They were sitting cross-legged on the floor of Pran's house. An assortment of dishes was arranged in front of them on bamboo mats. Pran's wife slipped in and out of the room like a phantom, her smile the only communication with her guests.

Conor leaned closer to whisper in Meg's ear. "Tired? Or is something wrong with the food? They don't expect you to eat everything, but if you can manage a taste of each dish, they'll love you forever."

"No, no, really, everything's wonderful," she replied. It was neither the time nor the place for her questions about his phone call.

He seemed satisfied with her answer and resumed his conversation in Thai with Pran. Moments later, Conor turned to her and suggested they bid good-night to their host. "We're getting up at daybreak, so Pran understands the party is over."

"Please thank him and his wife for me. I especially enjoyed the shrimp."

There were bows and nods of appreciation and approval all around and suddenly, Meg found herself standing at the foot of her bungalow in the dark. Conor leaned against the railing of the stairs.

"They liked you a lot," he was saying, "especially Lek. Did you notice her nails?"

Meg smiled absently. "Yes. Conor—" She broke off, reluctant to mar the evening with questions.

He leaned closer, his breath fanning softly on her cheek. "What is it?"

"Did you call somewhere else this afternoon?"

Conor stepped back. The slant of light from the open doorway of Meg's bungalow fell across his face. "Somewhere else?" he repeated.

"The clerk at the post office said you'd telephoned the States, too."

He looked away, but not before she caught the flash of anger in his face. "Is there some reason why I shouldn't be calling the States?"

She felt foolish then. "I . . . I just wondered if you were still pursuing the story angle. You know, about my father."

"We made an agreement about that, remember?" Conor faced her straight-on. The yellow light from the lamp inside the bungalow made his expression harsh and unpleasant.

Meg felt herself losing ground. "I just wondered, that's all. It's . . . it's very important to me—to keep this thing private, I mean."

"And I don't go back on my promises."

The edge in his voice angered her. "I was merely confirming our business agreement. You needn't be so defensive."

"Are you always so concerned about business?" He moved closer, placing his hands on her shoulders.

The tone of his voice was softer now, but his hands pressed firmly into her bare skin. "I like to keep things straight," she said.

His hands dropped to his sides. "Fair enough," he muttered. "See you in the morning."

Meg watched him stride across the shadowy court-yard to his own bungalow. Why do I insist on boxing myself into the same corner time and time again? she wondered.

Much later, she realized he'd still managed to avoid telling her about the telephone call.

THE EXCITEMENT of cruising down the Mekong River, the banks of Laos on one side and rice paddies of

Thailand on the other, faded after not much more
than an hour.

The sun forced Meg, Conor and Win, their guide,
to huddle in a sweaty clump beneath the small canopy
hastily constructed once they'd emerged from the
morning shade. The long, open boat chugged along at
a maddeningly slow pace. Its owner sat in the stern,
navigating by a twelve-inch pole attached to the out-
board motor. He chewed pensively on the wad of tobacco that bulged in one cheek.

Meg envied him his air of detachment. Sweat had
already soaked through the thin cotton shirt and shorts
she wore. Her skin felt as though it was crawling with
a million invisible bugs. Most likely is, she decided,
squashing a lone mosquito against her arm. Even
Conor and Win had given up their conversation to
stare with glazed expressions at some indeterminate
point in the distance.

She closed her eyes, trying to imagine what this
place must have been like when war was still going on
in Vietnam. What horrors this river had witnessed, its
murky waters churning with exploding mortars and
human flesh. Nausea rolled up from her stomach. Meg
groaned and hung her head between her crossed legs.

Conor was instantly alert. "Are you sick?"

"No...I don't think so. Just the heat, I guess."

He opened up an insulated shoulder bag and pulled
out a can of soda water. "Here, drink this."

Meg clutched the can, rolling it over her face, neck
and arms. She saw the concern in his face and was
suddenly overwhelmed by emotion. How could she
have had such suspicious thoughts about him?

"You're better off drinking it," he teased.

She flipped the top and drank greedily. Satisfied, she grinned over at him. If Win hadn't been crouching so close by, she might have been tempted to give Conor a thank-you kiss. Then she recalled the suspicion she'd felt last night and shook her head in defeat. Everyone has a price, they say. Can mine be a can of soda?

"What's so funny?"

"Nothing, really. What about you and Win? Aren't you thirsty?"

Conor spoke in Thai to Pran's cousin. "We'll wait until we get to Chiang Saen and have lunch there before driving out to the camp."

"Will there be a car there?"

"Apparently Pran's arranged a taxi. Chiang Saen's pretty small."

"Is this the way you traveled when you came before? The time you filmed the newsclip?"

Conor shook his head. "No. I flew to Chiang Rai. Flights are irregular and have to be booked well in advance unless you have special connections. That's why flying wasn't really an option for us this time. My crew and I drove up to Chiang Saen, but that way's longer."

"Have you thought about what we'll do after we get to the camp?" she asked.

"Not really. I don't want to anticipate too much."

Meg set the empty pop can down and turned to look at the edge of jungle on the Laotian side. Obviously Conor was trying to tell her not to expect too much. The problem was, she did.

THE TAXI driver waited patiently at the gate while a security guard scrutinized their permit and passports.

Finally, the guard waved them inside and the cab passed through the chain-link fence into the circular drive of the refugee camp's administrative building.

Building was a misleading term, Meg thought. A squat, corrugated-tin shed, a flagpole with the Thai banner, a flowering bush and a few palms comprised the reception area. When the taxi stopped, two uniformed soldiers exited the shed. Meg felt her heart rate pick up speed.

This is it, she told herself. All the hours of anxiety and the millions of questions racing through her mind were going to be answered at last. Trembling with anticipation, she literally stumbled out of the car. Conor reached out to steady her with his arm, tucking it reassuringly inside her own.

The permit procedure was repeated and questions fired in Thai at Conor. Meg stared about the compound during the exchange. It was impossible to picture her father standing here, on the very spot she'd seen in the film.

Beyond the shed were rows of barracks crisscrossed by lines and lines of laundry. A whole city of people and animals shifted among the structures. Some more curious types approached the link fence separating the inner camp from the reception area. Meg averted her eyes from the listless despair in their faces.

"Can I have the photograph?" Conor bent to ask Meg. Seeing her confusion, he gently explained, "The print I took from the video. Remember the close-up? Have you got it in your purse?"

"Oh, yes, yes. Just a sec." She opened the shoulder bag and pulled out a brown envelope.

The Thai soldier waited politely while Conor slipped
the picture out of the envelope and handed it to him.
He studied it for a long time. Then he slowly shook his
head.

"What's he saying?" Meg spoke up. "Why is he
shaking his head?"

Conor held up a hand to silence her. He seemed to
be arguing with the soldier. The faces of all three men
darkened with anger. Meg's frustration mounted.

"Please!"

The men looked at her expectantly, the intensity of
the moment gone.

"Will someone please just tell me where my father
is?"

Conor took hold of her hand and squeezed it. He
spoke again to the soldiers and then swung Meg about
to usher her back to the taxi.

"Stop it! I want to know what's going on."

"Inside," he hissed. The door closed behind him
and the driver circled toward the gate.

Conor held her face between his two hands. "Okay.
Those soldiers said they've never seen that man before. Wait...I haven't finished. I pointed out to them
that a picture can't tell a lie and obviously the man was
standing in front of their own station back there. They
insisted he was a stranger. Perhaps another journalist."

"That's ridiculous," she gasped. "You'd have met
him or known about him."

"Of course, but there's nothing to be gained by arguing with a Thai soldier, believe me."

Meg turned to stare out the rear window as the taxi
went through the gate. Her eyes filled with frus-

trated, angry tears. She wanted to leap from the cab and run back inside and shake the information out of the soldiers.

"Take a deep breath and relax," Conor was whispering.

"To hell with the deep breath. I'd like to go back and wring their necks."

He brought her head down to his chest and put his arms around her.

"I just don't believe them," she continued.

There was a brief pause and then Conor said, "Neither do I. The thing is, I don't know why they'd lie."

"What now?" Meg asked, straightening. The warmth of Conor's arms still clung to her and any signal from him would have coaxed her back. But he dropped his arm from the back of the seat. She felt a stab of disappointment, despite knowing he was simply following the lead she herself had set.

"The driver will take us back to Chiang Saen. Win's waiting for us at the restaurant. We'll have lunch before we make any serious decisions." He spoke to the cabdriver and spent the remainder of the short drive staring out the window.

Win was waiting patiently at a table on the patio of what appeared to be the only restaurant in town.

Conor paid off the taxi driver and ordered lunch before filling Win in on what had happened at the camp. Win's English was limited, but he made an attempt to convey his regret.

"Miss Meg, so sorry. These men bad people."

Conor watched as Meg managed a wan smile. "It's okay, Win. Maybe they're telling the truth. Maybe he's not my father at all. Maybe I should just go home and forget the whole thing."

The glass of beer on its way to Conor's mouth froze in midair. He was surprised by this sudden show of defeat. It seemed unlike her. Yet he couldn't help thinking this might be a way out. If he could persuade her to give up, he could report back to Gallagher that the trip had been a waste of time and the whole stinking business would be over.

Except that if she did give up she would return home, and—surprised at his own reaction—he didn't want that to happen.

Over the past couple of days, he'd seen a whole gamut of her emotions and attitudes and he'd been impressed by all of them. Challenged and exasperated, too. She had a solid sense of humor and was no complainer, in spite of her insistence on getting to the bottom of every issue. Yeah, he had to admit it, he was beginning to like her. A lot. Too damn much, in fact, for what he was supposed to be doing for Gallagher.

Lunch was eaten in the silence that fell after Meg's announcement. Conor watched her push the food around on her plate and guessed she was letting the events of the past hour sink in. If Win hadn't been there, Conor could have spoken more freely to her. Perhaps he would have given in to the urge to wrap his arms around her again.

It was strange how the sensation of providing comfort had pleased him. It was so long since he'd felt that special kind of warmth; not since the early days when Mi Mi had first moved in with him—until he'd blown everything by devoting himself to his job. By the time he remembered her, she'd already packed and left.

Meg broke into his daydream. "All right, what options do we have now?"

Conor felt his insides shine with an invisible smile. She was no quitter, he had to give her that. Even if she was going to complicate his life further.

"We might be able to get to one of the refugees in the camp. Win didn't go to the camp with us, so the guard won't know him. Perhaps we can think up a cover story to get him inside."

"What about a permit?"

Conor shrugged. "There are ways around that. Greasing the palm, as they say."

"Maybe we'd better ask Win how he feels about doing this."

Conor quickly translated for the Thai. Win wrinkled his forehead for a long, thoughtful moment before smiling agreement.

"We'd better find a place for the night and work out a plan there. The more privacy the better." Conor placed some money on the table and stood.

Win hurried off to book rooms at the single hotel in town. Meg and Conor stood in the middle of the paved main road.

Conor checked his watch. "I've arranged to meet Win here in half an hour. Would you care to see some of the sights?"

"A walk would be nice."

"Which direction?" he asked. "East to the river, west to the highway or south to . . . I don't know what lies south of here. Jungle, I guess." He was grinning.

"Can we follow that sidewalk along the river?"

"Let's go," he said, taking her left arm in his and heading east.

They'd only walked a few yards when a shout came from behind. A man was running toward them.

Meg saw Conor's frown, but didn't recognize the man until he was standing in front of them. It was one of the security guards from the gate at the camp.

He opened his mouth in a breathless, urgent rush of words.

Conor's reply was steadier, but intense. He gestured for Meg to follow them along the embankment to a bench. She noticed that it was hidden from the road by a clump of bushes and wondered if he'd chosen it for that reason.

The man was obviously anxious, alternately craning his head behind to the street and casting furtive glances at Meg. She was irritated at not knowing what was going on, but had the sense to be patient. Finally, Conor turned to her.

"This guy says he's seen your...well, the man we're looking for. I think he's legit."

"What does he say? About my...father."

Conor spoke again to the man, who was beginning to calm down. Then he looked at Meg.

"He wants some money for the information. Says he's putting his job in danger by coming to us."

"How much does he want?"

Conor talked briefly to the man. "He's asking for a hundred dollars, but I know he'll take whatever we want to give him."

"A hundred dollars! I don't know what to say, I've never paid a bribe before."

"Let me handle it. I'll try for fifty. That's more than enough." He took his wallet out of his pocket and handed the man a fistful of *baht* notes.

The man made a show of complaining, but departed as quickly as he'd appeared. Conor crooked his arm around Meg's. "Come on, let's head back to the hotel. Apparently some of the men at the camp were talking about our visit and the picture. They all know the man in the photo. He lives up with the hill tribes and visits the camp regularly. He's very well-liked and has done a lot of good for the people in the area as well as at the camp. The commander was trying to protect his privacy."

"Did you mention my dad's name?"

"I did. They've never heard the name. Everyone calls him Ghost Tiger. For the color of his skin. Also—" Conor paused "—to honor him. Ghost tigers being a rare commodity."

"Where does he live? Can we go there to . . . to talk to him?" Meg felt her fingers digging into Conor's arm.

"Well, he's told me the name of the tribe he's living with. The Karen people—one of the biggest and most politically influential tribes in the North."

"Can we go there?"

He sighed at the insistence in her voice.

"It'll take two or three days just to get there," he warned. "And there's no guarantee the man will be there or that he'll even be—"

"My father. I realize that. But I didn't come all this way to pull back at the first sign of difficulty. When can we leave?"

"Tomorrow morning. Win and I will get some supplies tonight."

Relief swept through Meg. She'd been afraid he was going to give her a hard time.

"One thing more."

The tone in his voice told her she wasn't going to like what he said. "Yes?"

"He says this Ghost Tiger is married . . . to a Karen woman."

Meg bit her lip and looked toward the river. I've just raised the lid on a Pandora's box, she thought. But there's no going back now.

GALLAGHER SWORE, reaching out an arm to the ringing telephone on his desk.

"Gallagher here."

"Colonel Noel Gallagher?"

"Of course, dammit. Who is it?"

"Brian Scott from the Worldways Travel Agency. You called about a booking to Bangkok."

Gallagher pivoted his swivel chair around, stretched out a leg and pushed shut his office door. "Right. What have you got?"

"I can get you on a flight tomorrow morning. Gets into Bangkok early Sunday morning their time."

Two days away. Gallagher flipped over his desk calendar. Tremayne had just called from Chiang Rai before dawn to say he and the Devlin woman were leaving for the camp. Treymayne had agreed to report back as soon as he'd confirmed a location for Devlin. Gallagher didn't expect to hear from him for at least another day, given the poor phone facilities outside Chiang Rai.

His mind raced with options. If he waited for Tremayne to call back, he might not get another seat on short notice. And there was no way he could book transport on a military plane. "Okay, reserve it for me."

"Will this be on a government warrant?"

"Christ, no!" he shouted into the phone. "And don't send the tickets here. I'll pick them up myself."

After the details were completed, Gallagher hung up and surveyed his office with a satisfied smile. He'd have time for one more visit to Cape Cod. He bet the Devlin woman was a dutiful daughter and had left a forwarding address of some kind with her mother. Besides, he wouldn't mind paying a call on Lydia Devlin again. Joe had always had good taste in women.

CHAPTER SEVEN

"MORE COFFEE, darling?"

Lydia glanced up from the morning paper. Jeffrey was standing at the counter, coffeepot in hand.

"No, thanks, Jeffrey. Two cups is all the caffeine I can handle in one day. I thought you were in a hurry this morning."

Jeffrey placed the pot down and sat in the chair next to his wife. "My meeting with John can wait. I'm more interested in what's been going on in this household."

She hid her face behind the paper and forced a casual note into her voice. "What on earth are you talking about?"

"Lydia." Jeffrey gently pushed aside the newspaper. "Something's on your mind. You've been wandering around this house in a daze for almost two weeks now. You've got dark circles under your eyes from lying awake half the night. No, don't argue. I'm the guy you're bouncing up and down in bed every time you toss and turn."

Lydia tried to smile, but couldn't still her racing heart. Not now, not yet. Please.

He waited for her to speak but when she simply continued to stare at him, her large blue eyes swimming with tears, he didn't have the heart to push. Jeffrey leaned over and kissed her.

"Look, whatever it is, I'm here to help. Remember that. I love you."

"Jeffrey...I... Darling—" she took a breath "—it's just anxiety about Meg. I'm fine, really."

Jeffrey knew there was no point pushing Lydia. Stubborn was her second name. If she and Meg weren't so much alike, they'd get along famously. "I just want you to know there's not a single thing you have to keep from me. Unless, of course, you're having an affair with the mailman."

She did smile at that. "You keep me far too content to stray. Besides, our mailman is a she."

He patted her hand. "Remember what I said. Now, would you like to drive into Boston with me? You can take a look at this bowfront chest John's found for the shop. Give me your expert intuition on its authenticity."

"No, thanks, darling. I know you two were planning an extended lunch at your brew pub. Go ahead. I'm fine. And give my love to John."

Jeffrey kissed her again before leaving the room. Lydia waited for the sound of the garage door closing, then gave in to the rare luxury of a good cry.

She allowed herself fifteen minutes of self-pity, then pulled herself together. Today was her day for aerobics class at the club and she had an appointment to get her hair done afterward. It wouldn't do to show up with red eyes. No point in setting abuzz the small group she and Jeffrey socialized with in Cape Cod. There would be enough gossip if Joe turned up alive.

That brought a quick stab of guilt. It wasn't that she'd ever wanted Joe to die; simply, that she'd gotten used to the idea of his being dead. And, for all of their sakes, she reasoned, he ought to stay dead.

I'm starting to use the same kind of logic Meg is prone to, she thought, and smiled. She knew she needn't worry about Meg. Jeffrey was right about Meg's judgment. In spite of her daughter's irritating habit of letting her emotions govern her actions, there was a solid core of common sense and intuition in Meg. As a child, she'd often boxed herself into impossible situations out of pride or stubbornness. Yet she usually managed to extricate herself without losing face. And she was certainly skilled at shifting responsibility for the whole affair onto someone else. Like her mother.

Lydia sighed. Still, she was worried. So many things could happen. The worst of which was that if indeed Joe was alive and Meg found him, her daughter's image of her father might be shattered.

Meg had just turned twelve when Joe went missing. The girl had worshiped her father with the fervent blindness of adolescence. It had been painful enough to witness Meg's grief after they'd received official notice of Joe's probable death. Lydia had never allowed herself to tarnish Meg's picture of her father.

Sometimes, after all the years of pretense, Lydia almost believed the fairy tale herself. Perhaps they *had* been a happy family. Perhaps, as Joe so often had accused, she *had* imagined infidelities. There was some truth to the adage that if you hear something often enough, you came to believe it. Lord knew, there had been many times in those days when Lydia had not known what to believe.

She forced herself up from the breakfast table. She didn't really feel like exercise class today, but knew she needed the diversion. The doorbell rang as she was tying the laces on her sneakers.

The déjà vu she felt when she opened the door was like a wallop to her stomach. Standing in front of her was a smiling young man in a dark uniform.

"Mrs. Haycock?"

She managed a faint whisper. "Yes."

"Sorry to trouble you, ma'am, but someone tried to call you last night. About a telegram. I've got it here, if you'll sign for it."

He must have sensed her fear, for he smiled reassuringly and added, "I don't think it's bad news, ma'am."

Lydia scrawled her signature and took the telegram. After she closed the door, she unfolded the envelope with trembling fingers.

The sender was identified in the top left-hand corner of the telegram as a Pran Sukrit, with an address in Chiang Rai. Lydia quickly scanned the message, noting that Meg's name came at the end of it. This Pran person—she remembered the name then, from Meg's telephone call—must have sent the telegram on Meg's behalf.

She told herself to relax and read the message again: "Mother. Going into hill tribes. Looking for man there called Ghost Tiger. Call few days. Love. Meg."

Relief overwhelmed her. Lydia was starting to walk toward the kitchen when the doorbell pealed again. She tucked the telegram into her pocket and headed for the front door. She wondered if she'd ever get to the club.

"Mr. Gallagher." Lydia wished she'd left the house five minutes earlier.

His eyes narrowed. He hadn't expected instant recognition. Had she been talking to someone? He tipped his gray fedora. "Mrs. Haycock, sorry to trouble you again. Could I step in for a moment?"

"Mr. Gallagher, I don't really know what you expect of me.

"As I told you the last time you called, my first husband—"

He brushed past her into the foyer. Lydia bit her lip. She didn't know whether to be afraid or angry. But she wasn't going to be intimidated by someone in her own home. Keeping the door wide open, she asked, "Why have you come back Mr. Gallagher?"

"Sorry for the intrusion, Mrs. Haycock, but after I spoke to you a few days ago, I tried to contact someone at the Pentagon about that news feature. As you might expect, no one there had any information. At least, nothing anyone was going to reveal." His bland face twisted into a grin. "You know what these government agencies are like. Give you the runaround every time."

"You didn't come all the way here to tell me you had no success."

Gallagher's eyebrows raised in surprise. "No, you're right. I came back because I've decided to go to Thailand myself." Her astonishment pleased him. Nothing better, he thought, than a good game of hardball. "You're probably wondering why," he continued.

Lydia cleared her throat nervously. "Frankly, I do wonder why you'd bother. Given the lack of evidence that the man you saw was Joe."

He paused, staring into her royal blue eyes. "That's what I came about. The evidence. You see, in my inquiries, I got in touch with my—and Joe's—old commanding officer, Tom Braithwaite. He had some interesting information for me. Apparently Joe was on a secret mission at the time he disappeared. Tom thinks he might have been working for the CIA. And Tom thinks that Joe's disappearance had something to do with a CIA cover-up. You may recall the bad press the CIA was getting in those days."

Lydia was too stunned to do more than nod.

"Well, I showed a copy of that tape to Tom and he's damn certain it's Joe. That was enough for me. I've booked a flight to Bangkok and I'm leaving tomorrow. Just thought I'd drop around to find out if you'd heard anything further."

Lydia shook her head. "Mr. Gallagher, that's impossible. Apparently the man in the documentary is known in the area."

Gallagher frowned. "You've heard from your daughter?"

Lydia hesitated, unsure suddenly if she ought to have spoken up. Then, deciding the truth might get rid of the man once and for all, blurted out, "Yes, I have. She's sent me a telegram to say she's gone looking for a man known as...as..." Lydia fumbled in her pocket and retrieved the folded paper.

"May I?" His tone was courteous but there was a flicker of impatience in Gallagher's eyes.

Lydia glanced quickly at the telegram and, ignoring his outstretched hand, pushed it back into her pocket. "Ghost Tiger, he's called. So there's no reason to believe the man is Joe at all."

Gallagher let his hand drop. Ghost Tiger. The name was familiar, but he couldn't quite recall which part of his past it belonged to. At any rate, he'd gotten more than he expected from this visit. He nodded politely and eased past Lydia out onto the veranda.

"Perhaps you're right, Mrs. Haycock. There's probably no point in pursuing the matter further." He turned and walked down the sloping drive to his parked car.

Lydia automatically closed and locked the door. She leaned against it, collecting the bits and pieces of her mind. It wasn't until much later that she had a chance to relax and review the morning's events. Something had been nagging at her all day and on the drive home from the beauty salon she was finally able to identify it.

That awful Gallagher man had mentioned talking to Tom Braithwaite. But hadn't Meg said that Braithwaite was dead? Why would Gallagher lie? And, too late, she realized what a gold mine of information she'd handed him. It was definitely time to talk with Jeffrey.

MEG PAUSED to wipe the trickle of sweat rolling down the back of her neck. The rice paddy they were struggling through seemed to go on forever. Conor and Win were yards ahead of her, marching on with a resolve she wished she could match. In the beginning, when they'd stepped out of the cab that had driven them as far as the paved road extended, she'd felt such eagerness and determination.

But the sun hadn't even nudged itself above the horizon and the trail had meandered through fields with crops vaguely reminiscent of those back home. Farmers whipping teams of water buffalo waved cheerily at them and Meg's heart sang with the certainty that she was going to find her father.

By midmorning, the trail had swerved down into a valley. Rice paddies stretched like emerald quilts as far as the eye could see. Win led them along one of the many narrow paths that transsected the soggy rice fields. Meg found that whenever her concentration wavered, her foot slipped into the spongy earth. They were scarcely a quarter of the way across one section of paddy and her shoes were already covered with muck.

She stopped to replace them with the rubber thongs Conor had advised her to buy in Chiang Saen. Then she tied the sneakers to the loop of her backpack. They would be easier to clean when the mud dried. A swallow of warm water from her canteen and she was ready. Conor and Win were specks in the distance.

The solitude of the trek gave her a chance to think. She knew the odds of finding her father were small, but Meg had a strong optimistic streak. Almost a perverse optimistic streak, she thought wryly. She began to picture their meeting.

What did you say to a father who had obviously abandoned you many years ago?

"Hi, Dad. So, what's new?"

Words chased each other around in Meg's head. She found herself unable to dwell on anything more than the relentless sun. When she caught up to the men, they were leaning against the trunk of the only tree in the entire rice paddy.

"We'll break here for lunch," Conor said. He was already unwrapping the sweet breads and spring rolls they'd ordered at the restaurant that morning. "Don't sit on the ground—it's too wet."

Meg bit back the sarcastic quip she had ready. It was too early in the trek to show physical defeat. And she guessed that Conor wouldn't be too sympathetic to whining.

She gobbled up the lunch in silence, drank some water and almost felt like a new woman. "How much farther?" she asked.

"Until?"

His deliberate obtuseness irritated her. "Until we get there," she snapped.

"We're heading for the Karen tribe at the far end of this valley. The guy from the camp said this Ghost Tiger was married to a Karen woman. If he's not there, we'll have to decide whether to go on or to head back to Chiang Saen."

"We go on," she said. "I didn't come all this way to stop so easily."

"The bottom line is that there may be other factors to consider."

Having made his point, Conor packed up the remains of the lunch. He and Win began walking. Meg slung her pack around her shoulders, pulled her sun hat down over her forehead and followed.

Time drifted by in a green haze, until the path came to a halt at the foot of a steep hill. Conor and Win had dropped their packs onto the ground, which was now dry and grassy. Both were taking huge gulps from their water bottles, by the time she reached them.

"Take a good long drink," Conor advised. "We've one more climb to make before we reach the village."

Meg looked around. She didn't see a soul, much less a whole village. "Where is it?"

"The other side of this hill."

She looked up—way up—and wanted to cry. "How high is that thing?"

"Only a few hundred feet, but in this heat . . ."

He didn't have to say anything more. If there'd been water to spare, she'd have poured it over her head. She swallowed primly, swishing the water around in her mouth before letting it drip down her throat.

Conor watched her with a bemused expression. "We're not in the Sahara, you know. There's plenty of water around."

"Sure, but it's either muddy and full of living things or hiding somewhere on the other side of that mountain."

He laughed. "I wouldn't even call this thing a foot-hill. In another hour we'll have a cold shower and a hot meal."

"You mean there's a hotel on the other side of that hill, too?"

Conor's burst of laughter boomed into the valley.

"What's so funny?" she asked. "Okay, I know it won't exactly be the Hilton but there'll be some kind of hotel. Won't there?"

Conor wiped his face with a square of cloth. "You'll see. Come on. Let's get the climb over with."

When Meg reached the crest of hill an hour later, she understood Conor's laughter. The village below consisted of no more than a dozen wooden houses, built on stilts in much the same style as Pran's, without the shady, flowering courtyard. It sprawled up the slope of a small hill. Chickens, goats and pigs wandered at will. Huge mud puddles covered the ground, along with the assorted droppings of the animals. A scattering of people wandered into the central open space of the village to stare in dumb astonishment at the visitors.

Meg felt as though she'd been airlifted in from some distant planet. People surrounded her, pointing and giggling. The children were more direct. They ran right up to her to touch her.

"Candy! Candy!" they shouted.

"Don't open up your pack here," Conor warned. "You might start a mob scene. We have to meet with the village's headman."

A few yards ahead Meg could see a bamboo house festooned with colorful banners. The sight cheered her. Perhaps this was the hotel.

But when they reached the bottom of the ladder stairway leading up to the house, a gray-haired man climbed down to greet them. He wore a sarong with one end brought up between his legs and tucked into the waist, creating baggy pantaloons. A fringed length of cloth was wrapped around his forehead and knotted. When he bowed his head at them, the fringe bobbed along with him. His cheek bulged with a plug of chewing tobacco.

Win addressed the man first, then introduced Conor. The three men chatted for a while and then Conor asked for the photograph.

Meg watched the headman closely as Conor handed over the picture. She saw a glimmer of recognition in his eyes, though his face remained impassive. After a few seconds, he passed the photograph back to Conor, shook his head politely and gestured toward the house. Win started up the stairs.

"Conor," she spoke up. "What's happening? What did he say?"

Conor answered in a low voice. "The headman says he's never seen the man in the picture before and that he's never heard of anyone called Ghost Tiger."

"I could have sworn I saw something in his eyes. I bet he's covering up."

"That's my assessment of the situation, too. However, he's also invited us to stay the night in his own house. A very hospitable gesture, I might add. Let's go inside, find out about cleaning ourselves up and then talk about our choices."

"Well, I'd rather have a word or two with this headman first," she grumbled. "But I'll go along with you for now."

Conor stood with one foot on the bottom rung of the steps. He shook his head in mock despair. "You talk so tough, Meg Devlin, but you don't look very tough." His index finger traced a line of dirt down the side of her face, ran along the rim of her jaw and halted at the faint dimple in her chin.

There was an expression in his eyes that raised goose bumps, in spite of the sweltering temperature. It was a look that wasn't hard to read, but one Meg hadn't seen in a man's face for a long time. Ignoring the suggestion in his voice, she asked, "Can you find out where the showers are?"

Conor let his hand drop. "I can try, but I've a feeling the facilities here are quite primitive."

They deposited their packs inside the single large room of the headman's house. An old woman crouched over a hearth at one end. Mats were rolled up against the woven-grass walls. Huge blackened pots and caldrons hung by hooks from the ceiling. One side of the room was partitioned from the rest by a tattered chintz curtain. A rooster pecked about for crumbs on the wooden floor.

"It's not the Hilton," Conor said.

Meg sighed. "It's not even Campgrounds of America."

"Get a change of clothing, your towel and soap and I'll find out where the facilties are."

"Great. Are we all ... do we all sleep here together in this room?"

"The headman has graciously given you and me the private quarters over there." Conor jerked his head toward the tiny curtained area.

She peeked behind the curtain. Though comparable to the average broom closet, the space was clean and bare. Two grass mats stood propped against the wall. Meg let her backpack slip off her shoulders.

"Well, home sweet home. It won't take me a second," she promised, searching for clean trousers, blouse and underwear. She pulled out items for shower and shampoo and placed them on the floor, all the while aware of Conor standing behind her. His presence was upsetting.

"Weren't you going to find out about showers?" she asked.

He gave a dazed shrug, mumbled an apology and let the curtain drop.

By the time she had risen from the floor, laden with her things, Conor had returned and set to work at his own pack.

"That's it?" she asked, cocking an eye at the items he grasped in one hand.

"I travel light."

On their way out of the house, Conor was stopped by Win. After a few words, Conor explained that he'd ordered dinner. "Chicken okay with you?"

"Great!"

They were almost at the edge of the yard when a loud squawking caught their attention. Looking back, Meg saw a young boy chasing a scrawny chicken while a handful of other children watched in amusement. The boy lunged at the bird and then stood triumphant, holding it in the air by its feet.

"Dinner," Conor said.

Meg grimaced.

"No supermarkets here. What you see is what you get." Conor turned toward a path leading into a thicket of trees.

Meg followed, wishing she'd asked for a vegetarian meal.

"Where are we going?"

"Thought you wanted a shower."

"Yes, I do, but . . ."

"It's around the corner up ahead, if Win's directions can be relied on."

Meg glanced behind her. The village was hardly visible through the trees. A few yards farther on, she bumped into Conor who'd stopped on the trail. Ahead was a small waterfall cascading from a handmade bamboo sluice. The water fell into a pool, which fed into yet another bamboo trough and so on down the hill.

"What's that?"

"Our shower, I believe. Looks like part of the irrigation system for the rice fields in the valley."

"At least it's wet." She wanted only to get out of her dirty clothes and wash her hair. "There's just one problem," she pointed out.

Conor had slung his towel over a fallen tree trunk. "What's that?"

"No dressing room, no walls."

He started unbuttoning his shirt. "I'll close my eyes."

"Why don't I trust you?"

The shirt gaped open. Meg tried not to let her jaw follow suit. She'd never seen him shirtless and wondered if she could resist cheating if he asked her to close her eyes.

"We could both turn around and sidle into the pool at the same time," he suggested.

"Sounds like some kind of strange folk dance," she muttered. "Why don't you get into the water while I turn around and then close your eyes while I get in."

"Too complicated."

"Conor." Exasperation edged her voice. She was desperate for a wash. "Give me a break and get in. I'm closing my eyes, starting now."

There was a rustling noise and then silence. Meg's ears strained, waiting for a splash. Nothing. She opened her eyes. Conor was standing directly in front of her, naked from the waist up.

"You peeked." His voice was low and husky. The smile had disappeared with his shirt.

"You were supposed to be getting into the water." Her rebuke was weak. Meg couldn't take her eyes off his chest. A narrow vee of black hair bisected his pectoral muscles.

"I thought it would be more fun if we helped each other. Sort of co-op bathing." Conor moved closer, raising his hands to the buttons at the neck of her cotton shirt.

She parted her lips to laugh, but all that came out before his mouth descended on hers was a faint gasp. Meg felt his tongue enter, sliding along the inside of her mouth before thrusting deeper. He pressed against her and she felt his hunger in the hardness of his body, the urgency of his hands as they slid under her shirt in a single, breathtaking motion.

Her mouth was sweet and salty. The nipples beneath his fingers stretched in desire. He thought he might burst.

"Conor," she murmured. "Please . . ."

He knew her heart wasn't in the objection. He knew from the way she arched her back and clutched at him that she wanted him to go on and on. And he would have, if the lilt of a child's giggle hadn't broken through the rushing sound of their combined breathing.

Conor froze.

"What? What is it?" The question slurred from Meg's lips as if from a dazed stupor.

There was an awkward refastening of clothing. The source of the giggle had disappeared into the greenery. Meg avoided Conor's face. She felt as though she'd been caught necking in the back seat of a car. She shook her head, realizing that she'd almost made a foolish mistake.

Conor finished buttoning his shirt and walked a few feet away to the head of the trail to the pond. He wanted to give her a moment of privacy. What a jerk he'd been, acting as though she'd been just waiting for him to move in on her.

When Meg caught up to him, he said, "Look, I'm sorry. I shouldn't have done that. It wasn't fair. You have enough on your mind right now."

Meg pushed back a long strand of hair that dangled across her forehead. "Don't be so quick to give yourself that much credit, Conor Tremayne." Then she strode on ahead of him.

Conor whistled an embarrassed tune. Put in my place. He sighed. Deserved it, too.

CHAPTER EIGHT

MEG STARED apprehensively into her bowl of soup. She could identify strips of onion and chunks of carrot. The strands of leafy things seemed innocuous but there was something else lurking beneath the light broth.

"Something wrong?" Conor asked. He was sitting across from her, cross-legged on a grass mat. Win and the headman slurped noisily a few feet away.

Meg shooed away the hen that wandered close to her bowl. There was something obscene about the chicken's curiosity about their meal. Recognizing a lost relative? Meg wondered. She scooped up some broth, catching a pale yellow claw on the edge of the aluminum spoon.

"Oh, my God, there's a foot in my soup."

Conor grinned. "Feel honored. You've been given the prized morsel."

"What do I do with it? And don't tell me to eat it."

Ignoring her question, Conor leaned over to address the headman. They chatted briefly before Conor turned backed to Meg and held out his soup bowl.

"I've just explained to the headman that you, as my woman, have decided to honor me with the claw. Spoon it into my bowl and bow your head to me, then to him."

"Is all this ritual necessary?"

"If you don't want to offend our host, it is. There you go, be the good little woman for me."

Meg bit down on her lower lip. She followed his instructions with a smile. The chicken's foot plopped into Conor's bowl.

"Don't ever use that expression again if you know what's good for you!" she hissed through her teeth.

A grin stretched across Conor's face. "I know what would be good for me, all right."

The heat in Meg's face was from more than the soup. "Don't let what happened a few hours ago turn your head."

"You know, there must have been two feet in the cook pot. Shall I remind the headman?"

"That's a low move, Tremayne."

The headman rose and signaled to the woman stooped over the hearth at the back of the room. She advanced shyly and bent to retrieve the dishes.

Conor began speaking to the men. There was a rapid exchange between the headman and Win.

"What's going on?" Meg asked.

"I've asked the headman if you can be part of the discussion and he's not very pleased about it. Perhaps it would be better if you listened and let me fill you in later."

"I suppose I've got no choice. At least thank the headman's wife for the dinner."

"I'll have to pass on the compliment to him, but she'll hear it."

Smiles and nods followed Conor's thank-you. The old man motioned them to sit in the doorway of the house. A faint breeze swept up the stairs, carrying with it the smokiness of village hearth fires. The night, though speckled with the yellow glow of kerosene lanterns, was as black as any Meg had ever seen.

Common sense told her to temper her annoyance at being shunted aside. She knew she couldn't communicate with the men and she also knew she could trust Conor to cover all the details. On the way back from the irrigation pond, he had explained that if the headman refused to tell them anything, they'd have to proceed farther into the hills. Somewhere, someone would identify the photograph Meg carried.

Anyway, she was content to sit and stare at Conor as he talked. She indulged in the memory of his hands on her skin and his lips on hers. In spite of the warm evening, she shivered. Since their return from the pond, she'd refused to dwell on what might have happened had they not been interrupted. There was no way she could afford to be sidetracked from her mission.

And yet she seemed unable to prevent the unexpected thrill of pleasure she felt merely brushing against him or watching him stretch his arms back in a yawn. Meg railed silently against the perversity of fate. Why now? she wondered.

"Meg? Meg?"

Startled, Meg looked up at the faces in front of her. "Pardon?"

"The headman suggests we return to Chiang Saen and ask the local authorities about Ghost Tiger."

Meg bit back her frustration. "You're not going along with that, I hope."

Conor gave a tight, half smile. "Is that a question or a statement?"

"I'm not going back to Chiang Saen. The police there won't be any more helpful than the man at the refugee camp."

He sighed. "I thought that might be your reaction. I've explained all that to the old man but—"

"Can't we just keep going?"

"Where?" He sounded frustrated. "We could spend weeks wandering these hills and still come up with nothing. There's no point heading off aimlessly without a lead."

"Tell him there's a reward for information about Ghost Tiger. Ask him to tell the rest of the villagers. Maybe someone will come forward."

"No one here is going to defy the headman. If he says he's never heard of Ghost Tiger, that's that."

A sense of helplessness overwhelmed Meg. She stared bleakly at the passive expression on the headman's face. How could she reach this man, so totally foreign to her own background?

"Conor, please talk to the headman for me. This is what I want you to say—word for word."

"Nothing to lose I guess. Go ahead."

"Tell him that . . . that I honored my father. That I remember my father as a kind and loving man. When he disappeared in action, I was twelve years old. His loss was a terrible blow. I . . . I . . ." Meg paused, forcing a calming breath into her lungs. She waited while the headman's wife placed a pot of tea and tiny bowls before them. The old lady smiled shyly at Meg.

The green tea was hot and Meg sipped carefully while Conor translated for the headman. Then she continued. "Tell him because my father's body was never found, I couldn't put my grief to rest. The spirit of my father haunts me.''

Conor nodded approvingly. Spirits were revered by the hill tribes. The eloquence of Meg's speech moved him. He knew she was speaking from her heart, as well as from her need to sway the old man. A sudden desire to wrap his arms around her in comfort overcame him. The feeling had nothing to do with physical attraction. And that fact alone surprised him.

But the headman wasn't persuaded. He rose and nodded a good-night. Conor turned to Meg. The disappointment in her face prompted him to place a hand on her shoulder. ''I'm sorry, Meg. You made a great pitch. There must be an incredibly strong bond to Ghost Tiger if the old man is willing to risk offending the spirits.''

Meg wearily massaged the bridge of her nose. ''To have come all this way only to reach a dead end...''

''Win and I think we should visit one more village on the long shot that someone from another tribe may have heard of Ghost Tiger. Not everyone will have the same principles of loyalty as the headman here.''

''How will we know where to go?''

''I've left that to Win. He'll find out the nearest compound to this one.''

''What do you honestly think our chances are of finding my father?''

The question was unexpected. He wondered if her iron determination was beginning to falter. Irrationally, he suddenly didn't want that to happen. He stroked the side of her cheek with the back of his hand. ''God, Meg, don't ask me to answer that.''

She brushed his hand aside. ''You already have.''

"Come on," Conor said, pulling her toward the open doorway. "Let's get some fresh air."

Behind them, the headman's house was in darkness but the pinpoints of lanterns flickered in the still night. They perched on the top step of the ladder stairs.

Meg shivered. A chill had descended on the hilltop. "The altitude," Conor explained. "Want to get a sweatshirt?"

"No, I'll be fine. It's so beautiful here at night when you can't see all the dirt and poverty of the village. Even the sky looks different than it does back home."

"It is different. The constellations aren't the same. If we traveled south of the equator, we'd see the Southern Cross."

Meg sighed. "I guess I'll soon be seeing all the familiar stars. I've only got another week left and I still have to get back to Bangkok for my flight home."

The reminder jolted him. Then he was angry at himself. Idiot, did you think your life was going to continue like this? Days—and nights—with her by your side?

"You're not thinking of giving up?"

Meg turned her head to look at him. "Haven't you more or less been suggesting that all along? There's nothing in this for you. Why should you care whether or not I give up?"

"Did this afternoon mean so little to you that you can ask that question? For Christ's sake, Meg . . ."

"Conor, I'm so confused and frustrated and despairing of ever finding anything—much less the truth—about my father." Her voice dropped to a whisper. "And I haven't forgotten this afternoon."

"Don't give up." He broke eye contact with her and stared ahead, his husky plea falling into the silent night.

MEG ROLLED in her sleep, half conscious of the faint stirrings of daybreak. She curled into the warm body at her side, giving in to the memory of Conor's hands and lips at the irrigation pond. She wanted to stay in the safety of dreamland, where passion was unquestioned. Where she didn't have to ponder those maddening tingles of desire for Conor or why she was resisting them so much.

She reached out a hand that froze, mid-stroke; moved farther and touched— God! A paw. Her eyes flew open. A mangy dog nestled in the hollow of her body lifted a reproachful face, rose shakily to its feet at her yelp and scurried away.

There was muffled laughter from the other side of the curtain. Meg pulled up the edge of it to face two youngsters, sitting inches away. They giggled, covering their mouths with grubby hands. Meg let the curtain drop and sank back onto the grass mat.

"Well," she muttered, "I suppose I can look forward to a few fleas now." Smiling ruefully, she dressed in yesterday's clothes. Laundry was obviously not an option or a priority on the trek. She folded up the sarong she'd used as a sheet.

There had been some biscuits left in the zippered section of her pack. Conor had given a couple to the headman, but Meg knew there were at least two packages left. When she pulled the pack toward her, a piece of brown paper fluttered up from the floor. Someone had scrawled a crude diagram on it.

"Strange," Meg murmured.

"What is? Cozying up to a mangy cur?"

Conor was standing partially draped by the curtain. His teasing grin eased into a question at the look on her face. "What is it?"

Meg handed him the paper. "I found this tucked under my backpack."

He studied the paper, then pushed it into his shirt pocket. "I'll show it to Win. It looks almost like a map and there are some symbols I don't recognize. Some kind of writing, perhaps. It's just possible we have a nibble here."

"Where's Win? Can you give it to him right now?"

"Hold on, he's still finishing his breakfast. Besides, we don't dare show it to him in the presence of the headman. I don't want anyone to get into trouble for helping us. Meanwhile, care for some breakfast?"

"It isn't chicken soup, is it?"

"No, just the cookies we brought and tea."

"Didn't we give some of those cookies to the headman?"

"Yeah, why?"

"That paper is part of the wrapping."

"It is? I hadn't noticed." Conor took the square out of his pocket to have a second look. "You're right."

"It probably doesn't mean anything. I'm sure these cookies are everywhere."

"They are in town, but not up here in the hills. Not many locals would pay good money for something like cookies. Come and get some tea. I'll show this to Win after we've said our goodbyes."

Their leavetaking was almost as grand as their arrival. Meg had wanted to leave some money for the headman's wife, but Conor deterred her.

"She'd be offended and the old man would only take it anyway. Everything in the house belongs to him. I left a couple packs of cigarettes and he'll probably share some with her."

"But I have to give her something. She did all the work."

"How about some candy or gum?"

In the end, Meg found a roll of Life Savers in her pack. The woman cracked a toothless smile at the gift. No language at all between us, Meg thought, and worlds of differences. Still, she'd felt a brief connection to the old woman. It occurred to her that perhaps the woman had left the note. Hadn't she been hovering around them all night, pouring tea and clearing plates?

Impulsively, Meg hugged her. Perhaps she'd never know who had written the note, but just in case . . .

A few children followed them until the last wooden house was out of sight. Meg paused to throw a handful of candies in their direction.

"That was a good diversion. Over here, we'll show Win the note."

Their guide frowned at the message on the paper. He spoke to Conor who translated for Meg.

"Win says the words are in the Karen dialect. He thinks the map refers to the Akha tribe, not far from here."

"Can he take us there?"

"That's the problem. He doesn't want to."

"Why not?"

"Some Akha people have a reputation for being outsiders up here and engaging in dubious activities. They're a rough lot, not nearly as sociable as the Karen people."

"What do you mean by dubious activities?"

"A main cash crop is the poppy."

"The flower? Oh, you mean—"

"You guessed it. Opium. Many tribes in these parts have smoked opium for a long long time. They continue to do so, in spite of all that the government does to discourage their personal use. Win doesn't want to have anything to do with them."

"Terrific. We get around one obstacle only to face another. What can we do to persuade him? Increase his guide fee?"

"That's a good suggestion. Money talks here as it does everywhere else."

He negotiated with Win and reported back. "He'll take us for a small bonus. Apparently, he's engaged and needs the money for a house in Chiang Rai."

"Great. How long will it take us to get to these Akha people?"

"We could reach it by sundown. But there is one more thing. People say some Akha used to be head-hunters a long time ago. Any reservations about going there?"

"None whatsoever."

Conor smiled. If Win hadn't been gawking close by, he'd have kissed that determined face. "Let's go then," he said, and fell into place behind Meg on the narrow trail, heading due east into the morning sun.

LYDIA CAREFULLY set the Florentine tray on the coffee table and handed Jeffrey his martini.

"Is it Sunday already?" Jeffrey put down the newspaper. There was a puzzled but teasing expression on his face.

Lydia gave a small laugh. He was referring to their weekly ritual of cocktails before Sunday dinner. The real joke was that Jeffrey quite often would break routine by mixing a drink before dinner and saying, in his breezy, offhand way, "It must be Sunday."

"It feels like Sunday."

Jeffrey returned his wife's smile, but he was quick enough to catch the the edge in her voice.

"Time for our talk?"

She shook her head in mock despair. "How could I ever keep anything from you?"

"Why would you want to?" Jeffrey moved along the sofa, closer to Lydia, and took her hand in his.

Lydia swallowed hard and began. "A couple of weeks ago Meg called me to say that she'd been watching the news on television. There'd been some special feature on one of those refugee camps in Thailand. She was upset because she thought she'd seen a man in the film who looked like her father."

Jeffrey was staring intently into her face, his eyes dead serious. "And?"

"We...we made some inquiries but didn't learn much. You may not remember, but years ago, when you asked me to marry you, I told you how Meg had reacted to the news of her father's disappearance. After she saw this documentary, she became obsessed with the idea that her father might be alive."

"Joe."

Lydia looked up from her sherry glass into Jeffrey's eyes.

"For God's sake, Lydia. What's with this 'her father' nonsense? You're talking about Joe. Right? And you're telling me that you think he might be alive."

Lydia nodded. Jeffrey's impatience with her was justified. Why *had* she been waffling about this for the past few weeks? What had she expected, after all? That Jeffrey would walk out the door? The notion was as ridiculous as the way she was feeling that very moment.

"Joe." She repeated the name and exhaled a long sigh. "Forgive me, Jeffrey, for being so foolish. It wasn't that I underestimated you. I just didn't want to face the possibility of his being alive, so I let myself deny it. Until now."

"Lydia, I can imagine how you must have felt at this revelation of Meg's. My God, it hurts me to think you kept it all inside when you could have—"

"Jeffrey, please, I already feel bad enough. I suppose I was being true to form, as Meg might say. But let me go on. This whole story has taken a serious turn."

Jeffrey's eyes narrowed. "Continue, then."

"A few days after our call to the Pentagon—we tried to contact Joe's former commanding officer—Meg was visited by the journalist who produced the documentary. Apparently she's hooked up with this man in Thailand and has gone off into the hills to look for someone called Ghost Tiger who may or may not be Joe and—"

"Whoa!" interrupted Jeffrey. "Backtrack to the part about the journalist and take it one step at a time."

Lydia did, and when she'd finished, Jeffrey didn't speak for a long time. Lydia played with the stem of her sherry glass, knowing he'd talk when he'd assimilated all the information.

Finally, Jeffrey rubbed his hands together as if warming them over a fire. "All right. It seems that Meg has been given this name, though there's little solid evidence that the man is Joe Devlin. But this fellow Gallagher bothers me. He's obviously concocted the story about wanting to reunite with a wartime buddy. But for what purpose? Does he know anything about this Ghost Tiger?"

"*Now* he does."

"What do you mean by that?"

"The telegram had just been delivered moments before he arrived. He was horrible, Jeffrey. There's something about him that repulses me. I . . . I wanted to get rid of him. I thought if he knew going to Thailand would be a wild-goose chase, he'd not bother. So . . . so I told him the man in the documentary was someone called Ghost Tiger and was probably very well-known there."

Jeffrey released a long sigh. "Where's the telegram now?"

"In my jewelery box."

"Will you get it for me?" As she rose from the sofa, Jeffrey held out a hand to stop her.

"We do know one thing."

"What?"

"We have to go to Thailand. Meg's on her own with a man neither of us has met and this Gallagher, equally unknown to us, could well be heading after her."

Lydia felt her face drain of color. "How could I have been so foolish? Why didn't I tell you from the start?"

"Don't." Jeffrey stood to hold her in his arms. "You're not alone in this anymore. And Meg's a very capable young woman."

"Oh, God, I hope so." Lydia buried her head in Jeffrey's shoulder and began to weep.

CHAPTER NINE

GALLAGHER CHECKED his watch for the fourth time since the hostess had disappeared with his empty dinner tray. Another three hours to go. He wished he'd been able to afford the Concorde and make connecting flights to Bangkok, but he didn't dare risk padding an expense account for this trip. He'd even paid the fare himself, rather than have to submit receipts. As far as anyone in Accounting and Personnel knew, he was taking a long-overdue vacation in northern Michigan.

Not that he hadn't considered making up some business reason to travel to Thailand. He had a couple of current files on drug smugglers that he could use to support a sting job with the co-operation of Thai police and CIA staff at the embassy in Bangkok.

But he decided he didn't want anyone asking questions about his movements there. That way, he was free to go after Devlin and finish the job properly, without annoying inquiries from Langley.

Gallagher pushed aside the curtain and peered out into the enormous black void beyond the plane. The closer he got to Southeast Asia, the more anxious he got. Years of analysis had failed to obliterate the rush of nauseating adrenaline, the dry mouth and loose bowels that each return to the East brought. He never traveled here if he could send a lackey in his place. Except for the visit to Tremayne right after he'd received the call about Devlin, Gallagher hadn't been to Thailand for at least ten years.

When he'd been released from the camp in the first exchange of POWs after the war, he'd spent a year convalescing in some fancy veterans' hospital. He supposed he should have been grateful that the Company pulled strings to get him the best care available, followed by top-notch therapy, both physical and mental. But after what he'd gone through in the jungles of Laos and then in the tiger cages of North Vietnam, he figured the Company owed him.

Over the years, he'd begun collecting exactly what he was owed. Skimming a little off the top on this account or that, setting up phony case files and even a few phony johns he was allegedly running in East Germany. Gallagher smiled as he recalled how the reunification of Germany conveniently terminated those johns, allowing him to establish other false case files in Latin America and what had been Soviet Bloc countries.

He had almost enough set by for early retirement to his fishing lodge in Michigan and his winter retreat in the Grand Caymans. But when the computer's warning blip alerted the Pentagon's information staff to advise Gallagher about the Devlin inquiry, all plans for retirement were put on hold.

Gallagher didn't care if he had to spend every cent he'd saved to catch his ex-partner. If he was really lucky, he might even get his hands on what Devlin had taken for himself. Yes, he thought grimly, letting the curtain drop and checking the time once more, he just might have it all—Devlin and the bullion. It was certainly no more than he was owed.

MEG HAD LOST complete track of time. They'd walked for hours through patches of jungle, up and down so many hills she was certain they were traveling in circles. Every vine, tree and bush looked identical to the ones they'd already passed. Even the strip of muddy water meandering in the valley below seemed to offer the same view each time Meg caught a glimpse of it through the trees.

Only once had there been a break in the monotony. The trail had widened at one point and the two men were more than twenty feet ahead. Conor glanced back every now and then. Making sure, Meg thought with some resentment, that she hadn't been snatched up by an ape swinging on a vine.

She gave a tight smile; he waved a finger and turned his back to her again. A long dark shadow slipped out of the bushes on one side of the path and slithered across it. Meg couldn't estimate how long the snake was, only that she counted to twenty before the tip of its tail followed the rest of it into the jungle on the opposite side.

"Conor!" she called, her voice tremulous at first and then stronger as the Conor and Win disappeared out of sight. Her legs refused to move. "Now I know how a rabbit feels when the hounds are near," she muttered aloud. "Conor!"

There was a moment's satisfaction when Conor dashed back to her, his face drawn with concern.

"What is it?"

Meg felt silly. Why had she called him so urgently? The snake, after all, had vanished. "There was a huge snake. It went across the path up there and I've never seen one so long before. I . . . I was afraid to keep going in case it was lurking about."

"Ready to pounce at you?"

The smirk on his face annoyed her. She was thirsty, hot and tired. She'd just been confronted by a reptile large enough to swallow a Volkswagen, and who needed this kind of male patronizing anyway? She brushed by him, but he caught her by the elbow.

"Look, it's hot and we've still got a ways to go. I'm sorry you were frightened but there's no point in getting all uptight about it. Nothing happened—you're okay. Besides—" he grinned "—you look damn tempting when you flare up like that. And there's no irrigation pond handy." His mouth hovered over her brow, lips nibbled gently across and down the bridge of her nose to her mouth.

In spite of her annoyance, Meg felt a rush of heat. Her lips parted and she took the soft underside of his lower lip between her teeth and sucked on it. She was aware of his low groan and probed his mouth with her tongue hesitantly at first, then more boldly as desire rose from deep inside. His hands came up to her breasts, caressing in a gentle, rhythmic motion, and she swayed against him, wanting him.

But he pulled his mouth away from hers and buried his face in the crook of her neck and shoulder. "God, if we don't stop now, we'll never make it to that village."

"Much less to the next irrigation pond," she added breathlessly.

Conor laughed, took her face between his two hands and pecked the tip of her nose. "You're a good sport, you know."

"A good sport? Makes me sound like some adolescent playing rugger at boarding school." She made a face. "Come on, then, mate." Meg adjusted her backpack, and plodded ahead of Conor.

An hour later, Meg's carefree mood vanished.

She'd never seen a real skull before—at least not outside a museum. Certainly never perched on the end of a pole in the middle of a jungle.

"What does it mean?" Meg asked, not that she wanted to know. What she wanted was to put a few miles between that skull and herself.

Conor and Win exchanged anxious glances. They'd come upon the gruesome find on a small trail that had veered off the main path.

"Win says the Akha village is just ahead. Apparently they're a rather inhospitable sort and traditionally have left warning signs like this one to deter unwanted guests."

"Wouldn't a simple No Trespassing sign do?"

Conor's teeth flashed in his sunburned face. "Win says this is very old. Not a recent guest."

"Well, that's a relief. I hope you warned them we were coming. Made reservations or whatever you do in this neck of the woods."

Meg's last comment sobered Conor. "Yes, well, guess we'll just have to take our chances and hope that the villagers have grown friendlier."

Win insisted that Conor lead the way. He's no fool, Meg thought, and stayed well behind both of them.

More and more posts appeared at the side of the trail, although there were no more skulls. Some sported bones and feathers, some the pelts of animals dead so long their skins were like strips of leather. She avoided staring at them. Her blood pressure was already soaring.

The trail ended abruptly in a clearing enclosed by a crudely-built rail fence. The collection of huts inside was as far removed from the village they had left as Jupiter was from Earth. The entire area was bare of foliage of any kind. The straw and baked-mud huts were assembled in haphazard fashion on skeletal wooden frames. A few water buffalo and some pigs and chickens scavenged in the muddy yard.

A toddler wearing only a black shirt screamed when he caught sight of the three strangers. His cry brought a handful of people out of the huts. They stared with a mixture of curiosity and sullen hostility. The contrast with the warm, spontaneous greetings of the Karen people chilled Meg and she unconsciously drifted closer to Conor.

Win called out something and a slight man slid down a bamboo ladder leaning against one of the huts. At his approach, the others moved silently into the clearing, surrounding the visitors.

Meg brushed against Conor's arm, unnerved by the unfriendly circle of faces.

"Keep a smile pasted on your face," he hissed in her ear. "Don't worry, nothing's going to happen."

But she couldn't keep the image of that yellowed skull from flashing into her mind. "Well, I don't see any giant cooking pots."

Conor's smile broadened. One of the women, as if she'd understood this exchange, cackled, exposing two rows of brown, stumped teeth.

"Win says this is one of the poorest villages in the hills. They want money to put us up for the night."

"What about my father? Are you going to show them the photograph?"

"All in good time. You can't rush these things. There's a certain protocol to follow. Right now, the headman has invited us for a drink in his hut."

"I'd rather have a shower and get out of these filthy clothes," Meg grumbled.

"Not a chance here. Did you notice how dry it is? We can't expect the same kind of accommodation we had last night. And certainly no irrigation pond."

She laughed at the rueful expression on his face. A young girl next to her mimicked the laugh and the others giggled.

"As usual, you've made a hit," Conor said, taking her by the arm.

The group of people parted for them to follow the headman up the stairs into his house. It consisted of one large room, similar to the one they'd slept in the previous night. But there the similarity ended.

The floor, made of uneven planks and covered with rush matting, was littered with debris. Chickens pecked about, a mangy dog scratched furiously in one corner of the room, and blackened pots coated with remains of numerous meals perched on the rocks of a small hearth. A black-and-white spotted piglet helped itself to leftovers from one of the pots.

"At least there's a dishwasher," Meg murmured. She felt a warning poke in the ribs from Conor. "No one can understand me," she objected.

"This is a serious occasion. Don't make me laugh."

The headman kicked at the pig, which ran squealing to the other end of the hut. He motioned for the three to sit down and barked an order to a woman crouched in the shadows beyond the hearth. She shuffled toward them carrying a battered aluminum tray with four opaque glasses and a bamboo gourd. There was no sign of interest in her face as she set the tray down on the floor in front of the headman and squatted a few inches away from Meg.

The headman held up the gourd with a flourish of pride, spoke rapidly and poured a thin, milky-white liquid into the glasses. He handed one to Conor, then Win and finally Meg, spoke again and downed his drink in one gulp. Conor and Win followed suit.

"Go ahead," Conor prompted. "It's a kind of beer made from fermented rice. Not too bad."

Meg peered down at her drink, noting the wisps of straw and tiny black specks floating in it. She closed her eyes and swallowed. The bitterness of the beer caught her behind the ears and she opened her mouth, gasping at the sudden sharp taste.

The headman thought her performance hilarious and insisted on seconds. Meg shook her head vehemently, to no avail.

"This round will go down easier," encouraged Conor.

"I'm afraid it'll meet the first round coming back up." But she managed to down the beer and this time kept her hand firmly planted on top of the glass.

Once the niceties of ritual had been observed, Conor asked Meg for the photograph. After examining it for a moment, the headman tossed the photograph back to Conor. Then he rose from the floor, spoke quickly to the woman hovering in the background and went out the door. The three looked at one another, mystified by his sudden departure.

"Well?" Meg asked. "I take it from the shaking of his head that the picture drew a big blank."

Conor pursed his lips in thought. "Yes and no. Could you see his face from there?"

"Not really. He was looking down at the photo and he sat in the shadow. Why?"

"He said he'd never seen the man in the picture before but his face and eyes said otherwise. I'd swear he recognized your father. The disturbing thing was—" He paused.

"What?"

"The look in his eyes."

"What kind of a look? "

"Loathing."

JEFFREY CARRIED the two suitcases out through the automatic doors of the airport and stood, dazed.

"Now what?" Lydia asked at his right elbow. "Flagging down a cab here could be a real challenge."

"Not to mention life-threatening," he murmured, eyeing the traffic speeding in and out of the terminal. He raised his right arm and held it aloft until a black car squealed to a stop in front of them. Jeffrey grinned at Lydia. "First rule of thumb when hailing cabs in big cities: Don't go to them, make them come to you."

An hour later, refreshed from a hot shower and a glass of iced tea, Lydia and Jeffrey stepped into another cab to take them to the U.S. Embassy. They'd decided to follow Meg's trail as best they could, knowing she'd gone there before leaving Bangkok. But the young American they spoke to at the embassy proved to be unhelpful.

"It wasn't so much his not knowing anything," Lydia said over dinner later at their hotel, "but he didn't seem to care. I thought embassies were supposed to provide assistance to their citizens abroad."

Jeffrey sighed. Lydia had been harping on the point ever since their return to the Inter-Continental. "Darling, I'm sure you're reading far too much into all of this. He admitted that Meg had been there inquiring about Joe. And he told us exactly what he'd said to her—that there was no Joseph Devlin listed in the embassy's register of Americans living in Thailand. What more did you expect?"

"If he could remember all that, surely he could remember where she'd decided to go from here."

He wiped a hand across his face. Jet lag was just starting to hit and he was ready for bed. "But we already know where she went, Lydia. She sent us the telegram. What does it matter if the fellow couldn't say what her plans were after leaving the embassy?"

"It wasn't so much what he said, but what he didn't say. If it wasn't for that young Thai woman who spoke to us in the reception area, we wouldn't even know how to get to Chiang Rai. Remember what she murmured just after she told us where to buy airline tickets?"

Jeffrey stared at Lydia, recalling the hurried, whispered words.

"She said another American came early this morning asking for Joe Devlin."

Their eyes met. Lydia spoke the name they were both thinking. "Gallagher. He's here already and a step ahead of us."

"WE HAVE TO talk."

Meg looked up from her perch on the top rung of the crude stairs leading to the headman's lodgings. She'd been watching the quick descent of the sun below the trees beyond the wall of the Akha compound.

Conor squeezed past to straddle the rung below her. Meg thought he looked worn-out. He'd been inside for the past half hour talking to the headman through Win. The talk had begun with negotiating the price of their meals and overnight stay. It hadn't been much of a meal and Meg suspected the curt tone in Conor's voice stemmed from the headman's attempt to gouge.

"What's up? Is he trying to wring another fifty *baht* from us?"

"I wish it were that simple. He wants us to leave now, before morning."

"What? Is the man crazy? I mean, it's not as if there's a Holiday Inn over the next hill."

"Something strange about that guy."

"Yeah, he knows when he's got a captive audience. That makes him as peculiar as any other shoddy businessman back home."

"Point taken. No, it's more than that. He's been cool ever since you pulled out that photograph. If he was trying to protect the guy, you'd think he'd just play dumb the way the Karen headman did."

"What are you trying to tell me?"

He liked her way of ambushing him with the nitty-gritty, even though it required him to think two steps ahead of her. Or try to. He let slip an ironic smile.

"Come on," he said, extending a hand to her. "Let's find a more private place to talk."

"Private? We're the only ones who can understand what we're saying. I don't think there's much of a privacy issue."

Conor's smile widened. "I noticed the moon is almost full. We can take a short walk around the compound fence."

"Is it safe? Aren't there wild animals out there?"

"I thought you were the camping expert. Really, we'll be fine." He cupped her elbow in his hand and led her around the collection of huts to the gate. Shadows of people and animals settling down for the night flitted in the dim glow of lanterns and moonlight.

Conor headed for a small rise of land immediately outside the gate. In spite of his amusement at Meg's question about wild animals, he'd had enough experience in jungles to know one didn't stray too far.

"There!" he said, patting the stubby grass next to him as he sat down. "Seems safe enough."

Meg folded her legs crosswise beside him. His slightly patronizing tone irritated her, but she decided to let the remark pass. At the moment, there were more important things to discuss.

"How come the sigh?" he asked.

"Just thinking about the last few days and how all of this has turned my life into a complete turmoil."

Conor wondered how she'd feel if she had to return to the States with no clue at all about her father. Or worse, if she found him. He didn't want to think about that.

"So," she said with a false brightness, "what's the game plan?"

"Win and I both feel that the headman knows the man in the picture and doesn't like him one bit. Now, for some reason, he seems anxious to get rid of us. At this moment Win is trying to persuade him to let us stay on till daybreak. There's no way we could find our way in the dark."

"Did the headman give any impression at all about where my... this man might be?"

"Nothing. Won't even talk about him. And we can't expect any of the other villagers to come forward like the one from the Karen tribe. I get the feeling the headman rules with an iron fist."

"Then what do you suggest we do?"

There was a long pause. "We don't have that many options. Obviously we can't just wander through these hills aimlessly. I figure we start our return trip to Chiang Saen tomorrow—"

"No! Not yet! I've still got another week or so of holidays and I could—I don't know—phone in sick or something."

"From here?"

"I'm not going back. You can do what you like, but I'll hire Win to guide me."

"Slow down. There may be another option. Win knows of another tribe not far from here. They're related to the Karen people in some way—I couldn't understand Win's explanation—but that fellow who gave us the information back in Chiang Saen did say Ghost Tiger was living with a Karen woman. It's a lead, even if tenuous."

Meg realized she'd pushed aside that bit of information. It hurt to think that her father had conducted some kind of cruel death charade for such a common reason as another woman. Yet there had to be an explanation for what he had done and why he'd been so secretive.

"Then . . . then could we follow that up before going back?"

Conor heard the quaver in her voice. He wrapped an arm around her shoulders and felt her head tilt back against it. With his thumb he gently stroked her right cheek.

"Sure," he whispered. He slid his fingers down her cheek to the curve of jaw to the soft hollow of collarbone at the top of her shirt. His pulse quickened. She was so smooth. He turned her face toward his.

Meg's eyes shone in the moonlight. Conor saw surprise there, but interest, too. He lowered his mouth to hers, taking her lower lip between his own, savoring her sweetness. He heard a low groan and realized the pleasured sound had come from him. Her arms came up, hesitantly at first, but then folded tightly around him. Her mouth opened wide for him.

The flood of desire carried away all the questions and doubts of the day. Conor covered her face with kisses, then along the yielding slope of neck and back to her mouth again, tasting all of her in a slow journey from lips and tongue, around the curve of her jaw and down again. When his mouth reached the hollow at the base of her throat, he began to unbutton her shirt.

He heard her sharp intake of breath, but the arch of her spine thrusting her breasts against him urged him on. The shirt fell open and he slipped his hand up to unclasp her brassiere with a deftness that he'd forgotten he had. Her breasts spilled out into the moonlight—silvery globes with hard, dark areolas. He bent his head, pressing his face into their fullness and sucked on a taut nipple.

Meg gasped, her fingers clutching the hair on his head. Her moan excited him more. His mouth moved from one breast to the other, his hands stroking circles around them while his lips traced a path down to the waistband of her shorts.

He pulled a hand away to fumble at the button and zipper of the fly front, found the lacy strip of panties inside and leaned her back onto the grassy mound.

"God, you're beautiful, Meg. So beautiful," he murmured. His lips and tongue swept across her flat belly, explored the soft indentation of navel and moved down to the top of her bikini panties.

"Conor," she was whispering. "Don't stop. Please, don't stop."

The plea was all he needed. He groped for the front of his jeans. "Meg, I want you so much. You feel so wonderful. I...I need you.... God, how I need you."

"Conor, I want you too, all around me."

Her panting roared in his ears, urging him on and on until she clutched frantically at his shoulders, digging in her nails, and cried, "Conor!"

The name echoed in the stillness and he sank into her warm softness until there was nothing but the gentle rhythm of their two bodies and the balmy night air pressing all around. A long, shuddering moan from Meg made him look down into her face. Her eyes, wide with rapture, met his.

"Meg, I—" But the way she looked up at him with such naked trust in her eyes stopped him. He lowered his face into the hollow of her neck and sighed. "You're wonderful."

Moments later, when they had shifted apart and adjusted clothing, he could sense her disappointment. Not in the lovemaking, he knew, but in him. She'd been expecting something more and he'd failed to give it to her. He wanted to say the words she needed to hear, those declarations of love he'd not made to anyone for a long time. But they'd lodged in his throat like bitter reminders of lost opportunities.

He hated himself when he saw the falseness in her bright smile but he felt the ghosts of others crowding behind him—Gallagher, his brother, Eric, and Mi Mi's face, when she'd said goodbye.

Meg leaned on his arm to get up and he touched her chin with the tip of his finger. "Meg," he began, his voice hoarse but gentle, "I won't ever forget this night."

She stared into his face a thoughtful moment before answering, "I hope not, Conor. I truly hope not." And then she walked ahead of him toward the compound gate.

CHAPTER TEN

MEG FELT as though she were in a ship, rocking on a stormy sea.

"Uhh?" Her eyelids flapped. The shaking continued.

"Time to rise and shine, sleepyhead. We're on our way."

Conor's smiling face leaned over her.

"God, it can't be morning yet. I just fell asleep," she groaned.

"Troubles? No regrets, I hope." His dark eyes were serious.

She smiled. "No regrets. Just...I don't know... restlessness, perhaps." She hesitated. "Maybe wishing it could happen all over again."

"Well, maybe if we were at the Holiday Inn or someplace..."

A voice behind Conor caught his attention. He smiled—a bit wistfully, she thought—and withdrew from the crudely-partitioned sleeping area they'd shared in the headman's lodging. Meg stretched her cramped legs and folded up the sarong she'd used as a ground sheet.

While she zipped up her backpack she heard a sudden swell of angry voices coming from the other end of the room. Pushing aside the tattered grass mat hanging from a ceiling beam, Meg saw Win, Conor and the headman huddled together, glaring at one another.

Maybe the headman's annoyed because we don't have time for bacon and eggs, she thought, smiling at the irony of the notion. After last night's dinner of meatless, vegetable-less soup, there was little chance of any food at all this morning. Her rumbling stomach still held out hope, but reason declared otherwise.

Conor turned at her approach. "Come on, we're out of here."

Meg realized the abrupt tone in his voice had nothing to do with her, although it was a cold splash in the face after his whispered endearments last night. But she refused to let the magic disappear so soon.

"What's up? Is he offended because we can't stay for breakfast?"

The trace of a smile crossed Conor's face. "He wants twice as much as we agreed on. Win's upset because he thinks the guy will get even with us somehow if we don't pay up."

"Well?"

"No way. We've paid him far more than he deserved. The rest is pure extortion. Let's go. And just ignore him as we leave. He'll make some threatening gestures, but it's all show for his family."

Meg noticed for the first time a cluster of youngsters watching them with inscrutable expressions.

"Why not just give him the money? Who cares? It's probably only a few dollars."

"That's not the point," Conor replied, leading her to the door.

As he predicted, the headman followed them down the stairs and all the way to the gate of the compound, haranguing them and gesturing wildly. A handful of villagers watched, their faces surly and resentful.

The three had just exited the gate when a stone landed a few feet from Win. He turned around sharply but Conor said something that persuaded him to keep moving. Their pace was so brisk that by the time they'd reached the end of the trail with the skull perched on the stake, Meg was out of breath.

The gruesome warning appeared to be grinning at them as if, Meg thought, it was chanting "Told you so!"

"And so you did," she muttered.

"What was that?" Conor spoke from behind.

"Oh, nothing. Though I must say, I didn't know you could be so stubborn."

There was a brooding silence. Well, Meg thought, back to reality already. She ducked her head to avoid a low branch, then set her sights on Win's back, concentrating only on the rapid stride of legs and maneuvering of feet over rotting logs and mossy boulders. They'd been walking a good hour when Conor called for a rest.

"Win isn't sure which direction the village is."

"What's that supposed to mean?"

"Just what I said. Win says the village is upriver from the Akha compound but we're not sure if our descent of that hill has put us ahead or behind that point."

"That's a pretty important difference, isn't it? I mean, it's not as if we can pull into the next service station for directions."

"Win's offered to follow the river upstream a bit to see if there's any sign of it. He thinks we should wait here, rather than go back. No point in all of us wandering around looking for one another in the jungle. This part of Thailand is unfamiliar to both of us."

The admission shocked her. "Then why is Win guiding us? Why is he heading off into the bush if he doesn't have the faintest idea where he is?"

"He's guiding us because we hired him because you're determined to find this man you think might be your father. And 'unfamiliar' doesn't mean complete ignorance. He knows which direction the village is supposed to be and he's taking an hour to check it out. If he's wrong, he'll come back for us and we'll head back to Chiang Saen."

The cool retort angered her. She turned her back on Conor and slumped at the base of the tree, drawing up her knees to her chest and resting her head on them. She didn't see Win go. Didn't even know if Conor was still there. And didn't care. Meg closed her eyes and let herself drift into exhausted sleep.

The sound that woke her was one she'd only heard in movies. It didn't belong in her troubled dream and certainly jarred in the sunny grove of trees—the cold, hard clink of ammunition cartridges sliding into place. A hand clamped down on her kneecap as her eyes flew open.

"Don't move. Don't cry out. It's all right," Conor said calmly from her side.

She couldn't see his face. All she could see was the circle of men in tattered camouflage suits. And of course, their collection of rifles and submachine guns pointing directly at her.

JEFFREY'S HANDS tightened on the steering wheel. He must have taken a wrong turn somewhere and driven into the middle of a Grand Prix race or something. Cars whizzed by on all sides, including the gravel shoulder. He wished Lydia had taken his suggestion that they fly, but she seemed to think they'd have more mobility if they rented a car.

"Darling, I know you're feeling a bit tense, but according to the last sign we passed, we should be arriving in Chiang Mai anytime."

"I don't know how you can read the signs. The language here looks like some kind of bizarre shorthand," he grumbled.

"It was in English—they do have a lot of tourists here, you know."

"I haven't noticed any on this highway. All the smart ones are up in the air, well away from this bunch of Formula One hopefuls."

Lydia sighed. She knew all the signs of irritation. Jeffrey so seldom let things bother him, she forgot he could even get annoyed. Unlike the other members of her family, past and present.

She wished the thought away as soon as it had surfaced. No matter how stubborn Meg could be, how pigheaded and self-righteous, she was her daughter, her only child. Whenever Lydia missed Meg, the image she conjured up in her mind was of a skinny twelve-year-old, slightly freckled, strawberry-blond hair that refused to be tamed and eyes reddened from long hours of crying for her father.

However this strange trip ended, Lydia vowed never to reproach Meg for taking off on such a pointless quest. She personally didn't believe for one minute that Joe was alive. Surely she would feel it if he were?

Well—she sighed again—I'll dab at her tears the way I did when she was twelve, bundle her up in the car and take her back home. Maybe she'll finally be able to put her father's ghost to rest. Lydia lay her head back against the seat and closed her eyes.

No, Joe couldn't be alive. If he were, his silence all these years would be unspeakably cruel. And no matter how selfish he'd been, he would never hurt Meg that way. Still, the whole matter of Noel Gallagher was peculiar. Just how did he fit into all of this?

"Lydia! Lydia, wake up, we're here." Jeffrey's voice brought Lydia back to reality.

"My goodness, it is certainly smaller than Bangkok. But rather quaint, don't you think?"

Jeffrey was too busy negotiating the traffic to gawk. Eventually, he pulled off onto a side street and took out the map the clerk at the Inter-Continental had given him that morning.

"The hotel that was recommended is on some side street, but we may have to ask directions. Of course, all the signs are in that chicken-scratch writing."

"Yes, dear, they haven't gotten around to changing the signs for you."

"Tsk, tsk. Such patronizing. How ill-mannered."

Lydia returned her husband's smile. Jeffrey had always been able to get away with mimicking her New England ancestors. They needed to be brought down to earth, he'd say. Now Joe. He'd been another matter altogether. Ranting, raving, belittling. Lydia shivered. Why was she thinking of Joe, all of a sudden?

"You can't be cold?"

"No. More like a goose walking over my grave."

Jeffrey put down the map and took her hand. "Darling, you're not to let that worrisome imagination carry you off. Meg will be just fine."

It's not Meg I'm worried about. "You're right. Of course, she's fine. You know...mothers. Shall we ask that man there if he knows the way? He looks as though he might speak English."

An hour later, they'd checked in and were eating a late dinner, courtesy of room service.

"How clever of you to find the hotel receptionist's father on his way home from work," Jeffrey marveled.

"Wasn't I, though?" They laughed. Then Lydia put down her plate and went to Jeffrey, who was sitting on the edge of the bed.

"I love you so very much," she said.

"Come here," he said, and pulled her down beside him.

MEG KNEW there was something else locked up in the dark. Something with four legs that scurried.

"What was that?"

Conor's hand squeezed hers. He pulled her closer into the circle of his arms, tucking his legs around hers. They were sitting on the dirt floor of a tiny hut that had offered a quick glimpse of bags of rice, wooden crates and blackened pots until the corrugated iron door had locked behind them. Conor guessed they'd been inside no more than half an hour. He also figured that right about now Win was just discovering they were gone. Not that it made any difference to what was happening here. Thirty minutes or ten hours. They were in trouble and it was his fault.

He'd gone over and over it in his mind during the long walk to this place. What he should have done, where they should have gone—with Win! his hindsight screamed—and why they should have paid what the headman had wanted that morning. Because surely that was why this ragtag guerrilla bunch had kidnapped them—to get what the headman was owed.

Sometime on that long walk he'd realized the men were Akha. Fragments of dialect mixed in with regular Thai were the clue, but his knowledge of the tribal language was too poor to be of any help. He'd badly underestimated the headman's anger.

"Conor? What's going to happen to us?"

He couldn't see her face, but he heard the edge of panic in her voice.

"I don't know. Once someone in charge comes along, I'm sure this misunderstanding will be all cleared up."

"What misunderstanding?"

"Well, once they realize we'll pay the headman what he asked for, they'll let us go."

"Isn't this an extreme way of collecting a bill?"

Conor hugged her closer.

"Meg, I don't know what this is about. The only thing I can come up with is this morning's fight about money."

He felt her pull away from him. "They've got our passports and wallets, Conor. If all they wanted was the money..."

She didn't have to finish the sentence. He'd been doing his damndest to avoid that uncomfortable bit of knowledge. "I don't know.... I just don't know," he whispered. He'd never felt so helpless in all his life.

A metallic clanging boomed in the hut. The door was unbolted and creaked open. Meg squinted. A dark figure stood in the strip of light falling into the hut.

Movement burst into the darkness. Arms grabbed at them, pulling them to their feet and pushing them outside. Voices babbled all around them and Meg's fear threatened to choke her.

She closed her eyes against the painful brilliance of sun. The heat and stench of sweaty bodies wrapped around her, almost as nauseating as the panic rising inside. Carefully, she opened her eyes.

The men, guns in hand, huddled around her. Conor stood a few feet away, his hands tied behind him. A short, pugnacious-looking man strode back and forth, yelling at him. Conor shouted back. One of the men raised the butt of a gun at Conor's head. Meg screamed.

The group froze in a deadly tableau. The man in charge walked over to Meg, looked her up and down, then turned to say something to Conor.

"Keep calm. Whatever happens, don't be afraid," Conor called out.

The butt of the gun struck him and he slumped to the ground.

"Conor!" Meg cried.

There was a lot of shouting then—at Meg and at the man who'd hit Conor. One of the men beside Meg grabbed her by the arm, another pushed from behind and before she had a chance to cry out, she was flung into the darkness again. The door banged shut.

The hollering outside went on for a few more minutes and gradually faded. The hut filled with wrenching gasps until Meg was too exhausted to cry anymore. And then silence—almost.

There. She drew herself up off the floor, standing on tiptoe, pressing against the wall of the hut. Again. Snuffling noises somewhere in the dark. Coming closer.

MAYBE SHE OUGHT to have stuck with the tap lessons. At least her repertoire would have included more than step-one-two, shuffle-shuffle. Her voice was long gone. She'd sung every camp song she could remember and then some, making up words to nameless tunes. Her feet were two cement blocks, but she kept them moving. One, two, shuffle-shuffle.

Not bad, she told herself, for someone who'd dropped out of class after ten weeks and almost twenty years ago. Of course, her rhythm was dragging a bit, but the footwork was keeping those four-legged creatures at bay. Also kept at bay was that other beast—terror.

Meg had never felt so alone in her life after those first few panic-stricken moments of thumping on the door, calling out for help. Such a waste of energy, she realized later. Energy she could have put to better use tap-dancing away the vermin.

Oh, she allowed herself a break here and there. But then she could hear the squeaks and snuffling of what was probably—with the way her luck was running—an entire rat colony. And she'd start moving her legs again, sometimes relieving the monotony by slapping the palm of her hand against the wall of the hut. And just when she was certain one more shuffle of foot on the dirt floor would be her last, just when she was so tired she had slid halfway down the wall, Meg heard voices murmuring outside.

At first she thought they'd come back for her. The door burst open, silhouettes of gun barrels hit the walls of the shed. It was twilight and streaks of crimson and orange spilled across faces and clothing, painting everything in harsh, neon colors.

Their shouting was just as incomprehensible as the commotion hours earlier, but the arms that reached out to her now were gentler. Someone handed her a canteen of water, someone else a packet of cookies. When her eyes had adjusted to the eerie light and the bile of fear had trickled back down her throat, Meg allowed a tiny part of herself to relax.

Then she realized how different these men looked. They wore navy trousers and baggy shirts instead of combat fatigues. The guns were the same, though, and that sobering fact kept her from celebrating release from the shed. Were they rescuers, she wondered, or just different captors?

CHAPTER ELEVEN

THE OLD MAN bowed politely, though there was no smile on his face as he ushered Jeffrey and Lydia through the gate. In fact, Jeffrey had spotted immediately the slight frown at his opening remark that he was looking for Meg Devlin.

But he kept these thoughts to himself while he and Lydia followed the man across the sunny courtyard to the base of what appeared to be a giant tree-house. The old man left them standing there and disappeared into what looked like a shed. Jeffrey peered up into the branches of the huge tree.

"What are you doing?"

Lydia's voice sounded peevish. She must be feeling as uncomfortable as he was. "Looks like something the Swiss Family Robinson might have constructed. There are no vines hanging around, so I guess it's safe to assume Tarzan isn't going to swing out of the bushes at me."

"Jeffrey!" she hissed. "Keep your voice down."

He smiled, recognizing distinct signs of tension. But the smile vanished when he saw the grim-faced man approaching them.

"Mr. Devlin?"

Jeffrey shook his head. "No, I'm Jeffrey Haycock. Meg is my stepdaughter. This is my wife, Lydia."

The man scarcely nodded at Lydia. Anger surged through Jeffrey. "Look, I'm sorry. Perhaps we should start all over again. My wife and I received a telegram from Meg just a couple of days ago. The sender was identified as a Mr. Pran Sukrit, with this address. Are you Mr. Sukrit?"

The man bowed his head slightly. "Yes, I am Mr. Sukrit. Perhaps if you have some identification—"

"Isn't this getting to be a little ridiculous?" Jeffrey demanded. "What happened to that Thai hospitality I've been reading about? Good God, my wife and I have traveled half the world in search of our daughter and you have the gall to ask us to identify ourselves. Who are you, Mr. Sukrit, and why did you send that telegram?"

"I apologize, Mr. Haycock. You are right. I have forgotten my manners. Please—" he turned to Lydia and bowed his head "—please follow me up the stairs to my home. We will have some food and drink."

Grateful she'd worn slacks, Lydia climbed up the ladder stairs with Jeffrey close behind. She'd never heard such anger in his voice, but the message had gotten through, it seemed. There were large cushions on a highly-polished teak floor. The man gestured toward a chair, but Lydia shook her head.

"The cushion will be fine, thank you."

"Will you have tea? Or perhaps something stronger?"

"Tea, thank you," Lydia answered.

"Mr. Haycock? I myself will drink a Scotch and soda. Would you care for one?"

"Thank you." Jeffrey regretted the grudging tone in his voice. He continued "Look, I meant no of-

fense. But if you knew the strain we've been through
these past few days—"

"Mr. Sukrit," Lydia interrupted. "Is there a particular reason why you wanted to make sure we were
really Meg's parents?"

"Yes, Mrs. Haycock. Only yesterday we had a most
unpleasant visit from another American. He, too, was
inquiring about your daughter."

Lydia felt a flutter of apprehension. "Was this person a . . . a Mr. Galllagher?"

"And what exactly did he want to know?" Jeffrey's voice sounded grim.

"He asked where your daughter and Mr. Treymayne went after leaving here—" Pran paused "—but
he already knew about Chiang Saen. He seemed to
know a lot of things. I think he came here only to
confirm—to be certain."

Lydia nodded. "Of course he knew. He came to our
house—in the States—pretending to be looking for his
former army buddy, Joe Devlin. Joe is Meg's father.
He went missing twenty years ago in Vietnam. I... It's
a long story."

Pran nodded. "Yes, Mr. Tremayne explained some
of it to me."

"Just who the hell is this Tremayne?" Jeffrey cut
into the conversation.

"Jeffrey!" Lydia protested, but Pran held up a
hand, smiling.

"Mr. Tremayne is my very good friend for many
years now. He has been a journalist here in Thailand
for almost ten years. He is a good man. Do not worry
about Conor Tremayne."

"Well, thanks for the endorsement, but we're not very happy about our daughter traipsing around a foreign country with a complete stranger."

Pran smiled. "Oh, Mr. Tremayne is no stranger to Miss Devlin."

"What do you mean?" Lydia asked.

"They seemed to be very friendly with one another. I think my old friend Tremayne may be in love with your daughter."

Jeffrey caught Lydia's eye and shook his head, warning her to keep calm. The old man returned with a tray of drinks. Good timing, thought Jeffrey. I could use one of those right about now.

Pran waited while they sipped their drinks, offering the tray of biscuits around. Then he said, "After leaving here, Mr. Tremayne and Miss Devlin went to Chiang Saen. They hired my cousin, Mr. Win, as a guide. I believe they planned to visit the refugee camp outside Chiang Saen and they may have to go into the hill tribes."

"But I don't understand why you sent the message for her. Surely nothing was wrong?" Lydia asked.

"No, no. There is no place in Chiang Saen to wire messages. Miss Devlin and Mr. Tremayne telephoned me the night before they left for the hill tribes. I agreed to telelgram the message to you. Your daughter did not want you to be worried.

"Where is it you said they've gone? Hill tribes? Who are they?"

Pran looked at Jeffrey. "Not to worry Mr. Haycock. The people in the hills live more primitively than we do in the city, but they are good people. I . . ." He hesitated, glancing at Lydia. "I believe Mr. Tremayne

said somebody from one of the hill villages knew
something about this man—Mr. Devlin?''

Lydia nodded. "Yes, Meg mentioned a man called
Ghost Tiger. Well, I suppose you know that because
you sent the message.''

Jeffrey finally broke the silence that filled the room
after Lydia's comment. "Mr. Sukrit, we don't really
know very much at all. Perhaps that explains our sense
of urgency. This man, Gallagher, gave my wife some
cockamamy story. We don't know who he is or why
he's so interested in all of this.''

"We don't even know if this Ghost Tiger is my—
that is—my daughter's father,'' put in Lydia.

Pran's expression was sympathetic. "May I suggest
something? If you can wait until tomorrow morning,
I may be able to get some information about this Gallagher. I have some contacts in the American Embassy in Bangkok. I cannot promise you much, but
there may be something to learn about Gallagher.'' He
said the name with distaste.

"That would be wonderful, Mr. Sukrit. And I suppose we should be making plans to travel to Chiang
Saen later in the day.''

"I offer my service as guide to Chiang Saen,'' Pran
said.

"Oh, my goodness, that's too much. We don't expect you to—''

"Please.'' Pran silenced Lydia's protest with a raised
palm. "I am very concerned about my good friend.
And I do not like this man Gallagher. I am not happy
about him following my friend. You will need someone you can trust, someone who speaks good English
for you.''

Jeffrey held out a hand. "Mr. Sukrit, my wife and I are honored to have you as guide."

Pran grasped the hand and gave a slight bow. "I will meet you at your hotel in the morning. About nine? We go to Chiang Saen, no matter what I learn about Gallagher."

TWO HOURS into the boat trip up the Mekong River to Chiang Saen, Lydia was beginning to understand, in a small way, why Joe had seemed so out of place on his leaves at home. Everything was so thick here; the heat, the humidity, the jungle. Time vanished on the river. She felt that if the boat floated too close to shore, it might vanish, too—be drawn into the dense foliage and lost forever. She couldn't imagine what it must have been like with planes buzzing overhead, the jungle erupting in explosions.

Soon after Joe had been reported missing, she'd gone to see one of the movies about the war, popular at that time. She'd sat through the movie twice; midway through the first showing, the tears had begun. Somewhere toward the end of the second run-through, her grief had left her almost catatonic. She exited the theater hating the war, hating the men who'd created it and hating Joe for disappearing before the awful mess of their relationship could be fixed. And she'd sworn she'd never cry over Joe Devlin again.

Lydia wrapped her arms around herself and lowered her head onto her knees, tucked up against her chest. When she lifted her head some time later, Jeffrey was sitting beside her in the bow of the wide, open boat.

"Did I fall asleep?" she asked.

"Sure did. Rocked the boat with your snoring."

Lydia smiled at the old joke between them. "So, no tape recorder to prove your allegations this time, either, I suppose."

Jeffrey shrugged. "Guess you'll just have to take my word for it again."

Lydia reached for the hand he extended to her. They sat in a companionable silence for a long while. Finally, she spoke.

"I was remembering those first few weeks after I heard Joe had gone missing. 'Presumed dead' was the phrase attached to the message. *Presumed.* A strange word, that. As if someone somewhere had sifted through all the facts to arrive at that conclusion. The reality was that if you went missing, it was highly unlikely anyone was going to take the time to look for you. Presumed dead was an easy way out of explaining your absence. And I suppose it made sense, given the conditions." She inhaled deeply.

"It's taken me a long time to accept that my devastation at the time was as much from fear of what would happen to Meg and me, as grief for Joe. Everything between us unraveled long before I received that message. But you know that." Lydia squeezed his hand and looked toward the riverbank. Somewhere from the stern she heard Pran chatting to the boatman.

"I've managed to come to terms with my own guilt about this ambivalence over Joe, but I regret not being more open with Meg. I keep thinking if I'd told her how things really were between Joe and me, she might not have had this terrible case of hero worship all her

life. She might not have set off on this . . . this quix-
otic journey.''

"I don't know that it would have made a difference, Lydia. You're being too hard on yourself. She
was only twelve, right on the verge of adolescence. It
was easy for her to develop an unconditional love for
a parent who was never home.''

"I realize that, Jeffrey, but . . . Well, what concerns
me most of all is . . . Just suppose for a moment that
this man, this Ghost Tiger, is Joe. I know the idea's
farfetched, but if he is Joe . . .'' Her voice trailed off.

GALLAGHER FISHED around in his trouser pocket for
a five-*baht* coin to give to the *samlor* driver. He covered his mouth when the three-wheeled vehicle roared
off in a belch of black exhaust. It had been a long time
since he'd been in a one-horse joint like Chiang Saen.
The place had a few taxis, but damned if he could get
one for the ten-minute ride out to the camp.

He slung his suit jacket over his shoulder and
walked up the paved drive to the refugee-camp gate.
Two Thai soldiers in beige uniforms leaned against the
tiny office door. They were smoking and laughing, but
straightened when they noticed Gallagher.

He knew they'd demand a camp permit and he
didn't have one. But he had something better—embassy credentials that his contact in Bangkok had arranged for him, along with top priority flight from
Bangkok to dumpy Chiang Saen. The CIA plant in the
American Embassy had been on Gallagher's own
payroll for a few years. Gallagher long ago decided he
needed someone in place to feed him information—the
kind of stuff that makes the embassy cocktail circuit.

A bit of imaginative bookkeeping was all it took and the whole business more than paid for itself. Gallagher never failed to be amazed at the gold mine of news that cropped up in social chitchat.

Then his pigeon did some nosing around, found out who filmed the documentary that the Devlin broad was asking about and whaddaya know? The guy even came up with the necessary leverage to persuade Tremayne to do some legwork for Gallagher. Emotional blackmail worked every time.

The guards finished clearing his papers on the security phone and opened the gates. They saluted smartly once they figured him for an American government official. Five minutes later he was sitting in front of the camp commander.

But there the papers proved worthless. The commander's English was poor to begin with and diminished as Gallagher spoke. Later, at the gate, he deliberately pulled out a wad of *baht* notes on the pretext of looking for cab fare. When the taxi arrived, he made sure the guards heard the name of a local tavern in Chiang Saen. He noticed them sneaking looks at one another while he climbed into the car. Not many people were above a bribe, Gallagher had learned long ago. The trick was in allowing them to take it discreetly.

He was on his second bottle of beer when one of the guards, dressed in street clothes, appeared at the other end of the bar. Gallagher tipped the bottle in the man's direction, and smiled.

IT WAS DARK by the time they reached their destination. Meg had no idea where they were nor how far they'd walked, except that she was bone tired. The walls of an enclosed compound suddenly appeared out of nowhere. The night erased all reference points. The compound could have been in the middle of jungle or on an open plain. For the last part of the walk, she'd felt as though they were marching down a gradual slope. She could smell the fetid odor of stagnant water nearby. A pond of some kind, she guessed. The gate of the enclosure creaked open and they entered silently, like thieves.

The soft glow of kerosene lamps flickered in the open windows of the scattering of Thai houses. Meg couldn't guess how big the compound was, but it seemed to be larger than Pran's in Chiang Rai. The place was quiet, but Meg sensed an air of hushed activity. She could also smell food cooking and her stomach rumbled in complaint. Her escort led her to the steps of a small bungalow on stilts and pointed up.

"I'd like something to eat before you lock me up again," Meg protested.

Their faces were impassive. "Well, I've been wanting to lose a couple of pounds." She headed up the stairs and stepped into the single dark room of the house.

The man who'd followed her up the stairs closed the door behind her.

"Damn!" she hissed.

"It beats the shed," came a tired-sounding voice from a corner. Meg whirled about. "Conor?"

"Here. About ten feet straight ahead. I'd meet you halfway, but I'm—"

The rest was cut off by Meg's arms wrapping around his neck, her mouth covering his shadowed face with kisses.

Later, after she'd had her fill of hugging, she listened as he filled her in on his adventures.

"I'd like to get my hands on the bastard who took my shoes," he began. "After they put you back in the shed, they made me walk—oh, about two or three miles, I guess. They had a camp tucked into the hills not far from the Akha village. In fact, I've a sneaking suspicion the village headman and the leader of that bunch are in cahoots."

Meg crossed her legs and moved closer to Conor. Doing so, her arm brushed his side. He grunted in pain.

"It's okay, just a few bruises. Maybe a cracked rib or two."

"God, Conor, what did they do to you?"

"Pushed me around a bit. I think they thought I was CIA or from some American-Thai drug-enforcement squad or something. I couldn't understand the dialect they spoke, but I did make out CIA a few times. I kept telling them I was a journalist, but they didn't understand me any better than I did them. I guess you've figured out that this lot here is a different bunch."

Meg nodded. "I can't decide if they're any better or not."

"Yeah, the accomodation's nicer, but the guys still have guns."

"How did you get away from those other men?"

"When we got to the camp I mentioned, one of the head honchos started asking me all these questions. I couldn't understand the dialect he was using but I did pick up the word CIA in the middle of his rambling speech. Anyway, they finally realized I didn't know anything and left me alone. I don't know how long I was locked up, but suddenly there was a lot of shouting and gunshots. The door flew open and this bunch came rushing in.''

"Do you know where we are?"

"It's a fairly large compound in a valley. The river's a few miles away. We passed it on our way. There are some farms in the area, so we must be near a community.''

"I thought I smelled stagnant water."

"Yeah, there's a marsh not far from here. What about you? They didn't... No one—''

Meg squeezed his hand. "I'm fine. No one mistreated me. But I was locked up for a long time in that shed. There were rats....''

Conor's arm brought her closer. The movement must have pained him because she heard a sharp intake of breath. "Be careful," she whispered, lowering her head into the space under his chin.

"God, Meg, I was so worried about you. Thinking about what I would do to those creeps if anyone touched you was all that kept me going.''

It was the first real admission of affection he'd made. Even in the midst of their lovemaking, he'd whispered her name, told her she was beautiful, so soft, so wonderful—but no word of caring.

There was a noise outside the door. Conor patted Meg's arm. "Stay here." He stumbled to his feet, gasping at the stabbing pain of muscles and blisters.

The door creaked open and the dim glow of a kerosene lantern swung into the room.

An old woman handed him a tray of food and watched him limp back to Meg. Then she sat the lantern down on the floor and left.

"Dinner?" Meg perked up, inhaling the rich, spicy aroma from the tray.

They ate in appreciative silence. The food was hot, tasty and wonderful. Their bowls were empty moments later. Meg reached for the teapot and poured another cup.

"I don't know why I feel better—we're almost prisoners here, it seems—but it's amazing how a good meal can take your mind off your problems." She paused and then, in a more serious voice, said, "Conor, what's going to happen to us? Why aren't these people talking to us? Do you think this has anything to do with Ghost Tiger?"

"It's a possibility, but I don't know why no one's bothered to question us. Maybe there's something going on between the first group and this lot. Some kind of territorial power struggle."

"Would it have anything to do with drugs?"

"This is the area referred to as the Golden Triangle," he said, "the convergence of Burma, Thailand and Laos. All kinds of drugs are grown, manufactured and smuggled out. The drug people in this part of the world are an unscrupulous lot. I can't imagine they'd let a couple of *farangs* wander around their territory."

"You mean . . ." Meg couldn't say the words.

"Yes. Lots of people have disappeared—permanently—in these hills."

188 GHOST TIGER

"What can we do?"

He admired the calm resolve in her voice. He wanted to wrap himself around her and make all the bad things go away. Maybe it was time to tell her about Gallagher.

"Come here," he whispered, his voice husky with emotion. He pulled her closer, ignoring the discomfort of her body pressing against his ribs. "I want to tell you a story. See . . ." He hesitated, looking at her.

"There were only two kids in my family. My brother's nine years older. My mother had some problems, I suppose, because they're always told me what a surprise my birth was. Anyway, I grew up with a big brother who was terrific. He was my hero. He always will be. Even now."

Conor paused, took a deep breath to rein in all the passion the memories aroused. "I was nine myself when Eric was drafted. He never dreamed of running away or looking for some loophole to save himself. He wanted to serve his country." He gave a harsh laugh.

Meg waited, fearing the slightest movement would stop him.

"He did. Served his country damn well and returned four years later—half a man, physically and spiritually. But he got a nice Purple Heart to compensate for missing legs. Of course, there was no job to go along with the medal. No girlfriend, either—she split, hours after he got back home." He stopped, averting his head to gaze at some unknown point on the other side of the room.

Meg reached up to kiss the hard, rough edge of his jaw. When he looked down at her, his eyes were bright with anger.

"The rest is cliché. A downhill slide to drinking, drugs—you name it, Eric did it. My father went bankrupt paying all the medical bills, not to mention the fines and bail money. He died of a heart attack three years after Eric got back. I was still in high school, trying to help out with part-time jobs. My mother took it all on—everything. She's quite a woman. You'd like her." He hugged Meg, bent down to kiss the tip of her nose.

"We had some rough years. Eric was in and out of veterans' hospitals, rehab centers, jail—" Conor shook his head. "There were so many demons to fight...." His voice trailed off.

There was a moment of silence before he continued. "By the time I was ready for college, I was ready to leave for good. I couldn't take it anymore. Couldn't take seeing my brother—my hero—crying or raving in an alcoholic stupor. I got a scholarship and left. My mother wanted me to go, but I felt awful leaving her to handle it all by herself. I wrote and telephoned, sent money when I was earning it, but weekend visits were all I could take.

"After I graduated in journalism, I wandered around Europe and the Mediterranean, followed what they used to call the 'hippie pipeline' through Afghanistan to India. When I got to this part of the world, I was curious. The war was over but there was the horrible aftermath of countries trying to pull themselves together. I had no desire to go to Vietnam, so I hung around Bangkok and came to love Thailand. It's a place of such contrasts." He uttered an ironic laugh. "Not unlike my own home. I got a job with the *International Herald Tribune* first, then moved up as foreign correspondent for an American newspaper. A few years ago I went free-lance and a buddy of mine—a Thai—and I teamed up to film a few documentaries. You've never seen any of them, I'm sure.''

''And Eric?''

Conor smiled at her. ''Eric pulled himself together. I don't know what the catalyst was—maybe meeting his wife, Marianne—but he did it. With a lot of help from his friends, as the song goes. He ended up in politics and has been councillor in our hometown— Fairview, Montana—for five years. The last letter I got, said he was running for mayor this year. He sounded—'' Conor searched for the right word ''—at peace with himself.'' Then he frowned.

Meg caught the shift in mood. She gave him a moment, and when he ventured no further, prompted, ''But?''

He took her face between his palms and turned it toward him. His eyes met hers. Meg saw the nakedness of his expression. She reached up a hand to stroke his cheek.

''A few weeks ago—''

The door swung open. The old woman shuffled into the room carrying a white enamel basin and a towel. A man holding a tattered black box followed her. They walked softly across the wooden floor, gave a quick half-bow to Conor and Meg and proceeded to pull back the sheet wrapped around Conor.

''What are you doing?'' Meg protested.

''It's okay,'' Conor reassured her. ''I've a feeling they're here to look at my feet.''

He was right. Meg wandered the shadowy room waiting for them to finish. She winced when she heard Conor's ragged breaths. There were more soothing sounds after that; water splashing against the sides of the bowl, the tearing of gauze and above it all, the soft murmuring of the old woman and her helper.

Finally they finished and Meg turned around when she heard them move toward the door. "Conor?" Meg tiptoed to the cot.

His eyes were closed, but partially opened at the sound of her voice.

A smile started in one corner of his mouth, then slipped. His head lolled to one side of the pillow. "Sorry...feel so tired all of a sudden. Must be the knock on my head."

His eyes closed. Meg stretched out her legs and leaned against the side of the cot. She watched him, thinking how vulnerable he looked in sleep. She could almost see the teenager in him. How painful those years must have been.

Meg tried not to think of her own family. Tried not to wonder if she'd ever see them again. What might have happened if she'd never made that first telephone call to the Pentagon? What if...?

The trail of speculation wearied her. It always ended in the same way. If she hadn't, Conor would never have ended up at her door with her cat in his arms. The idea that she might never have met him overwhelmed her with such dismay, she couldn't begin contemplating it. She *had* met him. She *was* here. With him. For now, that was all that mattered.

CHAPTER TWELVE

PRAN LISTENED politely while the commander of the refugee camp paced back and forth, obviously venting his frustration and annoyance at yet another interruption in his busy day.

Finally, Pran turned to Jeffrey and Lydia sitting next to him and translated. "The commander is very curious about all these questions about Joseph Devlin and Ghost Tiger. He said two other American people came asking these same questions, and another just yesterday."

"Gallagher," Jeffrey supplied.

"Perhaps so. The commander says he can only say what he has told everybody else. He does not know Joseph Devlin and he never heard of this Ghost Tiger. He says sorry, but he cannot help us."

Lydia twisted the handkerchief in her hands. "What now? Do we bribe him or what?"

Pran smiled and shook his head. "I think not. This man would be greatly offended. We must return to town and discuss."

Jeffrey helped Lydia to her feet. "Pran, please thank the commander for us."

Pran did so, bowing respectfully. He followed them out the door and into the waiting taxi. The car roared down the drive and through the security gates.

"I have doubts about that fellow, Pran. I think he was lying."

Pran gave a faint smile and nodded. "But of course, Mr. Jeffrey. Of course the man was lying."

GALLAGHER LEAPED back into the doorway when the taxi passed. Then, cautiously, he poked his head around the frame to see the cab pull up outside the single hotel in Chiang Saen. His hotel. He saw a Thai step out of the front and hold open the rear door. Lydia Haycock emerged, followed by a white-haired man. Damn!

He'd never have bet in a million years that Devlin's wife would follow him all the way to bloody Chiang Saen. The other American must be her second husband, Haycock. Couldn't think of his first name. The Thai he recognized as the snotty guy from Chiang Rai. Well, well. Hot on the trail. Were they after him or their daughter? Not that it mattered now.

He waited until the three vanished inside the hotel. Thank God he'd used an alias to register, although the clerk was bound to mention another American was also in town. Not many tourists wandered this far northeast of Chiang Mai. Gallagher knew he didn't have a lot of time to finish what had to be done. The arrival of the Haycocks complicated things, but as long as he kept cool he'd still come out ahead.

If only he hadn't stayed at the bar last night. Long after the security guard left, flush with his wad of American dollars, Gallagher sat, finishing a bottle of Scotch, planning every move and each word. He wanted to enjoy the expression on Devlin's face. He wanted to stretch out each delicious moment when

Devlin finally realized he hadn't come back just to get the gold.

Gallagher stepped briskly out into the street and hailed a taxi. He gave the man the written instructions the security guard had jotted down and sat back to enjoy the drive. All in all, Gallagher was pleased with the way things were turning out. He liked a challenge, and beating the Haycocks to the quarry was an unexpected one. He didn't know where the hell Tremayne and the Devlin woman were, but suspected they'd appear in Chiang Saen any time. All paths into the hills inevitably wound back to Chiang Saen. Unless they'd gotten lost and headed up into Burma, but the guard had said they had a guide with them.

It was ironic that Tremayne headed into the hills to look for Ghost Tiger when the man lived just a few miles outside of town. Gallagher had laughed long and hard at that news last night. Laughed until the tears came. The guard had admitted taking money from Tremayne for information but confessed to sending them off to the hill tribes where Ghost Tiger often visited his wife's family. Apparently he'd been too afraid to send them to Ghost Tiger's house down the road. That would have been risky on the heels of their visit to the camp.

But the man had certainly loosened up last night. Gallagher figured the results had been well worth the price of a bottle of Scotch in this flea trap.

The paved road that ran through Chiang Saen ended a mere ten kilometres north of the refugee camp. A narrow dirt trail veered west at that point. The cab-driver wasn't happy about venturing off into the bush, but a handful of *baht* notes persuaded him in the end.

Yessir, everyone has his price, thought Gallagher smugly. The old car rattled along for a few yards and stopped. A tree lay across the trail.

"Wait here," ordered Gallagher as he got out. To be sure, he waved a fifty-dollar American bill. The cabdriver nodded, switched off the engine and lit up a cigarette.

Gallagher followed the trail beyond the fallen tree. It looked as though it had been purposely chopped down and placed there to deter unwanted guests. The guard had been definite about the trail. Not far, he'd insisted, and you come to Ghost Tiger's compound. Somewhere in the dense greenery a monkey hooted. Gallagher jumped. It had been a long time since he'd been near a jungle.

The path was well used, in spite of the blockade. He wondered if that was a recent thing, then decided it must be. Trekking in supplies to the compound would be damn difficult on foot. There would probably be a guard posted somewhere in the area. He had his fake embassy papers to get past the guard. Devlin would be another matter. If he was lucky, he'd get close enough just to figure out the lay of the land, then he'd come back at nightfall.

A bamboo fence was the first sign of cultivated land. Gallagher slowed his pace, assuming a pose of someone unsure and nervous. His eyes shifted from left to right. To his surprise, the path led directly to a high bamboo wall. Gallagher approached it cautiously, peered through the crude slats to see a small clearing with two houses on stilts and a small shed. Chickens pecked in the dirt yard and a goat was teth-

ered to a post near the shed. There was no movement
or sign of human life inside.

Gallagher edged around the circular wall. A few feet
in front of him an old man dozed in the midday sun.
Siesta time for everyone, it seemed. A rooster crowed
from the other side of the wall. Gallagher grinned. No
guard, except for that geezer. Devlin obviously had
nothing to fear in this little haven he'd carved out for
himself in the Thai hills. Not yet, anyway.

By the time Gallagher got back to the cab, his shirt
was drenched with the sweat of excitement. He'd soon
be back—armed—with a little surprise for Joe.

"ANOTHER AMERICAN? Here?" Lydia's eyes met
Jeffrey's.

The clerk at the Formica counter that served as Reception nodded vigorously. "Yes, yes. A Mr. George.
Are you knowing a Mr. George from America?"

"No, no, I don't believe so. What room is he in?
Perhaps we could introduce ourselves," Jeffrey said.

"Room 26. Second floor. Down the hall from you."

They thanked the man and joined Pran, who was
waiting near the main door. He looked dismayed at the
information.

"This is not good news. We must talk, make plans.
Come, it will soon be evening. We will eat first, then
return to the hotel." As they headed out the door,
Pran suddenly stopped. "This man Gallagher, do you
think he is dangerous?"

Lydia thought for a moment. "I don't honestly
know. The first time I met him, he was quite pleasant. Almost bumbling. The second time, he seemed

more...intense. I can only say that there was something about the man I instinctively disliked."

Pran shook his head in agreement. "We eat now, then we discuss what to do."

They dined in one of the town's two restaurants, eating quickly and silently.

When Jeffrey had finished, he leaned back in his chair. "I can honestly say the Thai food I've had back home didn't compare at all to this, Pran. I only wish I could have enjoyed it more."

"When all of this is over, you and Mrs. Haycock must come to my home for a meal. My wife is a very good cook."

Lydia nodded politely, but her thoughts raced ahead. When all of this is over. When and how? She couldn't understand why Gallagher was so determined to find out if the man in the news feature had been Joe. She'd often suspected that there had been a secret side to her first husband. His jovial, extroverted nature with friends seldom carried over to their private lives. At home, he was moody and quiet.

Except for the single reference to Noel Gallagher in one letter, he'd never mentioned the man. Which certainly belied Gallagher's suggestion that the two had been friends. Whatever the reason for his interest in Joe, Lydia felt sure something bad lay ahead.

"Are you ready to go back to the hotel, darling?"

Jeffrey's face was concerned. He knew her so well. Lydia took a deep breath and nodded.

The main street of Chiang Saen was bathed in the bright pink light of dusk. Street vendors sold bowls of noodle soup and ice drinks and people milled about, enjoying the balmy coolness of evening. But Lydia was only aware of the hotel, the two-story stucco building across the street from the restaurant. Standing on the top step was Noel Gallagher.

She grabbed at Jeffrey's arm. "There he is! Gallagher."

Pran and Jeffrey froze, watching Gallagher jauntily descend the concrete steps and open the door of a waiting car. A Thai was sitting inside and spoke briefly to Gallagher before getting out of the driver's side. Gallagher got in and moved over, rolling down the window to speak again to the man. Then he drove off.

Jeffrey went into action. "Lydia, go back to the room, lock the door and stay there. Don't open it for anyone but Pran or me. No, don't argue. Pran and I are going to have a talk with that fellow and if we don't move now, he'll disappear in the crowd. Here's the key. Now go."

The urgency in his voice warned her not to protest. "Be careful," she called as the two men ran into the road after the Thai. Lydia clutched nervously at her throat as she briskly crossed the street to the hotel.

The difficult part was the waiting. Almost two hours later, there was a low tap at the door.

"Lyddie, it's me."

He hadn't called her that for years. When she opened the door, the expression on Jeffrey's face told her he was frightened.

"Where's Pran?"

"Coming. He's downstairs arranging a phone call to Bangkok. Apparently it's not such a simple matter in this neck of the woods. Oh, darling, it's so good to be here, holding you in my arms."

She tried not to be alarmed at his trembling. "Jeffrey, sit. Where's that Scotch of yours? I'm going to pour you a drink."

"No. Thanks for the offer, but we'll all need our wits about us. To figure out what's going on and what to do about it. Now, sit down here beside me. I've a lot to fill you in on before Pran returns."

"Jeffrey, you frighten me with that kind of talk. What is it? Nothing's happened to Meg?" Lydia's voice rose.

"I've heard nothing about Meg. But we must decide what to do about this Gallagher... this whole situation."

"For God's sake, Jeffrey, get to the point."

Her irritation seemed to help him focus. "Pran and I caught up with the fellow Gallagher was speaking to in the car. It seems this man is a security guard at the refugee camp. I'm sorry we took so long, but Pran wouldn't let me rush things. We had to invite the man for a drink, then beat around the bush so long I was almost ready to reach over and grab him by the collar and shake the story out of him. Thank God, Pran was there—"

"Thank God," Lydia murmured. "Go on."

"Gallagher visited the camp yesterday, chatted with the camp commander and came out all in a huff. He apparently bribed this guard to get the information he couldn't get out of the commander. Turns out Gallagher was asking about a man called Ghost Tiger—"

"Ghost Tiger? Not Joe?"

"That's what the guy said. He'd never heard of any Joe Devlin, but he sure as hell knew who Ghost Tiger was."

"And who is he?"

Jeffrey paused. There was such a deadly calm in Lydia's voice he could hardly believe it belonged to the woman who'd been his wife for the past sixteen years. She knows, he thought.

"The fellow said Ghost Tiger is a *farang,* a white man, who's been living here in the hills for years. He said the man is American, that no one knows very much about his past. Apparently he takes care of a lot of the refugees, visiting them, taking gifts and medicine. He's become something of a local hero. Anyway, Gallagher wanted to know how to find him and the man told him where Ghost Tiger lives. With his family."

Lydia caught the last sentence, added, it seemed, as an afterthought. She filed it away for later. "Where does he live?"

"Just outside of town. That's what was so ironic about the whole story. Meg and this Tremayne fellow have gone traipsing off to God-knows-where in search of Ghost Tiger and the man lives down the road." Jeffrey shook his head in disbelief. "I managed to persuade this guy to take Pran and me out to Ghost Tiger's place. Gallagher had rented the man's own car, so all three of us bundled into a cab. We got as far as the end of the paved road and the driver refused to go any farther. We had no choice but to turn around and come back to Chiang Saen. Unfortunately, there's no telephone at this Ghost Tiger's house so we've nothing to do but wait until tomorrow."

"Wait for what?"

"I don't know, to be honest, what our next step will be. Pran is calling the embassy again in Bangkok to

ask his friend there about Gallagher. He's obviously
gone visiting, but we can't just call the police. I mean,
for all we know, they're good buddies."

"Not if—"

"Not if what?"

"Not if this Ghost Tiger is really Joe. Jeffrey, I have
a very bad feeling about all this. I feel that everything—my life—is spiraling out of control."

Jeffrey took her into his arms. "Darling, don't give
in to that, please. I'm here, we've got Pran—everything will be resolved. One way or another."

MEG SHIVERED. The covers must have fallen onto the
floor. She raised her head and squinted blearily in the
ghostly light of daybreak. There were no covers, she
remembered, once the room came into focus. No bed,
either. Which explained the stiffness in every joint.

Conor's eyes flared open when she lifted a numb
arm from the cot. His smile was weak, but there was
a warmer glow in his eyes. "It's not quite the way I
imagined us waking up together."

Meg arched her back and stretched. "Good morning to you, too." She wanted to reach out and tousle
the knot of hair straggling across his forehead. Instead, she stroked it back into place. Conor circled her
wrist with his fingers and pulled her closer.

"I think I deserve more than a pat on the head," he
murmured. He propped himself up on one elbow and
pressed his lips squarely on hers.

The sound of the door latch drew them apart. Meg
rose shakily to her feet as the old woman reappeared
carrying a basin and pitcher. She placed the washing
utensils on the chest opposite the cot. A young boy

took up the rear, balancing a tray with teapot, fruit and bowls of boiled rice. The two came and left without a word.

Conor's eyes met hers. "Tea?" The hoarse longing in his voice cut the tension in the room.

Meg brought the tray over and put it on the floor beside Conor. She sat cross-legged next to the cot and poured the hot tea. "Perhaps it was a good thing we were interrupted."

"Perhaps," he agreed, though the hungry expression in his eyes said otherwise. He took a small, chipped cup from her. "Eat everything they've given us. You never know—"

The door creaked open. The sun had risen over the hilltops and streamed across the courtyard through the doorway. A tall, black figure poised on the threshold. Then a baritone voice cleared itself and spoke.

"Good morning. I hope you're enjoying the meal."

The man took two large strides out of the sunlight into the room. Meg felt her heart rise up into her throat. She recognized at once the snowy, leonine head and portly body—the man in the documentary.

"Perhaps I should introduce myself first and then you can tell me who you are and why you've been wandering in these hills," he was saying.

Meg heard the rustling of sheets as Conor shifted in the cot, but her eyes never left the man standing in front of her. She pushed herself up from the floor and took a step toward him.

"My name is Meg, and I believe you are my father."

CHAPTER THIRTEEN

MUCH LATER, Meg recalled other details. The quietness in the room, the range of expressions on his face as he approached her—even the lingering aroma of pineapple.

"Meg? My God, I can't believe it. You're...you're all grown-up."

There was such despair in the husky voice, Meg's inclination to quip 'It's been a while' vanished. She could only remain speechless.

It was Conor who came to their rescue, limping over to pull a chair up for the man who was now so shaken he, too, could only stare.

"Please, Mr., uh, Devlin, I guess it is, sit down. You've had a shock." Then he was at Meg's side, wrapping an arm around her shoulders although he knew she wasn't aware of him. "Meg?" he whispered in her ear. "Are you all right? Do you want to sit down?"

She looked at him, her eyes glazed with tears. "No, I think I'd just like to be alone with...with my father."

Then she went over to Joe Devlin, crouched down at his feet and rested her head on his knees. His own snowy head dropped down to hers and he began to weep.

Conor moved slowly toward the door and pulled it shut behind him.

Joe Devlin reached for a pack of cigarettes and lit one.

"I don't know where to begin," he said.

Meg sat down on the edge of the cot. She sensed his need for her to find a starting point, but her mind was in disarray. At the moment she was having difficulty putting together two connected thoughts. She wanted to say, "Just start at the beginning." But at *his* beginning or *hers?*

Joe took another long drag on his cigarette. "You must want to know why," he finally said.

It was a good start, she thought. Of all the questions racing around in her head, why was definitely at the hub. "Yes. Why? Then where and when and how and what. God..." Meg thought of her mother and Jeffrey, and for the length of a heartbeat wished—what?

That she'd never phoned the Pentagon? Never found her father? Never met Conor Tremayne? She buried her head in her hands. It was so complicated and not at all what she'd expected.

"It's a long story. I don't know if this is the place to tell it. Certainly, it isn't the time. Those men who took the two of you yesterday are still in the area. They're part of a drug-smuggling operation that's been under investigation for months now. They're dangerous men. You both were lucky your guide managed to find this village."

"I don't understand."

"The people here—they're Karen tribesmen—had organized a band of men to patrol the hills because for a long time the government did nothing about the opium trade in one of the nearby Akha villages. Then the smugglers set up their own little army and the government finally had to step in by sending a special squad to work undercover in this village. Luckily for you, your guide tumbled into the middle of the whole operation.'' Devlin reached over and butted his cigarette on one of the empty breakfast plates. He paused and stared at Meg.

''You've become a very beautiful young woman. I see that tangle of curls never did get tamed.'' A smile flashed across his face, then vanished. He looked away. ''How is . . . your mother?''

Meg took a deep breath. ''She's fine. As beautiful as ever. She's . . . she's married.''

He nodded his head, keeping his gaze fixed on some unknown point in the room. ''Of course. Happy, I hope?''

''Very.'' Meg paused. ''Why didn't you write? Or let us know you were alive?''

''As I said, it's a long story. I promise I'm not putting you off. But I think we should speak to your . . . What is he? Your fiancé? We should talk about getting back to Chiang Saen as soon as possible.''

''Conor. He's . . . he's a journalist. He's the one who made the news feature about the refugee camp outside of Chiang Saen. I saw you in it . . . on television.''

Devlin turned sharply toward her. ''News feature? Is that how you knew? God, I vaguely remember cameras being at the camp once, months ago. I didn't even realize I was filmed.'' He thought for a moment. ''That complicates things. If you saw me, then perhaps— Look, I've got my jeep here. We've got to get back to Chiang Saen. My contacts at the refugee camp have hinted that there's going to be some kind of raid in the area. I think that's why the Akha bunch were rough with your friend. They probably thought he was CIA working with the Thais."

"Where's Win?"

"Win? Oh, your guide. In one of the houses. He's fine. The people here were highly suspicious of you at first, but as I said, they're good people. I'll go and tell them we're leaving." He got up and headed for the door. Then he stopped and came back to Meg, still perched on the cot. His finger gently tipped her chin up.

"Meggie, love, I know there's no way I can ever hope to make any of it up to you. When I walked into the jungle twenty years ago, I knew it was for good. I've lived with that every day since. So...however it turns out between us will be on my shoulders. D'ye understand?" His voice, rough with emotion, lapsed into the cadence of his Irish parents. "I'll only say this for now—when I did walk away...it had nothing to do with you or your mother. I...I've never stopped loving you, and never once, in all these twenty years, stopped thinking about you." He turned away and headed for the door. "I'll send your friend in."

Meg wanted to call after him. She remembered running and jumping into his arms when he'd arrived home on leave. She remembered his strength and bigness, his black hair and laughing eyes. He was so different now—hair snowy-white, his bigness portly and barrel-chested, his face lined and tired. He was a stranger.

Daddy! She'd have loved to utter that childish yelp of glee once more. But so many other memories held her back. Memories of tears and lonely nights wondering when he'd come home. Or if. Memories of Lydia's drawn face, silent and closed up. Memories of Jeffrey, bringing his own brand of humor into their lives and hearts.

It wasn't until she felt Conor's hand on her shoulder that she realized he'd returned. His arms were open and Meg stood and walked into them. She closed her eyes and let his strength enfold her. She clung to him and felt safe.

"Are you all right?" he murmured after a long moment.

She nodded, too choked up to speak.

"Everything's going to be all right, Meg. Just take it as it comes, a single day at a time. You can't fix up all those years right away."

Meg leaned back to look up into his face. "You were right, you know, when you implied that maybe finding him wouldn't be what I expected. I don't feel the way I thought I would. I don't even *know* how I feel."

Her eyes were big and damp with tears, her lips trembling. She was so achingly beautiful, he wanted to close the door on the world and erase all pain from her face. He wanted to replace the pain there with desire and ecstasy and then the sweet calm afterward. Until he remembered Gallagher.

"Come," Conor whispered, taking her by the hand. "They're waiting for us." And he led her outside.

LYDIA OPENED her eyes. Fingers of gray dawn crept under the shutters. Sounds from the awakening world outside filled her head, chasing away the torments of the long, sleepless night.

"Jeffrey?"

"Hmm?" he mumbled. He was on his side facing the wall, his arm up over his head.

"Time to wake up."

Jeffrey muttered a complaint, rolled onto his back and rubbed his eyes. "Did you get any sleep?" he asked.

"Not much. You did, though."

Jeffrey propped himself on one elbow and looked down at his wife. "You make it sound like an accusation."

She bit her lower lip. "I'm sorry, darling. Just the complaint of a troubled night."

"Are you having second thoughts about what we decided?"

"You mean having Pran visit this Ghost Tiger and checking him out? No, you were right when you insisted that it's the only logical thing for us to do. But..."

Jeffrey sat up and pulled Lydia toward him. "But?"

"I'm trying desperately not to let my imagination run wild. You can't know how badly I just want to hire a guide and head into the jungle."

He chuckled. "I can't picture you ever doing that."

"Really? Well, you might be surprised to know that once, a long time ago, I was considered the wild card in my family."

Jeffrey's chuckle deepened. "You? A wild card?"

"In Bostonian society, with a father a respected judge and a mother a well-known socialite, my perverse choice of company was considered very wild. Bordering on uncontrollable. The only reason my parents consented to my marriage to an unknown, impoverished Irishman was that they knew I'd run off with him otherwise. And since I was an only child, my mother couldn't bear the idea of not putting on a flashy wedding. So, I married Joe Devlin and became an army wife. The transition from high society to that was quite a shock."

"I often wondered how you two paired up."

"Why didn't you ask?"

Jeffrey tilted her chin up. "Lydia, that question fell into the untouchable category. You had—and still have—a way of making taboo certain subjects. Joe Devlin was one of them."

"You make me sound awful."

"Not awful. Just—" he paused, looking for the right word "—formidable, I suppose. I never was really sure if it was grief or hate that closed off talk about Joe."

Lydia sighed. "I guess I have a lot of things to clear up when all of this is over. When Meg is back." She lapsed into silence.

Jeffrey lightly kissed the top of her head. "All in good time. What worries me now is this information from Pran's friend at the embassy."

"Yes. I knew Gallagher's story didn't jibe, but I never expected to learn he's in the CIA. What do you think Pran's friend meant by an investigation?"

"I'm not sure. It sounds like Gallagher is being investigated internally by the CIA. What was impor-

tant was the news that he's supposed to be in the
States. I imagine the fellow at the embassy was very
surprised to hear Gallagher is in northern Thailand.''

"Why is that important?''

"Well, it means that his presence here isn't sanc-
tioned by the Agency. If he's here on his own, on some
kind of personal quest, what's it all about? What's he
after?''

Lydia stared up at the ceiling fan, whirling slowly.
She felt hypnotized by the blades circling around and
around, like the questions Jeffrey was asking. The
same questions going around in her own mind. Questions too frightening to be answered.

CONOR AND WIN SAT in the rear of the jeep, clutching the top of the seats ahead of them. The ride toward Chiang Saen was the kind that locked jaws and
slipped disks. The chugging roar of the engine made
it impossible for Conor to catch the occasional word
that passed between Meg and Joe up front. From the
questions in Meg's eyes, he guessed that Devlin hadn't
yet told her the whole story.

He wondered what lay ahead of them in Chiang
Saen. No doubt it would be time for all of them to face
their own personal demons. At least all this bouncing
around kept him awake and alert. No more drifting
off into dreams of seduction. Back to the real world
with a vengeance, he thought. He had some decisions
to make about Gallagher. His orders had been to telephone Gallagher directly or to wire him through the
contact at the embassy as soon as he located Devlin.

Although Conor had wondered why Gallagher was
so insistent on finding Devlin and in such secrecy, he'd

only asked once. When Gallagher had contacted him that first time, Conor had angrily demanded to know why he was being blackmailed into helping find someone when Gallagher's own people at the CIA could have done the job in half the time.

Gallagher hadn't bothered answering. He didn't have to, once he'd laid his cards on the table—once Conor knew, there was no choice but to go along with the whole crazy deal.

Meg turned around and gave Conor a wan smile. She looked fragile and forlorn; not the spunky woman he'd shared the last few days with. But Tremayne knew she'd come around to accepting her father on whatever terms the two could arrange. She was that kind of person. He wasn't so sure how she'd accept him after he did what he had to do. If...

A lot hinged on that word. Perhaps if he knew why Gallagher wanted to find Devlin, he could decide what to do. If he could find a way to stop Gallagher from carrying out his threat to destroy his brother, Eric... God, it was impossible. He had to make some decision by the time they reached Chiang Saen.

Conor stared bleakly out the window. Vines and branches scraped the glass. Devlin had wisely left the top of the jeep up so the inside, though hot and stuffy, was at least protected from both sun and greenery. Conor wondered what kind of man Devlin was. What had made him walk away from his family, give up the life he had and disappear into the hills of Thailand? What exactly did it have to do with Gallagher?

THEY ARRIVED at the outskirts of Chiang Saen just after noon. It was the hottest part of the day and the town was deserted. Devlin pulled up in front of the hotel.

"Meg and I have agreed to meet later this evening at my place. I'll have the jeep waiting for you here about seven. That sound all right to you, Tremayne?"

Conor shrugged. "Fine. Perhaps the two of you would like some privacy."

In the act of climbing out of the jeep, Meg craned her head around. "I'd like you to come, Conor."

"Seven, then." Devlin paused, looking at Meg. He seemed about to say something, but shook his head and smiled.

The three watched the jeep continue along the road through the center of town. Win spoke briefly to Conor, then disappeared into the hotel.

"I'll settle up with Win," Conor said. "There's no point making him hang around now that we've found what we were looking for."

Meg was still staring down the road. When she turned in Conor's direction, he noticed the strain in her face. "Perhaps you should rest and be alone for a while," he suggested.

"Yes, I . . . I need to be alone. Will you come up to the room with me?"

Conor's smile was gentle. "Of course. I'll have the clerk send up tea and something to eat." He cupped her elbow gently in the palm of his hand and led her inside.

The clerk's eyes lit up when he saw them. "Please, Miss Devlin. Some people are here asking about you."

Meg stopped, her hand clutching onto Conor's arm. "People? Who?"

The clerk's smile broadened, anticipating pleasant surprise. "American people. A Mr. and Mrs. Haycock."

"Oh, God, no. Mother."

Conor looked at her and winced at the utter despair in her face.

GALLAGHER SWABBED the back of his neck with a small towel conveniently left beside the modern stainless-steel sink. In spite of the drone of the ceiling fan, the air inside the house was stifling. Ghost Tiger's house, he added with a tight smile. Or Joe Devlin's. Or Dan's—the name Devlin went by, here. At least, that's what his woman was screaming over and over until he shut her up with a piece of electrical tape plastered over her mouth and around her wrists and ankles.

He'd waited until the first light of day—that shadowy period of silent grayness when night sentries finally nod off to sleep and morning birds have yet to signal dawn. The old man dozing outside the fence had been no challenge and the two women who'd been sleeping peacefully were now securely tied up in a storage shed.

All that was left was to wait for Devlin. Gallagher had considered interrogating Devlin's woman, but she'd been so hysterical he figured he'd be wasting his time. She wasn't the type of woman he'd imagined with Devlin. Not classy, like Lydia Haycock; not even pretty, though perhaps she had been when she was younger. He suddenly remembered that day, twenty years ago, when Devlin had drunkenly confessed to having a Thai mistress.

They'd been sitting in the American-style bar in Vientiane—strobe lights, go-go girls, Jimi Hendrix wailing on a scratchy sound system—and his new partner says his Thai mistress may be pregnant and what is he going to do?

Pay her off, Gallagher had suggested, or give her money for an abortion. The expression on Devlin's face had chilled him. Even now, he could recall what Devlin had answered. "Guess you haven't heard what I've been saying, Gallagher. I love this woman."

What a sentimental fool, he'd thought. No, he and Devlin were obviously not in the same league. He'd heard so many reports about how tough and mean Joe Devlin was and here was the guy, practically blubbering in his beer over some Thai chick.

Of course, later he'd had a chance to see the other side of Devlin. That was the paradox about the man. Mean as hell, except for one tiny area that became a very damn big area in Noel Gallagher's life.

Gallagher tossed the empty beer bottle into the waste can below the sink. A pleasant surprise, the cold beer. Devlin's house in the compound came equipped with conveniences rarely found in rural Thailand—running water, albeit from a cistern, and a small refrigerator.

He paced back and forth between the kitchen and living area. The house was one huge open area partitioned by slatted screens. The layout made secrecy a challenge. Gallagher decided to wait for Devlin behind a screen opposite the main door. He propped a chair against the rear door leading down ladder stairs to a storage shed. His main concern was that Devlin might go into the shed before entering the house.

The security guard had said that Ghost Tiger had driven his jeep into the hills two days ago and was expected back today. Gallagher was gambling on Devlin needing to refresh himself before going on to the camp.

If he was lucky, he'd hear the jeep tackling the trail in from the paved road. He wondered if he'd hidden the guard's car well enough. Too late to worry now. The faint revving of an engine broke the midday silence.

A last check of the rear exit, then he hid behind the screen. The engine's throbbing grew louder and suddenly stopped. Gallagher tensed. His right hand reached down and unclasped the revolver from the holster strapped around his right calf.

There was a muffled shout below the house, followed by the thud of footsteps up the ladder. The door swung open.

"Tilan?"

There was a pause. Gallagher didn't dare peek around the screen. He knew Devlin would have to walk past the screen to come into the center of the room. His fingers curled tightly around the shaft of the gun. He'd already decided to take him alive. No way would he give up the need for revenge he'd carried on his back all these years.

Footsteps, cautious ones judging by the pacing, approached. When the first bit of arm appeared, Gallagher made his move. One long stride, left hand up to ward off a sudden shift from the man in front of him and one strong downstroke of the right hand. Devlin fell.

CONOR HUNG BACK. He was beginning to feel overwhelmed by family reunions. The threesome hugging
in the doorway of the hotel room blocked most of the
interior view, but Conor had managed a quick glimpse
of Pran sitting in a chair. Ah. He'd wondered how the
Haycocks had negotiated the complex trip from
Chiang Rai to Chiang Saen.

Meg was the first to break away. "Mother," she
said, looking suddenly behind her for Conor. "This is
Conor Tremayne, the journalist I told you about on
the phone."

Conor stepped forward to meet Lydia and Jeffrey.
He felt their appraisal of him—the many silent questions he figured they wanted to ask. Not that he
blamed them. If he were a parent, he, too, would want
to know the who, what, where and why of the connection with his daughter. Especially the what.

He nodded at Pran and saw the same questions in
his friend's face. The scene was uncomfortably reminiscent of the first time he'd stayed out all night and
come in, shoes in hand, to encounter his mother sitting at the kitchen table.

But the tone in the room shifted suddenly with
Meg's next sentence.

"Mother, we have to talk about something."

Tremayne watched the Haycocks automatically
close in on one another. He knew what Meg was about
to say and he sensed they did, too.

Lydia clasped Jeffrey's hand. "Yes, darling. Go
ahead, you needn't be afraid to say anything."

"We found him."

The pronoun needed no explanation. There was no
collective gasp, Tremayne noted, merely an exchange

of looks and a tightening of hands. Meg had come to his side and reached for his own hand. He liked the feeling of protectiveness that flowed through him.

It was Jeffrey who spoke first. "Then we should make plans."

"Well, yes," Meg began. "But perhaps Mother would rather get used to the idea for a bit. There's no rush."

"But there is—I mean, there may be a complication," Lydia said. She went over to the bed and sat down on the edge of it.

"We must discuss our plans now, Meg, because something has come up since you left. A man by the name of Gallagher has been asking questions about... about your father, and has come to Chiang Saen to look for him, too."

Conor stopped midstride on his way to sit next to Pran. It was only Meg's blurted response that gave him a chance to collect himself.

"Who is he? Why is he looking for Daddy?"

"We don't know," Jeffrey replied. "But he came to the house twice after you left for Thailand and has basically followed your trail right to Chiang Saen."

"Has he given you any information at all?"

Conor hoped nobody detected the anxiety in his voice. He noticed everyone turned toward him.

"I mean, well, did he say why he wanted to find out about Joe Devlin?"

"He gave some cock-and-bull story about seeing the documentary on television and being an old army buddy."

"Why do you not believe him?"

Jeffrey frowned. "Surely a bit fortuitous, don't you think? Besides, the second time he visited he wasn't as friendly. I'll trust Lydia's instincts on this one, Mr. uh, Tremayne."

Conor caught the puzzled look on Meg's face and the raised eyebrow on Pran's. He pushed on. "Where's Gallagher now?"

"Pran and I think he's gone to see Ghost Tiger. Or... Joe."

Conor was half-aware of Meg, sitting on the edge of the bed next to her mother and muttering, "I don't understand what's going on." Jeffrey continued to stare at him, defying him to offer a sound explanation for Gallagher's presence. Lydia gazed off into space—or the past, perhaps. And Pran sat calmly in the armchair, peering up at his friend with interested speculation.

Damn, damn, damn, was all that spun around in Conor's mind.

CHAPTER FOURTEEN

PRAN STOOD aside for Conor to enter the bar first. They had discreetly stepped out of the room, promising to return in half an hour. Conor knew from the dismay written on Meg's face that she'd hoped he'd remain, but he had seen enough family crises in his own life to know that sometimes blood *was* thicker than water.

After the waiter delivered two bottles of icy Tsingtao beer, he spoke. "Pran, I have to get out to Devlin's place as soon as possible."

His friend merely nodded. Conor knew Pran was too polite to ask questions, but he could see them in the man's eyes. He hated the deception he found himself enmeshed in.

"I need to meet with Gallagher and Devlin alone, before the others catch up to them. I can't explain right now how I know Gallagher, but I will someday. Trust me on it." He smiled across the table at Pran. "The other problem I have to deal with is what to tell the Haycocks about my absence. Any ideas?"

Pran pursed his lips in thought for a long moment. "In these cases, it is sometimes better to make a simple explanation. I can say that you had important meeting and will visit with them later. I will say that a

car is arranged to take Miss Devlin to see her father in
the morning. I will arrange this car myself.''

"Sounds okay to me. Devlin promised to send a car
for us tonight, about seven. It's only about three now
so I'll get to his place in good time to let him know the
change in plans. Anything else you can tell me about
his place? One way in, you said.''

"Yes. Mr. Jeffrey and I only went to the end of the
paved road. We could see the trail through the jungle
into the compound. The trail looked very bad. Our
driver refused to drive on it. I didn't see another
road.''

Conor thought for a long while. "I'm assuming
Gallagher is still there. The hotel clerk said he hasn't
returned. If I only knew why he couldn't wait . . .'' He
realized Pran expected him to finish the sentence and
the knowledge that he was being rude to such a good
friend galled him. "Pran, what exactly did your cousin
at the American Embassy say about Gallagher?''

"He said Mr. Gallagher is CIA personnel and also
when he called Virginia, they tell him Mr. Gallagher is
on vacation. Fishing in some place called Mish-ee-gan.
Mr. Conor, I ask you to be very careful of this man.
He is not good. Perhaps he is here because he wants to
hurt this Ghost Tiger. I do not know the—the—'' he
paused ''—connection, but it cannot be good. Not
good,'' he repeated, shaking his head for added em-
phasis.

Conor couldn't have agreed more. The whole damn
thing was definitely not good at all.

MEG COULDN'T STAY in the room another moment.
She knew her mother and Jeffrey wanted to be alone.

The other reason—the one she tried not to think about—was that she felt left out. Since her stunning announcement that she'd found her father, Lydia and Jeffrey had drawn together like iron filings to a magnet. Whatever the magic ingredient of their relationship was, it seemed to be holding them up, acting as a safety net against trouble.

But there was no such net for her. The whirl of emotions that she'd been swept into over the past two days wasn't slowing down at all. One moment she was on the verge of tears; the next, on the edge of anger.

She watched Jeffrey sitting with Lydia cradled in his arms. Not talking, just gently rocking back and forth. How she envied them that silent sharing of bad times.

The slender thread that connected her with Conor didn't seem to be strong enough for a net. Over the past few days, she'd shared many things with Conor. Insights and setbacks, danger and despair. Plus a few hours of whispered passion and excitement she'd not shared with any other man, not even David.

The basic materials were there, she knew instinctively, but not yet spun into a fabric that would hold. Their history together had just begun. Still, when she turned and walked quietly out of the hotel room, it was Conor she was seeking.

Standing on the steps outside the hotel, Meg realized that, as small a place as Chiang Saen was, finding Conor and Pran could take a long time. The collection of unfamiliar shops and buildings suddenly became a complicated maze of potential visiting places. Where had they gone?

She opted for the familiar, heading for the restaurant where they'd eaten the night before trekking into the hills. A few curious locals looked up from their afternoon-tea break. Meg paused in the doorway, then slapped her arms against her sides, frustrated. Perhaps they'd decided to have a beer somewhere.

Meg stepped onto the wooden boards that served as sidewalk and looked up and down the street. There was a bar in the hotel, though they might have gone farther. But it would be a starting point. She walked toward the hotel, searching both sides of the street for another possible drinking place.

People were just beginning to reappear from the customary post-lunch rest time so the street wasn't yet crowded. Half a normal city block from the hotel, Meg spotted Conor and Pran standing beside a taxi that was idling in the middle of the road. She shouted and waved her arm, but didn't get their attention.

When she saw Conor bend over to climb inside the car, she began to run. The car was heading in her direction. She veered off the boardwalk to try to flag it down, but collided with a bicycle rickshaw boy who was just dropping off his fare. By the time she disengaged herself from handlebars and the plump woman unloading her parcels, Conor's taxi was halfway down the street.

"Damn!" Meg turned to see if Pran was still standing in the road, but he, too, had disappeared. Then a beat-up-looking car chugged up to the stop sign on the other side of the street. Meg ran over to it, swung open the rear door and leaped inside.

The driver, whose head was bopping from side to side in time with the Thai rock group blaring from his radio, jumped when Meg poked him between the shoulders.

"See that taxi ahead? There, the black car going out of town. Follow it. Please!"

"No taxi," he shouted over the music.

"That taxi!" Meg hollered back, pointing toward the windshield.

The man's head swiveled to follow her finger, then peered back at Meg. She wanted to scream.

"Radio...too loud!" she shouted.

He reached over and switched it off. Then he smiled. "You American?"

"Oh, God! Please...yes, American. Now follow that taxi before it disappears."

The man's smile vanished. "This car..." He paused, searching for the vocabulary. "No taxi. This no taxi."

It was then that Meg realized there was no official identification certificate hanging from the front seat. "Please—" she fumbled in her pouch pack "—I'll pay you. Money." She held up a handful of *baht* notes.

"No, no." He shook his head vehemently. "Trouble for me. Trouble."

"Look, I have to follow a man in that car. I have to talk to him and I don't know where he's going."

"Follow a man?" He grinned. "Like cinema? American cinema?"

"Yes, yes. Like cinema."

"Okay, sure, you bet." He sat up and shifted into gear. The car picked up speed and reached the outskirts of town just as the taxi took the paved fork leading to the refugee camp.

Meg was too keyed up to sit back. She leaned over the front seat, resting her chin on her folded arms. The panic she'd felt trying to get the man to follow Conor's taxi suddenly evaporated. Now she was beginning to feel foolish.

She had no idea where or why Conor was driving out of town. He knew her father was picking them up in a few hours. Perhaps, for some reason, he'd decided to visit the camp again. But when the taxi passed the gate without slowing down, questions began to percolate in her mind.

"You movie star?"

"Huh?" She realized the man was talking to her.

"Movie star?"

"No, no, I'm not a movie star."

"Where you go? Nothing here—only village people. Not interesting for tourist."

She squinted against the glare bouncing off the rear bumper of the car ahead as it humped over a hill and vanished from sight. "Can't you go a little faster?" she asked.

"Faster? Sure, no problem. I like cinema. Chiang Saen no cinema. You go to Chiang Rai for cinema. You see movie star in America?"

Meg switched her gaze from the windshield to the man's expectant face. Just her luck to be stuck with a movie buff. His car crawled up the rise of hill, sputtered and died before reaching the top.

The man shifted into neutral, pulled the handbrake and shrugged. "Okay, no problem." He held up a reassuring palm, slid out the door and raised the hood of the car.

Meg climbed out and paced while he tinkered under the hood. Unable to restrain herself any longer, she leaned over his shoulder to look at the engine. She knew little about the workings of a car, but the patches of worn electrical tape wrapped around hoses and clamps were not a promising sight.

"Oh, no," she groaned.

He shook his head. "It's okay, no—"

"Problem. Right."

The hood clanged back into place and he gestured for her to get back in the car. Miraculously, it roared up and over the crest of the hill. He shifted into neutral, turned off the engine and let the car coast down. Meg gritted her teeth. She'd rather have given him the few cents he was saving on gas.

At the bottom of the hill, Conor's taxi passed them, returning to Chiang Saen. Meg's shout disconcerted her own driver, who stalled the car and couldn't get it going again.

She craned around, watching the taxi climb up and over the hill. Only the driver had been inside. Meg opened the rear door and stepped out onto the road. In the distance, there seemed to be nothing ahead but green.

"Where's the road?" she muttered.

The man stopped pumping the gas pedal. "No more road," he pronounced. "Road finished."

"Then where did he go?" She scanned both sides, dense with foliage.

"You go back now," the man suggested, revving the engine.

"No, there's got to be another road up there somewhere. Can you drive a bit farther?"

He was adamant, tired of the adventure. "Go back now," he repeated.

"Okay, you go back. I'm going to walk on a bit. Thank you very much. Let me give you some money."

He shook his head. "No money. You come with me. Not safe here walking on road. No good."

"It's all right. No problem." Meg smiled.

TWENTY MINUTES later Meg reached the end of the road. There was something bizarre the way the paving abruptly terminated, swallowed up on all sides now by jungle. Meg hummed a nursery tune, hoping to keep at bay the thought that she'd made a very big mistake.

The late-afternoon sun had sunk below the tree-tops, allowing only patches of light to filter through in a random pattern that shifted with each puff of breeze. Sunset in the tropics was a quick descent, twelve hours after sunrise. Already, the first cool air of approaching night was taking the edge off a steamy day.

Meg shivered, though more from anxiety than cold. One of the pools of pink sunlight bounced, reflecting metal in the dark bushes. She pushed her way toward it, uttering a silent prayer against snakes and other deadly creatures. Just off to the side, beneath a low-hanging banyan tree, was a parked car.

She walked around to the front of it. The hood was cool. There was a narrow track leading into the bush. Meg walked along it, breathing a sigh of relief when she came to a crude bamboo gate hanging askew. With mounting excitement, she realized that she might be on her father's property.

He'd mentioned casually that he lived on a farm beyond the refugee camp and that the road leading to it was negotiable only on foot or by the hardiest of vehicles. That was why he'd suggested driving them in his jeep, rather than having them arrange their own transportation. Meg didn't know why Conor was visiting her father, nor did she care, as long as she found the house before dark.

It was obvious from the deep wheel ruts on both sides of the track that it was used regularly. Someone had hacked at the creeping vines and branches from the trees and bushes fringing the track. Still, Meg's eyes shifted from left to right constantly as she walked. Once, a monkey hooted from deep within the jungle.

Conor had told her that most larger animals favored areas of the country where there was no human habitation. She hoped he was right. Still, she felt as though hidden pairs of eyes were tracking her every move.

Her stride picked up speed. A shriek pierced the blanket of greenery all around. She began to jog. Breathe in and out. That's it. Don't look around. Focus on the trail ahead. Faster now. Keep breathing. Steady. Calm down. Trail ending. There.

She sagged against the bamboo wall surrounding the compound, gasping in and out, slowing down the adrenaline charge. You coward, she scolded herself, afraid of your own shadow. The curve of the fence took her to the entrance of the compound. A spindly wicker chair leaned on its back two legs against the half-open gate.

Joe Devlin's jeep was parked adjacent to the gate in a place cut out of the foliage. Meg sighed with relief.

Her father would be surprised to see her. She hoped he wouldn't be upset. She suspected he'd wanted some time to prepare whoever he was living with that his long-lost, grown daughter would be arriving on his doorstep.

Meg tucked in her T-shirt and patted the wrinkles in her hiking shorts. She untied her ponytail and shook her head, freeing her hair into a cascade of tangled waves. Or frizz. She smiled, remembering her father's comment.

A memory flashed of Joe Devlin comforting her after she'd been teased by some neighborhood boys about her frizz. He'd said that some day a man would tell her how romantic she looked with her "wild locks."

Okay, let's go meet the folks. The main house stood in the center of the compound. There was no sign of anyone, nor any sounds of domestic activity. Meg hesitated. Everyone had to be here, she reasoned. Dad, his wife—family, too? she wondered—Conor and whoever owned the car out by the main road. Then she stopped, considering for the first time since she'd seen it, who *did* own the car?

The man they'd all been talking about at the hotel. What was his name? Something Gallagher? She wished she'd paid more attention, but at the time her mind had been swarming with words and fragments of questions and explanations. She did remember that her parents, especially Jeffrey, had seemed concerned. But only because no one really knew him. An old buddy of her dad's interested in finding him. That was it.

Meg took a few steps forward and stopped again. Perhaps everyone was at the far end of the compound. Because she hadn't driven in, no one had heard her coming. And of course, no one was expecting her. She tilted her head back and raised a hand to the side of her mouth to call out.

But another hand found her mouth first.

PRAN WAS SITTING with his back to the door. In the crowd of black-haired heads, it had taken Jeffrey a few seconds to pick him out. Then, grasping Lydia's hand, he wound his way around the tables packed with diners. Busy waiters skittered in and out of the crowd carrying large trays of food and cold drinks.

"Excuse me, Pran, but Lydia and I—"

Pran turned around and rose, simultaneously patting at his mouth with a napkin and pulling out the empty chair next to his. "Mr. Jeffrey, Mrs. Haycock! I have been looking for you. Please, may I introduce my cousin, Mr. Win? This is the man who took your daughter and Mr. Conor into the hills."

Jeffrey and Lydia nodded, then sat down.

Pran signaled a waiter. "Would you like a cold beer, Mr. Jeffrey? Something cold to drink, Mrs. Haycock?"

"Please," said Jeffrey. "By the way, have you seen Meg and this Tremayne fellow?"

"That is what I needed to talk to you about. Mr. Conor asked me to advise Meg that Mr. Devlin's car would pick her up in the morning, rather than this evening."

"I don't understand," put in Lydia. "Did Meg make plans to see my...her father tonight? She didn't say a word about this to us!"

"Easy, Lydia." Jeffrey patted Lydia's arm. "She left the room almost right after you and Tremayne. I assumed she'd met up with the two of you somewhere."

Pran shook his head. "I did not see your daughter. Mr. Tremayne and I had a beer in the bar of the hotel and then I went with him to hire a taxi."

"Why?"

Pran hesitated. "Mr. Conor had to go somewhere. He said to tell you and Meg that Mr. Devlin will call in the morning."

Win began to speak rapidly in Thai to Pran. Jeffrey drank from the bottle of beer the waiter had just placed in front of him.

Pran looked away from Win to Jeffrey and Lydia. "My cousin tells me that Ghost Tiger planned to meet with Mr. Conor and Miss Meg tonight. He was sending his jeep to pick them up at the hotel at seven."

"Seven now," muttered Jeffrey.

"Yes, but Mr. Conor asked me to tell you the plans would be changed."

"And how did Mr. Conor know the plans would be changed?" demanded Jeffrey, unable to keep the bite of sarcasm out of his voice.

Pran glanced at Lydia, then to Win before replying. "Mr. Conor did not explain. He said only that he must meet with Ghost Tiger first and that he would ask him to change the plans."

"What reason would Mr. Tremayne have to meet with . . . with Joe?" Lydia's voice sounded shaky.

"I do not know, Mrs. Haycock. I am sorry to say, I do not know."

A pall settled over the table. Lydia gazed down at the steaming plate the waiter had just delivered.

"So, Tremayne has gone to see Devlin. What about Meg?" asked Jeffrey.

"I have not seen Miss Meg since this afternoon."
Pran spoke to Win again. "My cousin says he has not
seen them since they arrived at the hotel. Mr. Conor
gave Win some money and told him he could return to
Chiang Rai."

"Well, if it's just seven now, we can presume that
Meg is probably waiting at the hotel for her father and
Tremayne. She won't know that the plans have been
altered and she's probably been in her room this whole
time, bathing and washing her hair and whatnot."
Jeffrey purposely made light of the situation for Lydia's sake, not mentioning that he'd tapped on Meg's
door before they'd left for their walk.

Lydia gave a wan smile. "Of course, Jeffrey. All this
fuss for nothing. But perhaps you and I ought to return to the hotel and let her know. So she won't
worry."

They excused themselves, insisting that Pran and
Win finish their meals. Pran said he would have the
waiter package up their own uneaten dinners and bring
them back to the hotel with him. When he arrived,
scarcely twenty minutes later, appetites had not been
restored.

"She's not here," Lydia blurted when she opened
the door for Pran.

IT ALL HAPPENED so quickly. The hand clamped hard
over Meg's mouth, and the arm tight across her chest
yanked her backward. She struggled, plucking vainly
at the fingers splayed across her lips as she was
dragged into a dark enclosure. But when she was
turned around, embraced in a hold vaguely familiar

and the hand was removed, she gave out a string of epithets.

"You shock me," whispered Conor.

Meg punched at his chest. "What the hell is going on? And why are we hiding in this— What is this? It smells like a barn. Where's my father?"

His finger lightly touched her lips. "Shh! Sit down here. Okay, on my lap if you're squeamish about a bit of dirt."

"It doesn't smell like dirt," she hissed, "and I want to know what's going on. Now."

A four-legged animal shuffled behind the bamboo wall they were crouched against. Sounds of munching filled the pause before Conor answered.

"Okay, me first. Then you have a hell of a lot of explaining to do about why you're here."

"You've got a nerve, you know that? I mean, we had an arrangement with my father and then, next thing I know, you're disappearing in some taxi with me running after you—"

He chuckled. "Is that how it went? You followed me here?"

"You said you were going first."

"Yes, right. Okay, um— Look, Meg, there's something I need to tell you but it'll have to wait for a bit. Just remember that, okay? I need you to remember I said that."

Meg's irritation gave way to anxiety. "What's going on, Conor? Is it my father? Has something happened to him?"

"No—at least I'm not sure. I just got here. The place is in darkness and there's no sign of anyone around. But I think there *is* someone here."

Meg craned her neck up and around. "In this barn?" she whispered.

"No. I think your father has a visitor."

"Then let's go and see." She stood and Conor quickly pulled her back down.

"Wait. They may not want to be interrupted. I want you to stay here while I go up to the house and have a look around."

Meg thought for a moment. "Look, Conor, talk like that just makes me scared. I mean, this isn't the movies. God, between you and the guy who drove me here I feel like I'm in an episode of 'Twilight Zone' or something. I'm not staying in this barn, I'm coming with you. And it's ridiculous to be sneaking around. My father did invite us here, remember?"

"All right, there's no point arguing. Just let me go first, okay?" He got to his feet and held out a hand. They huddled in the doorway of the shed and looked across the compound yard to the main house.

The house was built of bamboo and teak. It was a fancier version of the houses in the Karen village they'd stayed in their first night in the hills. The steps leading up to it were permanent wooden ones, rather than the makeshift bamboo ladders the hill tribes used. The side of the house facing the animal shed had four full-length window frames, inset with slatted wooden blinds similar to those in Pran's house. Except these blinds were closed.

As they hesitated in the doorway, a soft light flickered from between the slats of the blinds. "Someone's home," murmured Conor. He started to walk toward the house, then turned back to Meg. "See that other hut just below the house, at the rear?"

She nodded.

"Let's head for it first, because I want to approach the house from behind."

Meg felt her eyes widen. "Conor, cut it out. Let's just walk up the steps and knock on the door. For heaven's sake!"

"Just humor me, okay, Meg?"

The dead-serious tone stopped her. She tried reading the expression in his eyes, but all she came up with was an impenetrable blackness.

"One more thing," he said. "Whatever happens, just play along with it. Don't give in to panic or fear. Be cool."

"All right," she whispered, already sensing the first awakenings of fear flapping in her chest.

Conor hunched over and ran for the hut at the rear of the house. Meg followed, feeling at any moment that someone was going to holler "Cut!" She joined him at the closed door of the hut. He motioned for her to keep silent. She waited, watching his eyes dart from side to side, up the stairs leading to the back door of the house, then back to the hut. They passed over her in a dismissive sweep that chilled her.

Then he pulled back the sliding metal bolt of the door to the hut and gestured toward it.

"What?" Meg hissed. "I'm not going in there. Forget it."

"Don't be silly. We're going to wait in here until dark. Come on."

Meg hesitated. A demon of suspicion whispered in her ear. "You first."

"Sure." He took a step into the dark interior of the hut.

Meg followed him. Suddenly he stood aside, forcing her to go ahead of him. There was a quick scuffling from behind and the door closed.

She pulled on the handle, but he was already bolting it from outside. "Conor! You...you bastard! Open this door!" She banged her fist on the wooden boards.

Conor's muffled voice came through the cracks. "Shh! Meg, I'm sorry. It's better this way. Just wait for a few minutes. I'll be back."

Frustrated anger raged through her. Trembling, she leaned against the door. Relax, calm down. Deep breath, in and out. There. Feeling better already. Save your anger for when he opens that door.

Once her eyes had adjusted to the inside of the hut, she realized that the gaps between the bamboo afforded enough light to see. He'd better come back before dark.

Meg stepped away from the door. At least it wasn't a barn. She pictured herself walking into the staff room when she returned to school.

"So Meg, what did you do in the spring break?"

"Oh, spent a lot of time locked up in various sheds."

She froze. A noise somewhere. Inside. She waited. There. In the corner, behind those big basket things. Meg strained to identify it. It wasn't a squeak; more a low grunting sound. She tiptoed to the corner, grasped the edge of one of the baskets and heaved it aside.

Two faces, mouths gagged, stared up at her. Two women—arms and ankles trussed—with frightened, beseeching eyes.

CHAPTER FIFTEEN

LYDIA SAT, trying not to wring her clenched hands. She could see herself in the mirror opposite the bed. The normally smooth chignon was loose, tendrils of hair escaping constraint. Much the same as her normally calm self. She could even sense the giddiness of hysteria lurking, ready to pounce and take control of her. Control. What Meg had once referred to as Lydia's second name.

Not anymore. Nothing seemed to apply anymore. The dead arisen. Jeffrey's jocularity replaced by a sobering intensity. Lydia's calm rippling into a storm. She stood, went over to the chest of drawers and poured herself a shot of Jeffrey's duty-free Scotch. Downing it in one gulp, she turned around and saw Jeffrey's raised eyebrows.

Good for him, she thought, grateful for his silence. "All right," she said, "it's going on eight o'clock. We know that Meg isn't here. We know that Mr. Tremayne—do we call him Conor yet?—anyway, he's gone to see . . . Joe. Is it possible that Meg has gone there, too?"

No one answered at first. Then Pran said, "Miss Meg did not know that Mr. Conor went to see Ghost Tiger. Perhaps she is looking for him in town."

"I don't think so," cut in Jeffrey. "Meg's too impatient to spend a lot of time searching around. I think she came back here, found us out, waited until seven and then left to look for Tremayne. When she didn't find him, she probably decided to hire a taxi to drive out to Devlin's place on her own."

"But we were here moments after seven. Surely we couldn't have missed her so easily."

"I don't know, Lydia. As I said, this is all conjecture. Now we have to decide whether this matter is urgent enough to call in the police or not."

Silence greeted this last statement. There was something too awful, too final about calling police. Lydia wanted to believe events had not taken such a desperate turn.

An unexpected tapping at the door made her jump. Jeffrey reached it in one quick stride and flung it open.

"Oh," he said, the word falling in disappointment. Win was standing on the threshold. "Sorry, Win, we thought you were Meg. Come in."

Pran and Win began speaking to one another in Thai. Pran turned to Jeffrey and Lydia. "My cousin says he has found a man who drove Miss Meg out to Ghost Tiger's house."

"How? What happened?" Lydia walked over to Pran.

"I asked my cousin to find the taxi I hired for Mr. Conor. To ask him about Miss Meg. The man said another car followed him to the end of the road. He knew the man who owns this car. You see, not many ordinary citizens own cars in Chiang Saen—"

"Yes, yes," interrupted Jeffrey, tempted to shake the news out of him.

"Win found this man, the man who followed Mr. Conor's taxi. He said he took Miss Meg to the end of the road and she got out of the car. He said she refused to return to Chiang Saen with him."

"And he just left her there, in the middle of nowhere?" Jeffrey's voice rose in disbelief.

Pran nodded. "Miss Meg told the man to go."

Lydia and Jeffrey looked at one another. "Well, I hate to say it, but that sounds like Meg." Jeffrey sighed. "Pran, please thank Win for helping us."

After Win had left, Lydia asked the question everyone had been thinking. "What do we do now?"

"We have a couple of options," Jeffrey replied. "We can assume Meg is with her father and Tremayne and things are just fine. Or we can speculate that this Gallagher fellow is there, too, and..." The sentence trailed off.

"We don't really know very much about Noel Gallagher," Lydia reminded, "except our own intuition that he's up to no good. I know Joe didn't like him. Perhaps that isn't enough reason to question his credibility. Perhaps it's just as he said—that he saw the news feature, too, and was curious to find out if the man really was Joe."

Jeffrey disagreed. "A normal person would make phone calls and so on to find out, but definitely wouldn't fly over here. No. Gallagher has some interest in this beyond curiosity about a former partner. Especially one he didn't get along with."

"Please, Mr. Jeffrey, perhaps if I may suggest? This is not my business, but perhaps I may help."

"Pran, you've already helped us more than we can ever repay. What do you have in mind?"

"I think we should visit this refugee camp again. The commander there was not helpful to us before, but I think this was because he was protecting Ghost Tiger. If we go to him and tell him Ghost Tiger may be in danger, perhaps—"

"You're right," Jeffrey interrupted. "It's worth a try. At this point, we've got nothing to lose."

"No," whispered Lydia bleakly. "Nothing to lose." *Only everything.*

MEG WAS PARTWAY through untying the gag around the second woman's mouth when the door of the hut was unbolted.

The beam from a flashlight focused on her. She shielded her eyes from it and stumbled to her feet. "Conor! Quick, over here. Help me!" Her concern about the women had erased her anger at Conor. When he failed to answer, she moved toward the doorway.

He stood, flashlight in hand, transfixed by the sight in the shed. There was an impassive, remote look on his face that made her stop.

"Meg—" The name sounded as if it had been wrenched from his throat.

A movement behind him shifted her attention.

"Introductions are in order, I believe."

The voice was a strange one, and slightly unpleasant.

Meg paused. The man standing in the shadows moved closer. She looked at Conor again, but he was still staring at the two women, one of whom had begun to keen in a low monotone.

"Miss Devlin, I suppose," continued the man. "Please, come out. So unnecessary to hide in here. I watched the two of you leave the barn. Come. Your father is waiting for you."

Mention of Joe Devlin freed Meg of the spell. She moved toward the voice.

There was enough spillover from the flashlight for her to see that the man was shorter than she was, wearing a rumpled white shirt, tan trousers and holding in his extended hand a very large gun.

"The name's Noel Gallagher," he went on, the courtesy in his voice jarring against the low moaning from inside the hut.

"What's going on?" Meg's question, calm to her ears, echoed in a flutter of panic inside.

"We'll discuss all of that up in the house where we can be more comfortable. Now, come along. Don't worry about the women. They'll be fine. Conor will lock up after."

Conor? Meg whirled about to see him slowly close the door and slide the bolt across. Conor?

"I'm sorry you were so rudely locked up. I apologize on behalf of my friend and partner."

"Partner?"

Conor avoided making eye contact with Meg.

"Conor, what's this all about? How do you know this man?"

"If I may interrupt, Miss Devlin, time is precious. Conor will be happy to explain our connection once we're inside. Please—" He gestured with the gun to the stairs leading up to the house.

Meg felt Conor's presence behind her as she led the way up. Another time, she'd have been reassured,

knowing he was there. Now it took all her self-control
not to spin around and demand an immediate explanation. When she stepped into the large, shadowy
room, she paused.

"Straight ahead, your father is at the far end."

Meg walked the length of the room, heading for the
open kitchen area. She moved hesitantly, peering from
side to side for her father. When she reached a painted
lacquer screen folded out to section off the kitchen
from the rest of the room, she stopped and looked at
Gallagher.

"Don't see him yet? Go ahead," he said, motioning to the screen.

Meg stepped around the side of the screen and
gasped.

Joe Devlin sat, mouth gagged and bound by a long
yellow nylon rope to a straight-backed bamboo chair.
The rope circled around him several times, looped behind and through the back of the chair, which was
tilted on its two rear legs against the wall. Meg observed the course of the rope from the back of the
chair on an angle to the trigger mechanism of a shotgun, which was wedged between a wooden trunk and
the wall and aimed directly at Devlin.

She didn't need a guidebook to figure out the
treacherous path of the rope to chair, leaning precar-
iously on two legs, to the cocked trigger of the gun.

"What have you done to him? And who are you?"

Gallagher smiled. "Why, I used to be your father's
partner—way back in the old days. And believe me,
this small bit of inconvenience is nothing—I repeat,
nothing—to the years of hell that your father put me
through."

Meg backed away from the madness in his face. She looked at Conor, but he seemed lost in another world.

Then there was a muffled grunt from Joe Devlin. "No, don't move!" Meg cried out. "Please! Don't worry, everything will be all right."

She tried to keep calm, to let her mind get to the task of deciding what to do. A quick glance at Conor leaning casually against a sideboard, his arms crossed as if he were putting in time at a bus stop, told Meg he'd be no help.

Intuition advised her to keep Gallagher talking. He was all wound up anyway, unpredictable the way madmen are. So she sauntered away from the screen and the sight of her father to the center of the room.

"Don't you think I have a right to know why you've done this to my father?"

"Oh, you will know why. We have all the time in the world and I intend to savor every second of it."

"Why don't you let her go? She has nothing to do with any of this," Conor interjected, sounding almost bored.

Meg didn't dare risk looking across the room at him. She didn't want to begin to consider the role he'd played in the surreal scene taking place.

"Please don't start getting sentimental on me. I hired you to do a job and you've done it. Thank you and butt out." Gallagher dismissed Conor with a wave of the gun, then turned his attention back to Meg.

"What job?" Meg stared at Conor.

"It's a long story," he began, only to be interrupted by Gallagher.

"And it's my story," Gallagher stressed. "Sit down, relax, and I'll tell you about it."

"You're wasting time," Conor objected. "Let her go. You got what you wanted."

Gallagher waved the gun in Conor's face. "I've waited too long to get it over with like that." He snapped his fingers, then pointed at Devlin with his free hand. "My former partner hasn't begun to suffer yet. Perhaps I should start with his daughter. How would you like that, eh, partner?" He moved closer to Devlin and smirked.

Joe uttered something inaudible and jerked his head back. The chair wobbled so slightly, Meg thought she might have imagined it. A ripple of movement rolled along the rope, flattening to a soft vibration.

"No!" screamed Meg, jumping to her feet.

Conor restrained her from leaping toward Gallagher. "Don't! You'll only make things worse. Let him have his say. Then he'll untie your father."

Gallagher tilted his head back and laughed. The harshness of the sound echoed in the large room. "Such gullibility, Tremayne. Did you think when I asked you to find Joe Devlin it was so we could look at old war snapshots together?"

"Asked you to find Joe Devlin?" The disbelief in Meg's voice focused on Conor. "You?"

"Precisely," Gallagher replied for Conor. "I hired him to help you find your father, knowing all I had to do was follow behind. He was all too willing to help."

"You bastard," muttered Conor, edging closer to Meg. "Don't listen to him, Meg. He's been black-mailing me—my brother—you remember, don't you? Eric was—"

"Back in your corner!" Gallagher ordered, pointing the gun at Conor. He placed a hand on Meg's shoulder and lowered the barrel of the gun to the back of her neck. Conor backed away.

"Very good," continued Gallagher. "Now for my story. Come, my dear, sit down. I'll explain why I've come all this way to make sure that Joe Devlin expiates his crimes."

"What's my father ever done to you?"

Gallagher's face darkened. "Only taken my life from me. And my gold." His voice rose to a violent pitch.

LYDIA KNEW at once that their second visit to the camp's commanding officer wasn't going to be a repeat of the first one.

Granted, the same curtain had fallen over his face when Pran uttered Ghost Tiger's name. But then there had been a subtle flicker of interest when Noel Gallagher's name was mentioned. As Lydia finished explaining that Gallagher was probably at Ghost Tiger's compound that very moment, the commander raised a single finger to the sentry at his office door.

It all took a matter of minutes. Not wanting to lose face, the commander admitted through Pran that there was an American living nearby. A Mr. Daniel Freeman. Perhaps he and his men ought to visit Mr. Freeman to ensure that everything was all right.

The part Lydia had a problem with was his order to stay at the refugee camp. She and Jeffrey objected strongly, but to no avail. Pran advised them to be patient.

"Pran, why couldn't we just follow in our taxi?"

Pran shook his head firmly. "The commander is a powerful man in this region. He will have us all arrested if we defy him. Your embassy may come to your assistance, but unfortunately, I . . ."

He didn't need to finish the sentence. After the whole thing was over, Jeffrey and Lydia would return home. Pran had to keep on living there. "Pran, I'm sorry, I was being selfish. Of course, we'll wait here."

An hour later, there was still no word. A soldier had brought in tea and biscuits, but everyone was too tense to eat or drink.

"I don't think I can take a second more of this," hissed Lydia. "What's keeping them?"

Jeffrey shrugged, feigning an indifference he didn't feel. "Well, it may be a long way into the place from the main road. Perhaps you ought to use this time to decide—"

"What?" she asked when he stopped midsentence.

He hesitated and then, clasping her hands in his, said in a low voice, "Lydia, when all of this is over and Meg is safe with us again—don't interrupt, I know she will be—I want you to know if you need some time alone—away from me—to take all of what's happened in and try to decide—"

"Nonsense," Lydia interrupted. "I love you Jeffrey. Nothing else needs to be said."

Jeffrey reached out his arms to her. Then the door swung open and he knew immediately, from the expression on the face of the soldier standing in the doorway, that something had happened.

MEG BIT her lower lip, stifling a nervous giggle. There was something of the carnival fun-house in Gallagher's twisted face, looming inches above hers.

"Since you're so bent on telling your story, why don't you get it over with Gallagher?" drawled Conor from the bamboo chair opposite Meg's. One leg was slung across the other and his fingertips thrummed softly on the wide arm of the chair.

Meg bit down harder on her lip, though this time it was to restrain herself from rushing at Conor. She didn't know what was true and what wasn't, about his part in all that was happening, but she sniffed betrayal in the air. She sneaked a glance in her father's direction and turned back to Gallagher, perched on the edge of a low table.

"Yes, please tell me," she whispered appeasingly.

The crease in Gallagher's brow smoothed. He took strength from the submissive tone in her voice. "It all dates back to more than twenty years ago. The Vietcong had the edge and things were falling apart in Cambodia and Laos. Still, there was money to be made in this part of the world and everyone on two legs was heavily into getting a share.

"At the time, no one back home realized how involved the CIA was over here, but we knew. Didn't we, Devlin?"

The question was rhetorical, for Gallagher didn't even bother looking at Joe. From the distant expression on his face, Meg guessed he'd taken a sudden leap back in time.

"There was a very unstable coalition government in Laos then. The king and the Commies. Quite a team, eh?" He raised an eyebrow at Meg, as if expecting her to comment on this irony. Then he abruptly frowned. "The team fell apart, though, and the king wanted a safe trip out. That was arranged, but it seems that the guy was a bit absentminded. Left behind some gold bullion he couldn't really live without.'' Gallagher's face broke into a wide grin.

"So I got the job of carrying it out. They linked me up with another CIA operative in Chiang Rai—you guessed it!'' Gallagher exulted at the dawning realization in Meg's face.

"Your father, the so-called war hero.'' Gallagher half turned his head in Joe's direction and smirked.

Meg saw her father's legs twitch. His eyes smoldered above the gag across his mouth.

Conor unfolded his legs and stretched. "How much more of this do we have to listen to, Gallagher?''

The question was too much for Meg. She turned to face Conor. "I trusted you.''

The quaver in the reproach made Conor look down at the floor. He wasn't certain where his charade was taking him, but he couldn't risk looking Meg straight in the eye. He'd lose it then for sure.

Gallagher's voice peaked in a falsetto of sarcasm. "Oh, my, like that was it? Mixing business with pleasure—and on my time, too.'' Then the tone shifted. "Your papa owes me, darling. I've come a long way and waited a long time to collect. And not just the gold.''

"You can see my father isn't a wealthy man. Let him go!'' Meg begged.

"And leave out the best part of the story? Don't you want to hear how your daddy betrayed his country, much less his partner?''

A movement from Devlin caught Gallagher's eye. "Guess you wouldn't want your daughter to know how we'd planned things, eh, Joe? How we talked that night in Luang Prabang about going AWOL with the king's gold. Take early retirement, hide out in the hills till the war was over. No one would ever think we were still alive. It would've been so easy!'' He shook his head, rubbing the bridge of his nose with his gun hand.

Conor saw an opportunity to move but Gallagher lowered his arm and aimed the revolver again at Meg.

When he spoke, his voice was a frightening whisper. ''Then he did it himself, the bastard. And took my share, too.''

''It's a lie,'' Meg hissed. ''You're making it all up.''

Gallagher's free arm shot out to grab a handful of Meg's hair. Her cry brought Conor to his feet.

''Leave her alone, you son of a—''

''Stay where you are.'' The tip of the revolver rested against Meg's temple. ''Get up,'' he ordered Meg, cupping her elbow and assisting her to her feet in a bizarre display of chivalry. His breath was hot and sour in her face. ''I think it's time to have your papa tell us where the gold is. That's a good girl, come along with me. This way. Back up. Don't worry. I won't let you fall.''

Meg's legs wobbled. Turned around, she faced Conor head-on. He was standing now, fists clenched at his sides. His face was pale and tense as he watched Gallagher back Meg toward Devlin.

Pain radiated from the crown of her head where Gallagher fiercely gripped a mass of her hair. Unable to move her head, Meg's eyes shifted left to right, trying to get a sense of how close they were to her father. Gallagher's breath fanned the nape of her neck, his wiry body pressed into her back in a perverse intimacy. She caught a glimpse of Conor sidling along the wall in the same direction. What was he doing? she wondered. Did it matter? Did anything matter anymore, except maybe living?

And she would, Meg vowed. Survive somehow, deal with the rest later. She winced as Gallagher jerked her head back farther. Pain, she could handle. It was thinking that was unbearable. At least, thinking about the why. And right now, being pushed crablike across the room by a madman, she had to think quickly about the what and the how.

It all happened like a choreographed stunt. Meg fell out of step, her right foot landing squarely on Gallagher's. He lurched forward, lowering his gun hand and instinctively raising his forearm wrapped beneath Meg's chin. She opened her mouth wide, sinking her teeth into the scrawny flesh of Gallagher's arm.

Gallagher bellowed. In the split second before he could grab her again, Meg saw Conor dashing to her father. Her heart plummeted. Then she was back in Gallagher's grasp.

"Let her go, Gallagher." The hoarse voice was no more than a rasping whisper.

Joe Devlin, still in his chair, was pulling the tape away from his mouth. The length of rope stretching from the chair to the shotgun dangled onto the floor. Conor was crouched next to Devlin, unwinding the rope from the barrel of the gun.

"Stand back, Tremayne, away from Devlin. Against the wall. That's it. Good. Now, who do I get rid of first? Any preference, Miss Devlin?" he gasped angrily in her ear.

"No!" Meg cried.

"You came for me. Let them go."

"Don't move again, Devlin, or I'll start with your daughter. That's better. Where's the gold?"

Devlin shook his head sadly. "The gold's where it's always been. Where it belongs."

"Cut the dramatic bullcrap. I want it. It's mine. I earned it sitting in that stinking Communist jail for two years waiting to be rescued."

"Consider yourself lucky you made it back, Gallagher. A lot didn't."

"Lucky!"

Meg jumped at Gallagher's shout. Her father sat calmly in his chair, with Conor standing behind him. His attempt to save her father redeemed him somewhat, though all the unanswered questions clamored inside.

The sun had long gone down and the lamp's dim glow threw strange shadows on the mat walls. A strobe of light pulsed suddenly on one of the surfaces. Gallagher and Meg turned in unison to its source. The beam streaked across the room again, like a searchlight probing the night skies.

Muffled voices could be heard outside the house.

"It's too late, Gallagher," Devlin said. "You were always bad with timing. That's why you got caught in the first place. Too slow to get to the door of that bus. Put the gun down and let her go. I'll talk to the police for you."

"No way, Devlin. You're reading me wrong again. Just the way you did years ago. The gold is only part of it. The real part is making you pay. If I have to take her out with me, I will. I'll go to hell laughing."

Gallagher pulled Meg to the door, kicked it open and pushed Meg forward.

The beam of light settled on them, poised at the top of the stairs.

"I'll kill her if anyone tries to stop me," hollered Gallagher.

Meg heard running footsteps below and voices shouting in Thai. Slowly she and Gallagher descended, the light tracking their every step. They'd just reached the last step when a shout came from above. Devlin stood in the doorway.

"Stop now while you've got the chance, Gallagher."

"I've got the chance and I think I'll take it, Devlin." He raised the gun and, stretching his right arm, aimed it at Devlin.

"No!" screamed Meg. She swung her arm sharply backward, jabbing her elbow in Gallagher's face. The gun fired and in the millisecond before all hell broke loose, Meg saw her father topple backward.

CHAPTER SIXTEEN

MEG HIT the ground. She couldn't breathe. Her face was pushed into the loamy clay of the compound yard and a heavy weight lay on top of her. Starved of air, she began to hyperventilate. The shouting around her ebbed into a blackness flowing over and through her. She felt herself drifting.

Until she was wrenched from the cocoon of earth, lifted and flung, choking and gasping, onto her back. Faces hung over her, all unrecognizable save one. Conor. His face set, lines drawn from the war chart of the last few hours.

She coughed again, spitting up dirt and bile. Someone threw water into her face and she sputtered to a sitting position.

"What is this, a trial by fire or something? God!" Meg tried to stand but only made it to her knees. Conor eased her back onto the ground. Then she remembered. "My father!"

"He'll be all right. Gallagher caught him in the shoulder. Take it easy. Catch your breath. I'll be back in a second. Someone wants to talk to me."

Dazed, Meg looked about her. Men in uniform moved about the compound, pausing every now and then to call out to one another or huddle in small groups over glowing cigarettes. Their silhouettes bobbed against the walls of the house and fence like puppets in a shadow play.

Meg felt utterly alone. She wrapped her arms protectively around herself, as if to stave off the memories of the night. But Gallagher's words flew at her, nipping away at her emotions until she could no longer think about any part of what had happened that night. All she wanted to do was to sink into a dark place without memory, without feeling.

Gallagher. Where was he, she wondered? Lurking about or fled into the night? Panic fluttered inside her.

"Conor!" No one answered. A few curious heads turned her way. "Conor!"

Maybe Gallagher was waiting somewhere. There. Behind one of those bushes. Was that shadow moving her way? "Conor!"

Then he was crouching at her side and whispering in her ear. His hands stroked her cheeks, brushing the hair away from her face. "It's okay. It's all over, Meg. All over."

"Where is he? I thought I saw him peering at me from that bush over there." Meg pointed shakily toward the compound wall.

"There's no bush over there, Meg, only one of the police cars. He's gone. He's dead. One of the policemen shot him."

"Somebody pushed me to the ground. I remember almost suffocating."

There was a pause. "It was Gallagher. When he was shot, he fell over on top of you."

"Oh God!" Meg brought her hands up to her face and began to weep.

Conor cradled her in his arms and rocked her gently. He wished he could erase the events of the night and start over with a clean slate. But how far back would he have to go? To the very beginning, he figured, when he'd first knocked at her door with her cat in his arms. The impossibility of it shook him. Yet before the night was over, he knew he'd have to tell her.

"Where's my father?" Meg murmured.

"Inside. They've made him comfortable and stopped the bleeding. His wound doesn't look too serious, he's not in shock or anything. They've called for an ambulance."

"And the women in the shed?"

"They're inside with your father. One of them is his wife, the other his mother-in-law, I think. They found an old man tied up in the barn, too. Lying only feet away from where we were hiding at the beginning."

In the silence that fell between them, Conor searched for the words to explain what had happened. He worried about Meg's ability to handle any more revelations, but was afraid that the inevitable police business would further delay his talk.

Talk. A simple word for what he had to say, for the picture he needed to draw of his life and all the events that had led him to the hills of northern Thailand with a woman he now knew he loved.

"What do they know about Gallagher?" Meg finally asked.

"There was no ID on him, but I've made a statement to the commander in charge."

"And what about your statement to me?"

He should have known there'd be no easy way out with Meg. That was what had attracted him to her from the beginning. He took a deep breath. "Do you want to hear it now? Here?"

"Why not?" There was an edge of challenge in her whispered reply.

He couldn't help feeling defensive. "Meg, you've been through an awful lot, I just thought you might want to wait a bit. Until you're feeling up to it."

"Conor—" she raised her head to look him straight in the eye "I may never be 'up to it,' but I have to hear it. I have to know that not everything was a lie...." Her voice trailed off in the night.

"Then let's find a place to talk away from this confusion." He stood, holding out a hand, which she took. The boxed shape of a military ambulance idled outside the gate of the compound. Men hovered around its open rear door.

"I think they're taking your father now. Do you want to see him before they leave?"

Meg hesitated, sensing a farewell scene at the moment might be more than she could handle. Conor had said her father would be all right. Tomorrow would be soon enough.

"I don't think so. Could you find out where they're taking him, so I can see him in the morning?"

She watched Conor walk over to the gate and talk to a man who seemed to be in charge. She wasn't sure she was 'up to' the talk at all, or if she ever would be. But it seemed to her that she'd been living in a state of denial for a long time. As far back as the day she'd heard her father was dead, although that obstinate refusal to believe was now vindicated. As if it matters now, she thought bitterly. Being right was certainly no liberation.

Then there was her relationship with David, built on more denial. Denial that he really didn't love her as much as she'd loved him. Perhaps even denial about how she really felt for him. Had her feelings been wrapped up in some image—the attractive packaging of the perfect couple?

Meg sighed. It was all too complicated. Take everything one step at a time. Right now, the most important step was finding out the truth.

Conor returned with the information that Joe would be taken to the local clinic in Chiang Saen. "I'd suggest going inside to talk," he added, "but since your father's gone and the women are inside recovering from their own ordeal—"

"No," Meg interrupted. "I don't think it would be a good idea to introduce myself to them now."

"The commander has offered us his jeep to sit in, until they've finished up here. They'll drive us back to town."

"Okay." Then she remembered her mother and Jeffrey. "Has someone called my mom?"

"I believe so. Come on, we may not have a lot of time." He led her to a jeep parked outside the walled yard.

Inside, Meg felt a chill. Shivering, she rubbed her hands up and down against her arms.

"Here," Conor said, handing her a jacket someone had left in the rear seat. "What you really need is a shot of brandy."

"What I need is a shot of the truth for a change," she mumbled.

"Right. Okay, here goes." He inhaled, paused and began to talk.

"I first met Noel Gallagher a few weeks ago. I'm not sure of the date, but right after that feature on refugee camps was aired in the States. Apparently the instant you called the Pentagon, some built-in warning system Gallagher had installed on the computer there triggered a chain of events. I guess you could say a chain that led to this very night."

"What kind of a warning system?"

"He programmed something into Joe Devlin's file so that if there was ever an inquiry about him, Gallagher would be the first to be informed. It was his way of keeping a check on your father, on the off chance that someday someone might come up with information about Devlin."

"Sounds pretty iffy to me."

"Gallagher was obsessed with your father. You saw that tonight. He spent the last twenty-odd years fantasizing what he'd do if Devlin ever surfaced. Then bingo! Joe Devlin's daughter phones out of the blue, claiming to have seen her father on television.

"It was a long shot, but Gallagher had to follow it up. He got a copy of the tape and reviewed it over and over until he, too, was positive the man in the background was Devlin. Once he learned I'd filmed it, he flew to Bangkok to meet me."

Conor rubbed his face wearily, recalling that fateful day when he'd heard Gallagher's recorded message on his home answering machine. If only he'd never called back. If only...

He shook his head. Too late for that, he reminded himself. "Gallagher met me on the pretext that he worked for a publisher and was interested in putting together a book on refugee camps. I was between assignments and met him in a bar in Bangkok. Five minutes into the meeting, it was obvious he was no publisher. I'd have left then, but he started telling me this story about a man who'd gone AWOL and was accidentally filmed in my documentary. My curiosity was aroused.

"When he got to the part about what he wanted me to do—to contact you and pump you for information about your father—I decided I didn't want anything to do with the guy. I told him I wasn't a private detective and started to leave."

Conor waited a moment before going on. "Then he pulled out a letter he had. It was from a man in my brother Eric's platoon in 'Nam. I don't know how in hell Gallagher had gotten hold of the letter—it had been written years before—but it pretty much threw into doubt Eric's role in the skirmish that landed him in a wheelchair for the rest of his life. The same skirmish that earned him a medal for bravery.

"God! I couldn't believe it at first. I remember tossing the letter back at Gallagher, telling him what a crock it was. Then Gallagher started pulling out of his briefcase other papers documenting what the letter claimed. The guy who wrote the letter was killed in some freak accident before he could carry the matter any higher."

"Maybe it wasn't true, whatever the man said in the letter."

"That's what I kept telling myself. One night, a few days later, I finished off part of a bottle of Mekong whiskey and called my brother."

There was a slight pause. "As soon as I mentioned the name of the guy who'd written the letter, my brother started to cry on the phone. Said he'd not only lose the election, but everything—the whole damn life he'd finally made for himself. I couldn't listen anymore."

"You hung up?" There was disbelief in her voice.

"Yeah. I told him not to worry, I'd take care of it."

"But Conor, why didn't you talk to him? Find out if it was true?"

He turned his face to hers. Illuminated in the pale streak of moonlight, he looked haggard. "I was afraid it might be true. I heard the fear in my brother's voice."

"But there might have been circumstances... God! It all sounds so vague. Surely—"

"Dammit, Meg, I've gone over this a million times in my head. You're right. I should have called Eric back and demanded to know the whole story. But I didn't. Instead, I did what I'd been doing for my family for years. I took charge. I took care of it."

The statement was a chilling insight. Meg recalled what he'd told her that night she met her father. She could see in her mind's eye the adolescent Conor, coping with a grieving mother and a bitter, invalid brother. "Go on," she whispered.

"I told Gallagher I'd contact you in Boston. After I met you, I called him to say you had no definite information about your father. Then you left for Thailand and Gallagher insisted I follow you."

Meg frowned. "And I thought you were interested in making money from the story."

"I've never been blackmailed before, Meg. It's not a pleasant experience, believe me. Once you fall into the trap there's no way out. Yes, in the beginning I did lie. I led you to believe certain things. But afterward, after I knew . . . I knew . . ."

"What?"

"That I was falling in love with you. Dammit, Meg, look at me. In love with you. It's been so long since I've loved someone, and suddenly I found myself faced with all kinds of moral dilemmas."

"You seem to have handled them well," she retorted, unable to stop herself.

"Meg." His voice was husky with fear. "I never betrayed you or your father to Gallagher. The only time I contacted him after meeting you in Bangkok was when we reached Chiang Rai. I told him we were heading to Chiang Saen and the refugee camp. That was it. I had no idea he'd follow us here. I don't even know how he knew about Ghost Tiger." He waited for her to speak. Finally, in a low voice, he added, "I'm not sure of the moment when my attraction to you turned to love. But it happened. The last few days have been hell for me."

Meg brushed aside his hand. "They haven't exactly been wonderful for me, either, Conor. I'm sorry about your brother. I can even understand how you got involved in this. But if you'd told me about Gallagher at the beginning, at least we might have been prepared. My father might not have been shot."

"Christ, do you think I haven't blamed myself for all of that? Do you think I wasn't going through hell watching Gallagher torment you the way he did? I don't know if telling you might have stopped all of that from happening. Hindsight is always clearer than foresight.''

''But you could have told me anytime about Gallagher. It would have made all the difference to me and how confused I was about you. We could have worked together. Instead, you wanted to go it alone just the way you did after you spoke to Eric. Damn you, Conor, when are you going to start including other people in your agenda?''

He winced at the truth in her rebuke. Toughing things out on his own had been a lifetime trait. He'd always figured it was the manly thing to do.

The darkness inside the jeep was strafed by a blue light atop another vehicle arriving at the compound. Meg half turned to peer out into the night. The truck braked to a halt and the passenger doors swung open. Lydia and Jeffrey jumped out.

Oh God, she thought. Not now. She turned back to Conor. She saw the plea in his eyes but was suddenly overwhelmed by the need to distance herself from this man while she considered everything that had happened. ''The thing is,'' she whispered, ''I can't help thinking that the main reason you didn't tell me at the start was that you were afraid I'd turn against you. That—''

''Yes,'' he broke in, his voice sounding miserable. ''Some of that is true. I wanted you almost from the beginning. Wanted to be with you. To touch you. To make love to you. I was afraid I'd never get the chance if I told you everything.''

Meg fumbled for the handle of the jeep door and pushed on it. ''I knew it,'' she said and climbed out into the night.

"Because I loved you," he shouted after her but she was gone, running toward her mother.

Conor slumped back onto the seat. "Damn." He had a sickening sense that the flash flood of events begun when he'd first met Gallagher in a Bangkok bar had now swept Meg away from him.

MEG TAPPED ON her parents' door.

"Come in," Lydia's voice rang out.

Her mother and Jeffrey were sitting at a table in their hotel room, sipping coffee and reading newspapers amid the remains of their breakfast of fruit and rolls.

The sight was so domestic and normal Meg had to remind herself she was still in Thailand. She checked her watch. She'd slept almost twelve hours since her arrival at the hotel with her parents.

"Breakfast?" Meg walked over to the table. "I'm famished."

"Here. We saved you some." Lydia smiled as she handed her daughter a plate laden with fruit and a roll.

"Thanks. Don't tell me there's coffee, too?"

Jeffrey poured a cup from a vacuum jug. "No cream, but there's canned milk."

"Where did all this fabulous stuff come from? I feel like I'm eating at the Serendipity Café."

"You couldn't get fruit like this in Boston," Jeffrey asserted, helping himself to another wedge of pineapple.

"True. So—" Meg glanced up from splitting her roll "—no butter or jam?"

Jeffrey grinned. "You'll have to rough it awhile longer, kiddo. At least until we get back to Bangkok."

Bangkok. Meg stared down at her plate. Back to the real world. Away from here. Away from Conor. She felt a lump rise in her throat.

"Something wrong?" Lydia put down the three-day-old newspaper Jeffrey had found in the hotel lobby.

Meg shook her head. "Just thinking about going home. There's—there's a lot to do here, first." She met Lydia's gaze.

Lydia knew what her daughter was referring to, but it was Jeffrey who articulated the unspoken thought they all had in mind.

"You'll want to go and see your father."

Meg smiled at her stepfather. "Now I know why I love you so much."

Jeffrey beamed, flushing a bright pink. He was suddenly at a loss for words.

"Pran will know about Joe," Lydia said. "Last night the police told us they'd taken Joe to a clinic here in town. Pran has gone to the police to retrieve your passports and things taken by those drug smugglers."

"I'd forgotten all about that stuff."

"You did have a lot of other things on your mind. I'm sorry we didn't get a chance to talk last night, but Jeffrey and I both felt you needed to get right to bed."

Meg's smile slipped at the reminder of last night. She wondered how Conor had gotten back to town. Probably with the police. As soon as her head had hit the pillow she'd fallen into a deep sleep. In fact, she'd managed to avoid giving Conor more than five minutes' worth of her thoughts since she'd awakened. But it had taken all of her willpower to blot him out. One step at a time, she reminded herself. First Dad, then Conor.

The knock at the door changed her plans.

"Come in," called Jeffrey.

When Conor strode into the room, Meg's first impulse was to run out. Instead, she ducked her head to read the newspaper folded next to her cup of coffee.

"Hello," Lydia greeted, obviously puzzled by Meg's abrupt silence.

"Morning." Conor waited for Meg to look up at him but she remained engrossed in the paper.

"Would you like some coffee?" Lydia's hand reached out for the jug.

"Uh, no, thank you." He'd seen a frown cross Meg's brow at her mother's offer. "I, uh, wanted to say that a flight has been arranged for Mr. Devlin. They're taking him to Chiang Mai this afternoon."

"Why?" Meg looked up.

"The local doctor decided your father should have some tests to make sure there's no muscle or nerve damage. The clinic here isn't equipped to offer X rays or physiotherapy. Stuff like that." He stopped talking, but his glance never left Meg's face. She looked so vulnerable, staring up at him with waifish eyes. He'd give anything to have her simply get up and walk into his arms.

"Can I see him?" she asked.

"Yes, that's why I came."

Meg rose to her feet. "Mother, do you mind? I . . . I have some questions I need to ask before he leaves."

"Of course, darling, I expected you to see him. Perhaps Mr. Tremayne will go with you to the clinic."

"It's Conor, ma'am, and I'd be happy to."

Meg excused herself, informing Conor she'd meet him in the hallway in five minutes.

"So, uh, Conor—" Jeffrey seemed nonplused by Meg's obvious coolness "—I suppose you'll be heading back to Bangkok. Pran was telling us that you've been living there for some time."

Conor wondered what else Pran had been telling them. Then he felt ashamed. It wasn't Pran's fault everything between him and Meg had fallen apart. He had only himself to blame.

"Yes," he replied. "I've been in Thailand almost ten years, though I'll probably be visiting the States in the next few weeks. Some unfinished family business," he explained. He paused, then added, "You're probably wondering about my part in all of this."

It was a moment before anyone spoke. Jeffrey and Lydia exchanged glances. "Frankly," said Lydia, "we are. But I have faith in Meg's intuition about people. If she trusted you enough to head into the jungle to look for her father, then I know your part, as you say, must have been a positive one."

Conor was shamed by the remark. The problem was, Meg had trusted him, too. Still, Lydia's vote of confidence, in view of what had happened, overwhelmed him. "Thanks," he murmured, "I only wish..." His unspoken thought drifted into the room.

"Perhaps," Lydia suggested with a gentle smile, "you ought to see if Meg's ready now."

Conor returned her smile. "Yes. By the way, Pran has Meg's passport and backpack. He asked me to invite you for lunch at the same restaurant you were at last night.''

''Fine,'' Jeffrey said.

Conor excused himself and left the room. Lydia and Jeffrey looked at one another for a moment before Lydia finally spoke.

''I think that young man's in love with Meg.''

CHAPTER SEVENTEEN

MEG SPOKE only once during the short walk to the clinic.

"Thank you for telling me about my father."

"I thought you might not want to wait until you returned to Chiang Mai to see him."

She picked up on the "you" in his statement rather than the "we" it might have been.

When they reached the clinic, he said, "I'll wait outside."

"You don't have to."

His eyes flashed in annoyance. "I do have to, Meg. We need to talk."

"Suit yourself." She shrugged and went inside.

It was a small clinic. People were crowded on the wooden benches that formed a square around the waiting room. There was a reception desk and a nurse smiled politely at Meg.

"Mr. Devlin?"

The nurse's smile became perplexed.

"I mean, Mr. Freeman." Meg used the name she'd heard last night.

The nurse motioned to a door opposite and Meg passed through into a narrow corridor. On her left was an examining room where the doctor was peering down a child's throat. He glanced up, smiled and pointed to a closed door at the end of the hall. Meg tapped on the door.

"Come in."

The voice sounded weak. Meg hesitated, then turned the knob and entered.

Joe Devlin was lying propped up in an old-fashioned iron hospital bed. Gauze bandages were wrapped around his left shoulder and his left arm rested in a sling. The smile that appeared on his face was hesitant, almost shy.

"Meg."

"Hi, how are you? I . . . I wanted to see you before they took you to Chiang Mai."

He simply nodded, motioning to a wooden chair next to the bed. "Care for a drink? There's a flask of tea on the chest over there."

"No, thanks, I just had coffee at the hotel. Pran managed to find us a terrific breakfast."

"Good. I'm glad someone's looking out for you . . . all."

The significance of the added word gave Meg courage to get to the point. "I hardly know what to call you, it's been so long since I said the word *Daddy*."

He flinched at the obvious wistfulness in her voice and looked away, out the small window opposite his bed. "Call me whatever you feel comfortable with. I'm hardly in a position to make requests."

Meg sat down in the chair and reached out to touch his right hand, resting on the counterpane. "How about Father? It sounds more grown-up, anyway."

Joe turned from the window to meet her gaze and smiled. "You're a special girl, Meg Devlin, you always have been. I...I just hope people tell you that on a regular basis."

"They do, they do." She had a memory flash of Conor saying much the same thing, mere days ago. Seemed like another lifetime already.

"Before I tell you my story, I want to say up front that most of what Gallagher said last night was true." He paused for a moment and Meg knew he could see the hurt disappointment in her face. "I figured I should get that straight right away. I don't want you to harbor any more illusions about me."

"I missed you terribly. I loved you more than anything. Those feelings weren't illusions."

Joe averted his eyes. "It started out much the way Gallagher said. I was working for the CIA and had been for almost the last half of my so-called military career. I can't even remember when or how I was recruited. Anyway, I'd been posted in northern Thailand for a year when my last assignment came up.

"I wish I could draw a picture for you of what it was like here, then. Perhaps you'd understand better the desperation, the corruption of the times. I wanted out of it all. I realize now I'd wanted out for a long time. I hope that explains my behavior a little bit. Especially at home, with your mother." He looked up into Meg's face.

"Lydia and I had a whirlwind courtship. I was madly in love with her and she with me. But it wasn't long before we both realized our mutual attraction had more to do with rebelling than with a lasting kind of love. Her parents were old Boston society and mine were what they used to call shanty Irish. A bad mix in Boston at the time. But we didn't care. We flouted all their dire predictions and got married anyway. You were born the same year I shipped out for my first tour of duty in Vietnam.

"I don't need to go into the details of our marriage. Surely you saw for yourself things weren't going well. I was seldom at home. I was drinking. I was doing everything but being a good husband and father."

He raised a palm at the protest he saw in her face. "No, if you search your memory, you'll agree. The more disenchanted I became in my job, the worse things got when I was on leave. Then I met Tilan." He stopped to point to the carafe of tea. "Pour me some, will you?"

Meg picked up the jug with trembling hands. She wished it were something stronger. "Here," she said, passing him a glass.

Joe sipped the lukewarm drink, took a deep breath and continued. "I'd been undercover in the hill tribes for a year. Tilan is from the Karen tribe and I worked closely with her father. In exchange for his information about Communist sympathizers in the region, the CIA kept him and the Thai government informed about the drug trade. A tidy arrangement that Uncle Sam encouraged.

"During my stay with the Karen people, I came to love Tilan. She's younger than I am and was still unmarried because she wanted a love match. Her father, the chief of the tribe, loved her enough to agree. For some damn reason that I still can't figure out, she fell in love with me.

"We didn't have a lot in common, but in the year I stayed with the hill people, my admiration and respect for them grew. Their lives are so basic and generally, very peaceful. I...I suddenly felt myself becoming part of that peace." He stopped to gather his thoughts.

Meg noticed the flush of emotion spread up to the roots of his white hair. For the first time since she'd met him two days before, she saw how the years had aged more than the color of his hair. He seemed frailer than he had hours ago. He's only human, she realized. Just an ordinary man.

"That sense of peace within myself wasn't a feeling I could ever recall having, not even as a kid," he went on. "Tilan and I became lovers—secretly, at first, because her father wasn't that liberal. She told me she was pregnant just about the time Noel Gallagher contacted me in Chiang Rai."

Meg hadn't considered the possibility of stepsiblings.

Reading correctly the expression in her face, Devlin said, "There're a brother and a sister—much younger than you. The boy's in university in Bangkok," he said with pride. "And the girl works for a travel agency in Chiang Mai. She's engaged."

"It's...it's hard to take all of this in." Meg shook her head. There was such a tangle of feelings to sort through, possibly a lifetime's worth.

Devlin's smile was mixed with sadness. "I'm sorry you've got to deal with this at all. I can't help thinking it would have been better if I'd stayed—"

"Dead?"

"I'm not letting myself off the hook, Meggie, believe me. Let me finish first, before you judge."

"I didn't come here to judge, only to find some answers."

"I know, I know." He sighed. "I was in a dilemma because I'd foolishly not told Tilan I was married. She expected me to arrange things with her father. God, it was awful." He paused to sip his tea.

Meg couldn't help thinking that it couldn't have been as awful as learning your father was dead. But she kept silent, knowing she had to hear it all, no matter how painful.

"Gallagher met me in Chiang Rai with a new set of orders. I couldn't believe the government would approve such a hare-brained scheme. Smuggling gold from Vientiane, through the countryside of Laos to northern Thailand—all for a two-bit king whose name no one could pronounce.

"But there were all kinds of nutty schemes in those days. I never liked Gallagher from the start. Couldn't put my finger on it—he just seemed untrustworthy. Our first night in Vientiane we went to a go-go bar to get drunk. We knew our mission wasn't exactly high-risk, but there were some nasty things going on. I made the mistake of spilling my personal life to Gallagher. Not about you and your mother, but about Tilan and the baby.

"He thought I was asking him for advice. Typical of the guy! Suggested Tilan visit a doctor in Bangkok—get rid of our problem, he'd said. What a bastard he was." Devlin shook his head at the memory. "I put him in his place right away. Then he started talking about how money would be the answer to both our problems. He'd been toying with a crazy plan to steal some of the gold we were carrying.

"I reminded him we'd have two sets of govern-
ments looking for us and told him to forget it. But the
idea got me thinking.

"Well, we made it to Luang Prabang okay. It's a
fairly small town north of Vientiane. Lots of hippies
there in those days, touring the opium dens. We spent
a couple of days hanging out. The road was closed
because some bigwig had been killed in a Pathet Lao
ambush. Our last night there, some deadbeat-looking
guy knocked on my door, instead of Gallagher's. Said
he was looking for the Yank who'd been offering a lot
of money to do a job.

"'What kind of job?' I asked. He shut up then,
figuring he'd gotten the wrong guy. But I asked him
ever so nicely and managed to get the information I
wanted. CIA training came in handy."

Meg shivered at the picture he'd conjured up.

"It turned out," Devlin continued, "that Gallagher had a little surprise planned for me. Course, the
fool picked someone on drugs—not the most reliable
help." He gave a harsh laugh.

"Gallagher said you took the gold."

"I did. I decided I'd pull the double cross first. I
stayed awake all night, working things out, making the
decision that would change my life."

And not just yours, Meg added silently.

He glanced up at her, reading her mind. "Don't
think it came easy. I wrestled with it all night, but
knew it was the only solution. The last time I'd been
home, your mother and I had separation papers drawn
up. It was a mutual decision. Didn't your mother ever
tell you that?" he asked, puzzled by the look on Meg's
face.

"No," she whispered. "She didn't. I . . . I suppose she would have, but . . ."

Devlin pursed his lips. "She probably got word about my disappearing first and decided what was the point."

Meg could only nod. She recalled all those scenes accusing her mother of not caring about how Meg had felt for her father. Lydia had cared. Too much.

"So," Devlin said, "in the end I decided to make a new life for myself here in Thailand. Except for you and Lydia, I had no family of my own. Your mother was already in the process of starting a new life—" he paused "—but there was you." He stopped then, overcome with emotion.

Meg felt she ought to say something to console him but remembered her own grief. What a mess it still is, she thought miserably. How so many lives can be affected by a single, selfish act.

Devlin blew his nose and waited until he was composed. "Sorry, it isn't fair that you have to put up with my guilt, too. I want you to know—" he looked her straight in the eye "—there is guilt. Terrible guilt that would often take over my every thought. There were days when I couldn't get out of bed. I suppose now it was a kind of depression. Then, in time, I rationalized that I was better off dead. At least you'd be saved the pain of a divorce."

"At least I'd have had a father," Meg whispered.

"Yes, you're right about that. Like I said the other day when I first set eyes on you, Meggie, there's not a thing I can do to change those years. I can never make them up to you. I hope, in spite of what I did, that you went on to have a happy life. Did you?"

The unexpected question jarred Meg back. Faced with it, she had to agree that she had indeed had a happy life. That, despite the ups and downs of adolescence and her pained confusion about her parents, the years with her mother and then with Jeffrey had glowed with security and love. She couldn't begin to imagine how her life might have been without Jeffrey for a stepfather.

"I've had a great life. My stepfather is wonderful. I love him very much."

Devlin nodded and turned his head toward the window. "Good," he announced after a moment. "That helps. Getting back to Gallagher, I decided to double-cross him for two reasons.

"To beat him at his own game was part of it. The gold was a minor part. The main reason was my own need to get out of the war, to extricate myself from what the war was doing to the people here.

"Back home, everyone was so removed from it. They didn't see their land or whole families destroyed the way people did here. When the Communists gained control of first 'Nam, then Cambodia and Laos, millions of refugees fled to Thailand. I decided the king's gold should go to those people whose lives had been ripped apart.

"I sneaked into Gallagher's room the day we were leaving. He'd gone to finalize arrangements for the trip to Ban Houie Sai. I substituted some metal scrap for the gold ingots, tied it all up in the same neat packaging, and gambled that he wouldn't have time to check on it before we reached Ban Houie Sai.

"We set out on a local bus, but it was stopped by some guerrillas about fifty kilometres outside Ban

Houie Sai. They were searching all the luggage on board, looking for weapons. We knew if they found the gold, we were as good as dead.

"I ran into the woods, thinking Gallagher was right behind. Something happened—he fell or was shot— but I kept right on going. The rest you heard last night. He was taken prisoner and held in various camps until a prison exchange was done a couple of years later." Devlin wiped a hand across his brow.

"I guess that explains his hatred for you."

"Yeah, and his craziness, too. Hell, even if I hadn't planned on taking the gold, there'd have been no point going back for him. Then they'd have had two pris- oners—and the gold."

"You shouldn't feel guilty about that. He would have done the same."

"Oh, I know, I know. It's just that as I get older, I can't help thinking how, sooner or later, we pay for our sins."

There was a long silence. Meg didn't know what to say. The nurse poked her head around the door, said something to Joe and vanished.

"They're ready to take me to Chiang Mai. Is there— do you have any questions for me?"

Meg averted her eyes from the beseeching look in his face. "No, not yet. It'll take a while for everything to sink in. I . . . I'm not sure what my plans are. Mother and Jeffrey want to return to Bangkok as soon as possible."

They both avoided the topic of Lydia. What did her mother plan to do? Meg wondered.

"Perhaps, would it be expecting too much to ask you to . . . well, keep in touch?"

Meg's plans for finding her father hadn't carried her this far. "I'm not sure. I'll have to think about it." Nothing in life is simple anymore, she thought. Impulsively, she added, "Probably."

Tears shone in his eyes. He reached out his right hand to squeeze hers.

Meg bent over to kiss him on the cheek. "Bye for now, Dad. Take care."

Then she left the room, not trusting herself to look back.

The last person she wanted to see after leaving her father was Conor. But there he was, dwarfing the patients sitting with him on the bench.

"Meg," he said, standing when she walked into the waiting room. "I know my timing stinks, but there's unfinished business to deal with. Pran's having lunch with your folks, then he's coming with me for another interview with the police and the camp commander."

"I thought Pran already met with the commander. Conor, I really don't want—"

"He did," he broke in, "and the commander has made a report to the police here. But there are higher authorities in Bangkok who have to be answered to. Once Gallagher is officially identified, the American Embassy is going to want an investigation."

"Well, let them go ahead."

"Part of that investigation may reveal that Daniel Freeman and Joe Devlin are one and the same."

"Isn't there a statute of limitations on going AWOL? Wasn't there an amnesty?"

"Not for the king's gold."

That stopped her in her tracks. She hadn't considered her father might be in trouble.

"We've got to talk, now. We have to come up with some kind of explanation."

She looked into his dark, insistent eyes. "You're good at that, aren't you?" The taunt popped out without warning.

"At what?"

"At getting the story right," she said.

A dark flush spread up to his forehead. His jaw tightened. After a silence during which Meg was certain she could hear the tiny pulse at the base of his neck beating, he said, "How would you know, given that you haven't really been listening to anything I've said?"

She had to give him credit for that. He wasn't one to back off from confrontation. Anyway, his question was irrelevant. He'd had plenty of opportunity the past few days to set the record straight. More talk would only mean more circles spinning inside her already reeling mind.

"Well?"

God, she thought, there was no stopping the man. "All right." She heaved a laborious sigh. "But I have to meet with my mother before they fly my father out."

Meg strode past Conor through the clinic door.

CHAPTER EIGHTEEN

MEG SAT ON the edge of the bamboo chair in Conor's hotel room. The room was identical to hers, though its neatness made it difficult to believe someone was staying in it. Not like her own room down the hall, spilling over with clothing and toiletries. Another basic difference between us, she realized.

She waited while Conor ordered lunch. There'd been no point in telling him not to bother. Her appetite had disappeared along with a lot of other things. Things like trust.

He replaced the telephone receiver and stared at her. Looking for courage, she wondered, or inspiration?

"Why does my father have to figure into this at all?"

He frowned at the sudden non sequitur.

She explained. "Can't the commander just say that Gallagher was wandering the hills and was shot by drug smugglers? I mean, that's what happened to us. Only we weren't shot."

From the look on her face and the way she stressed the "we," Conor figured she was thinking he himself ought to have been. Or perhaps he was being too sensitive.

She did have a point, though he doubted the CIA would buy the fact that one of their own had been touring the hill tribes. Besides, Pran had said his friend at the American Embassy reported Gallagher was supposed to be fishing in Michigan. Quite a change in holiday plans.

He reminded her of that. "Won't they think it odd that Gallagher ended up in northern Thailand? In the hill tribes, for God's sake?"

He sounded a touch irritated. "Didn't Pran also say his friend thought Gallagher was being investigated for something?" Meg countered.

Conor pursed his lips in a silent whistle. "True. Maybe that's the angle we should focus on. We'll find out what's happening when we meet Pran."

There was a tap at the door. Room service. Conor took the tray and pushed a handful of notes at the clerk. He set the tray on a table, but neither one made a move for it.

Instead, Conor walked over to the window and peered out. "I've been thinking about what you said last night," he began.

"What did I say?" So much had been said in the past twenty-four hours, she could only summon the feelings rather than the actual words.

"When you told me I should have called Eric back after talking to Gallagher." He shook his head at the memory. "I suppose I figured I knew best. Now I realize how badly I underestimated Eric's ability to handle things on his own. I called him this morning." Conor turned from the window to face Meg.

"I . . . I feel worse than a jerk." He hesitated, then went on. "Eric had been expecting me to call him again. He even rang me in Bangkok, but I'd already left for the States. He did some investigating on his own. Found out that the letter was fake. But the reason he fell apart was that he knew deep inside that the gist of what was in the letter was true. He hadn't handled the operation that day well at all and that fact alone might have cost him the election. At least, that was how he reasoned it.

"Anyway—" Conor shrugged "—it's all been fixed up. Sort of." He grinned wanly at Meg. "At Eric's end, that is. He's told his wife and my mother. There's no great scandal to protect—only a screw-up under very difficult circumstances that happened a long time ago. Unlike—" he paused "the major screw-up here, committed by the other brother."

Meg sensed his eyes on her, willing her to make everything all right again. She wanted to, but there were too many emotions battling inside her.

Her silence said it all. "Well," he finally spoke, "I'm heading off to see Pran. I guess you'll want to be alone after your talk with your father. If you decide to leave before I get back, the keys are on the table."

She heard him move toward the door and click it tightly behind him. "Damn," she murmured. "I can't seem to get anything right these days." Meg picked up the key from the table and moved stiffly toward the door.

LYDIA'S ROOM WAS unlocked and Meg slipped quickly inside. She'd returned Conor's room key and had managed to make it back upstairs without bumping into him again. All she wanted to do right now was to crawl into a hole somewhere and try to sort out her life. A simple task.

The irony of the thought brought a smile to her lips that her mother noticed immediately.

"Meg! What is it? You have a strange expression on your face. Come here." Lydia tossed the magazine she'd been reading onto the floor and reached out an arm.

"Where's Jeffrey?"

"I left him and Pran to pay the check at the restaurant. Then they were going to see about getting a seat on the weekly flight to Chiang Mai and connect from there for Bangkok."

Meg frowned. "You're thinking of leaving today?"

"It's today or waiting another whole week, Pran says." She got up to fuss with the collar of her blouse in the mirror. "What about you? You are coming back with us, aren't you?"

"I . . . I don't know. I suppose I really haven't had time to think about when we'd leave. I . . . I thought we'd be here for a couple of days."

Everything seemed to be moving too quickly now, pushing Meg forward in an impetus of emotion that she felt powerless to handle. If they left that afternoon, when would she have a chance to be alone again with Conor? Perhaps Conor wouldn't want her to stay behind now, after her refusal to speak to him moments ago.

I think I've blown it, she thought, overwhelmed with such misery she turned to leave the room.

"Where are you going?" Lydia asked, turning away from the mirror. "What's wrong, Meg? Are you upset because you've just come from seeing your father?"

"No." Meg sighed. "Not really. It...it was something else."

"I think we'd better sit down and have that talk we ought to have had years ago. Come, let's sit down over here."

Meg followed her mother to the tiny sitting area of the room. God, she thought, another talk. Next thing you know, someone would suggest taking the whole family on one of those television shows to air our secrets in front of millions of viewers.

"Well, why not?" she muttered aloud. "I've heard so many stories today, what's one more?"

"Are you intending to be sarcastic, dear? Or is that fatigue speaking?"

"Sorry, Mother. It is fatigue and, I don't know, it seems that suddenly I have to deal with so much emotional...stuff!"

"Have you and Conor had an argument?"

Her mother had always been eerily prescient, Meg thought. "No, not an argument. You have to talk to have an argument and we seem to have difficulty doing that."

"You sound bitter. I had the feeling that you cared a lot for him, that you might even have been lovers."

The word shocked Meg. Not because it had come from Lydia's mouth—after all, she and David had lived together for almost two years—but that her mother had articulated what had been in Meg's mind since she'd heard about Conor's involvement with Gallagher.

Yes. They had been lovers. Briefly. Only once, as a matter of fact. Almost twice, Meg amended silently. And it seemed to her that lovers shared far more than bodies. They shared thoughts, secrets, hopes and dreams—above all, fears and insecurities. That's what she'd always thought lovers were about.

Once she'd thought she and David had shared those things. Until the day she discovered the sharing had been unilateral. With Conor, after those first awkward days, there had been an easy mingling of thoughts and expectations. Or had there? Perhaps she'd been deceiving herself all along.

"Meg?" Lydia was looking across the table at her, concern in her face.

"We *were*," Meg mumbled. She bent her head to pick at the threads on the batik tablecloth. "I did love him, Mother, and I know that sounds unbelievable, given that I've only known him a couple of weeks, but there was something—right from the beginning. I can't explain it."

"You don't have to. Remember that day we stumbled into Jeffrey's antique shop in Cape Cod? The same thing happened to me. Before we even left the shop."

"No kidding. Really?"

"Did you think I was actually interested in that glass hurricane lamp?"

Meg laughed. She vaguely remembered the two of them standing almost head-to-head, staring at something on a table for a very long time. "And you still had the nerve to bargain with him?"

"I had to delay leaving somehow. And I certainly didn't want that lamp!"

"That's why we had to drive up there again the very next weekend? Because you wanted to exchange it—"

"But I really wanted to see him again."

They laughed. "Poor man," said Lydia. "He never had a chance."

"I don't think he wanted one, Mother. I mean, a chance to get away."

There was a long pause. "This is hardly the same," Meg explained. "You see, Conor betrayed my trust. He knew Gallagher all the time and let me think he was coming with me because he was interested in my story. He never said a word to me, not even after..." Her voice trailed off.

"Why don't you tell me about it?" Lydia asked gently.

And Meg surprised herself by doing just that. When she'd finished, Lydia thought for a moment before speaking.

"I can see how you must have felt hurt, even let down. But surely 'betrayal' is a bit harsh? If Conor erred, it was in simple judgment. He had a decision to make and he went with protecting his brother. He never gave Gallagher any real information, especially after he realized he cared for you. If you give him the benefit of the doubt, you see that he would never have betrayed your father to Gallagher. It was Gallagher's unexpected arrival here that complicated matters. Otherwise, things might have turned out very differently."

"But that's the point, Mother. Things didn't turn out differently. Why couldn't he have just told me?"

Lydia reached across the table to pat Meg's hand. "Darling, you're railing at the impossible. What's done is done. You can't go through life saying 'What if?' We have to deal with our lives the way they unfold. We don't always have time or opportunity to consider all the options." Lydia paused, then, in a lower voice, said, "Tell me about your father."

The abrupt change in topic startled Meg, though that had been her reason for visiting her mother. She wondered how much she ought to tell Lydia. Then she looked into the gray eyes meeting hers, unafraid. Why hadn't she realized that about her mother before?

Meg repeated Joe's story in full. When she'd finished, Lydia walked to the bedside table to pour herself some tea from a carafe. She appeared calm, but her hands were trembling. Lydia returned to the chair next to Meg, sitting down and pulling it closer.

"And what did you think of all of that? How did you feel when you heard his story?"

It was the first time anyone had asked her that and Meg felt tears start. For once, someone was asking her how *she* felt. "I haven't had time to let it all sink in. At first, before he'd even finished, I felt hurt. I can understand why he did what he did on an intellectual level, but not emotionally."

"Do you feel betrayed?"

"Yes, I suppose I do. I keep thinking back to those days when we first found out. How much it hurt."

"You used to accuse me of not caring," Lydia said, "because I never wanted to talk about him. But it was because I didn't want to let you know how things really had been between us. Telling you about our plans for a divorce wouldn't have brought Joe back. You'd only have resented me for trying to shatter your image of him."

"I see that now. But why didn't you tell me later, when I was grown-up?"

Lydia's smile was wan. "There you go, asking why again. Because we began a life with Jeffrey and I didn't want to go back to that other life again."

"They're flying him to Chiang Mai this afternoon. Will you see him?"

"I've decided not to. Does that bother you?"

"No... I think I understand."

"I laid to rest my feelings for Joe many years ago. There's no reason to see him now. I don't expect—nor do I want—him to ask for my forgiveness. He did what he felt he had to do. I wasn't the person whose life was changed by that impulse. At least, not until I met Jeffrey." Her face shone with love. "I don't need to see Joe, Meg. Your father made his decision years ago. I made mine when I married Jeffrey. I know Jeffrey would understand perfectly if I wanted to see Joe, but the fact is that I don't."

Meg took a deep breath and came out with what was on her mind. "Mother, I have to apologize to you. All those years of thinking the nasty things I did. Not giving you credit for being the kind of person you are."

Lydia's smile warmed. "Darling, you were just being a kid. Some day you'll have children of your own and will find out for yourself. Now, are you going to pack for the trip back to Bangkok? Or are you going to stay on for a few days?"

"Stay on?"

"With your young man. To tie up loose ends, so to speak."

"I'm afraid it's too late."

"Don't ever say that if you love someone. You have to make it not be too late."

"I don't feel I can forgive him quite so easily."

"Do you forgive your father?"

"I . . . I don't know."

"You have a right to be angry. He betrayed your trust that he'd always be there as a father for you. Tell me, did he say he was sorry?"

Meg shrugged. "I can't remember."

"Did he ask you for forgiveness?"

She shook her head. "I don't think so. No, not really, but I know he felt badly."

"But he didn't beg you to forgive him or tell you how he'd been cruel and unthinking?"

A whisper. "No."

"I'm sorry, Meg, but that sounds exactly like your father. He was always very self-centered, always above reproach."

"You're not painting a very nice picture of him."

"Sometimes he wasn't very nice. He just was who he was—Joe Devlin."

"Not a hero," Meg murmured, recalling Gallagher's taunt.

"No, but not an archvillain, either. Just an ordinary man. Do you still love him, knowing all of these things about him?"

Meg looked at her mother. "Yes, a part of me does. Not the way I love Jeffrey, but yes. I feel love for him."

Lydia smiled. "And was Conor's so-called betrayal anywhere as large as your father's?"

"Of course not, I—" Meg stopped, getting the point.

A key turned in the lock and the door swung open. Jeffrey and Pran stood in the doorway.

"Oh!" Jeffrey's exclamation echoed in the room. "Shall we come back?"

Lydia and Meg exchanged knowing smiles. "It's all right, Meg and I've just finished our little chat. Now, what have you and Pran arranged?"

"No seats on the weekly flight but we managed to hire a plane to take us to Chiang Mai about five o'clock. We can stay overnight there and take the commercial flight to Bangkok tomorrow."

"Wonderful!"

Then Jeffrey turned to Meg and said, "Pran said he'd send on the things you left at his place in Chiang Rai."

Meg looked from her stepfather to Pran. She felt herself being swept up again in other people's plans. "Fine," she began, "though I'm not sure yet what I'm going to do."

Jeffrey, a puzzled expression on his face, said, "What do you mean?"

Lydia explained. "Well, Meg doesn't have to be home for a few more days. She may want to stay on and..."

"Ah, I see." Jeffrey looked from mother to daughter, shaking his head. "In that case, I suppose there's not a lot of packing to do."

"I'm not sure yet," Meg interjected, "what I'll be doing. I just wanted you and Mother to know I may not be coming back with you. But perhaps I will, I...I just don't know."

Then Jeffrey remembered Pran, still standing patiently on the threshold. "Good heavens, Pran, forgive all this family chitchat. Meg, Pran would like to talk with you."

Pran stepped forward. "Please, Mr. Conor asked me to speak with you, Miss Meg. Perhaps in the bar downstairs, so your parents can prepare for their trip?"

Meg frowned. Now what? she wondered. "Sure. I'll be back in a few minutes, Mother."

Jeffrey checked his watch. "It's almost three now. We have to be at the airport by five, which means leaving here about four-thirty. In case you decide to come with us after all."

Meg smiled. "Okay."

She and Pran were almost out the door when Lydia stopped her. "Darling, think over what we talked about very carefully. Don't make a decision you'll regret."

"What's that supposed to mean?" Jeffrey broke in.

"Nothing, Jeffrey. Mother will fill you in. Bye for now."

Meg's eyes darted left and right in the hallway, expecting to see Conor burst out of his room at any moment. When they walked into the bar and there was still no sign of him, she felt disappointed.

Pran ordered two lime and soda waters and summarized his morning meeting with the camp commander. "There was no need to meet again with you and Mr. Conor. Unless, of course, you would like to ask your own questions to the police. Or perhaps you would care to hear the information I have first?"

"Yes, of course, Pran. Please, go ahead."

"My friend at the American Embassy has learned that Gallagher has been investigated for fraud. I don't know the details—something about expense accounts and taking money from the government for himself.

They have just discovered he had a secret bank account somewhere.''

"And what about his presence here? What have the police told the embassy about . . . about everything?'' Joe Devlin's name, unspoken, hung suspended between them.

"Early this morning I talked with the commander at the camp and the chief of the local police. They do not care about this other American—Gallagher. They think he was a bad man and they have no serious interest in finding out about him and why he was here.'' He stared meaningfully at Meg.

"But what about my father?''

"Miss Meg, I believe you have spoken with your father. Mr. Conor said you went to visit him this morning. I do not know his story—only the little bit the people here have told me.'' He paused to sip his drink.

Meg waited impatiently, knowing Pran's style was to be slow, always polite and as discreet as possible. She also knew she had much to learn about the art of listening. If she'd been better at it, things might have turned out differently. She caught herself, then. No what-ifs, as Lydia had said.

Pran continued. "The people here do not know much about your father's past. Nothing, really. No one can say when he arrived, only that he has been here a long time. They know that he used to operate a tour-bus company, years ago, when the war was still happening in Vietnam. There were rumors that he was CIA, but in those days, stories about CIA were common. Almost any American living in Thailand, especially outside Bangkok, was considered CIA.

"He stayed with a Karen tribe, in the hills near here. Sometimes he would go away on business, they said. To Bangkok or the United States. Maybe other places." Pran sipped his drink again, then asked, "Do you mind me telling you these things? Forgive me, please, because I did not ask your permission."

Meg smiled. "Pran, I want to hear. I need to hear. Do you understand?"

He nodded. "Yes, too much secrecy is not good for the soul."

"Hmm," Meg agreed vehemently. "Go on, please."

"The people here came to respect your father. In time, they learned that he was not like many of the other Americans—here only to take and enjoy. He lived with the people and they could tell he was interested in their lives. After he married his wife, he moved in with the tribe and did not go away on business trips anymore. Much later, the people learned that he was a wealthy man.

"He did not show his wealth in the usual way. He continued to live a simple life here, but if someone needed money for medical treatment or to dig a new well, your father would always help. Some people took advantage of his generosity. Others were cynical, thinking he would ask something in return. But he never did.

"Later, he began to go again to Bangkok on business. But not as often as in the past. I suppose he kept his money in a bank there. He began to work with the refugees in the camp, translating for the international-aid workers who came from the big agencies. Because he was so private, people began to call him Ghost Tiger."

Meg nodded, overwhelmed by this further picture of her father. His way of seeking absolution, she thought. It helped, knowing he'd tried to make up, somehow. "What I'm worried about is the American Embassy asking questions. If they investigate, won't my father also be part of that?"

Pran frowned and Meg realized he didn't know all of Joe Devlin's past. She wasn't sure that she wanted to talk about it, or that she even had a right to.

Then he added, "The police here have long suspected Mr. Freeman, or Devlin, was hiding. They respect him so much that they no longer care about his past. They only want to protect him. That is why they allowed the embassy to believe Mr. Gallagher was shot while dealing with drug smugglers in the hill tribes."

"They reported that?"

"Not exactly. They simply did not mention Mr. Freeman. You know, the police can be discreet when they need to be. Sometimes, it is a matter of simply not giving all the information. I did not question the commander about this decision. Perhaps it would be best for all of us not to ask too many questions."

Meg chewed on that advice for a long moment. "Yes, I understand. I am relieved, for my father's sake, that things have turned out this way." Then, trying to make the inquiry sound casual, she asked, "What are Conor's plans now?"

A confused expression crossed Pran's face. "But Miss Meg, have you not spoken with Mr. Conor? I have offered you both my guesthouse outside of Chiang Rai. It is very private and a beautiful place. There is a cook and a caretaker. I thought you and Mr.

Conor would like some time to recover from the hardship of your trip in the hills."

"He didn't mention it to me."

"Ah! But I have only talked to him about it—just before Mr. Haycock and I returned to the hotel. We met Mr. Conor in the restaurant." There was a twinkle in his eye. "I have never seen my good friend Mr. Conor so happy since he has met you."

Meg felt a blush creep up the back of her neck. Nice of him to tell me so himself, she couldn't help thinking. Then she remembered her talk with Lydia. Would she have listened to him?

She stood. "Pran, thank you for everything you have done for me and my family. We can never hope to repay you."

His face looked blank. "Pay? Please, Miss Meg, such deeds are above that. We do what we can for people we care for. This surely is a philosophy you have in the States, too."

Meg smiled. "Yes, of course. Only sometimes, we need to be reminded." She'd have liked to lean over and kiss him on the cheek, but hesitated to break any of the strict Thai rules of etiquette. Instead, she held out her hand. "Thank you."

He nodded, shaking her hand. "Please consider my guesthouse. It will be a good place for you and Mr. Conor," he said as she headed out of the room.

Still waters sure do run deep, Meg thought, realizing how intuitive Pran's parting remark had been.

SHE WAS HALFWAY across the hotel lobby, dodging members of a tour group that had just arrived, when she spotted Conor exiting the front door. Frozen with indecision, jostled on all sides, Meg watched him descend the steps to the sidewalk.

Why hadn't he come to her right away with Pran's offer? Told her himself what Pran had said? How good it would be for them to be alone. But would she have listened? Meg shook her head in disgust. God! She'd been behaving like a child.

She began to move toward the hotel door, bumping past a couple on their way to the registration desk. Sorry! Rude noises from behind. Then she was outside, standing at the top of the steps. There was no sign of Conor.

Her mouth went dry with panic. What if she never found him? She dismissed the notion. She looked up and down the street, bursting with traffic now that siesta time was over.

There. Wasn't that his head, bobbing in a sea of others? Walking her way.

Meg moved slowly down the steps, sideswiping more tourists disembarking from the bus parked in front of the hotel. Conor paused, standing in the middle of the boardwalk across the street. He seemed perplexed, as though he wasn't quite sure what his next move would be. Then he turned back to face the hotel. Catching sight of her, he smiled and waved.

Meg waved back and began to run, dodging a trickle of cyclists and pausing impatiently in the center of the road for a taxi to pass. Then she was on the other side, standing in front of Conor and, unexpectedly, speechless.

"Meg," was all he said, but his eyes signaled much more. His hands came up, hesitated, and settled on her shoulders. "There's so much I want to say. Things that got swept aside in all of that confessing." The smile on his face was uneasy.

"I saw Pran," she said. "He told me about Gallagher and—"

"And about his offer?"

She nodded.

"So, what do you think? About Pran's offer, I mean. Would you be interested—I mean, I know you have a lot to think about, but is there a chance—" He stopped, his dark eyes searching hers, the back of his hand gently beginning to stroke the side of her face.

Meg reached up to place her hand on his. "I think it would be very rude to turn down such a generous offer."

A relieved smile creased his face. "God, Meg . . . I love you so much. I want to be with you here and always. Anywhere. You tell me where we can be together and I'll arrange it. I'll change jobs, I'll settle down with some newspaper back home—"

"Conor!" Meg was laughing, but her eyes filled with tears. "For God's sake, one step at a time. You're beginning to sound like me." She raised her hands to his face and brought it down to hers. "First, this," she murmured, placing her lips on his.

After a long moment, she pulled back slightly. "Now this." She tucked her arm in his, leading him across the street. They were at the foot of the stairs leading into the hotel.

"I think we can manage a very quick goodbye to Mother and Jeffrey, don't you? For appearances?" She grinned up at him.

He seemed dazed, but quite willing to let her make all the decisions.

"Then—" she paused a beat "—one more kiss to last until we can finally lock our hotel-room door. We'll arrange our trip to Chiang Rai tomorrow."

Conor wrapped his arms around her. "Whatever you say. You are now my official tour guide. Lead me on."

Meg stepped into his embrace. "Oh, I plan to," she teased. "On to guesthouses and planes and back home to my cat."

"That cat." He shook his head. "Quite a calling card."

Meg grinned, faking a seductive purr. "Quite an unexpected visitor." She raised her mouth to his. "Now, for that kiss..."

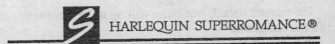

COMING NEXT MONTH

#594 THE PRINCESS AND THE PAUPER • Tracy Hughes
Jessica Hartman's beloved father was gone, leaving maddening
instructions in his will. In order to inherit her share of the ailing
company that bore her name, she would have to work side by side
with her estranged half-brother. Like it or not, she would have to
confront the forbidden feelings Cade ignited in her.

#595 NOT QUITE AN ANGEL • Bobby Hutchinson
Sometimes private investigator Adam Hawkins thought
Sameh Smith was from another planet. In her endearingly clumsy
way she helped derelicts, street kids and prostitutes. But she was
also a mystery. She had no personal history prior to April 1994,
and Adam was determined to find out why.

#596 DANCING IN THE DARK • Lynn Erickson
Alexandra St. Clair Costidos wanted her son back. His influential
father had spirited him away to an impregnable Greek island to
punish her for leaving him, and the law could do nothing. It was
time for drastic measures. Alex hired mercenary John Smith to
help her, but even if she regained her son, she was in danger of losing her heart.

#597 THE YANQUI PRINCE • Janice Kaiser
Reporter Michaela Emory thought it was time to take some risks.
How else could she have wild adventures and meet the man of her
dreams? Suddenly, she got the chance to do both when she flew to
South America to interview the legendary Yanqui Prince. A mod-
ern-day Robin Hood, Reed Lakesly was renowned for his courage
and charisma. Suddenly Michaela had more adventure and passion
than she'd bargained for....

AVAILABLE NOW:

MILLION DOLLAR SWEEPSTAKES (III)

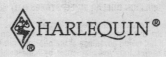

HARLEQUIN®

Weddings, Inc.

Harlequin Books requests the pleasure of your company this June in Eternity, Massachusetts, for WEDDINGS, INC.

For generations, couples have been coming to Eternity, Massachusetts, to exchange wedding vows. Legend has it that those married in Eternity's chapel are destined for a lifetime of happiness. And the residents are more than willing to give the legend a hand.

Beginning in June, you can experience the legend of Eternity. Watch for one title per month, across all of the Harlequin series.

HARLEQUIN BOOKS... NOT THE SAME OLD STORY!

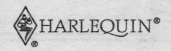

Harlequin proudly presents four stories about *convenient* but not *conventional* reasons for marriage:

- ◆ To save your godchildren from a "wicked stepmother"

- ◆ To help out your eccentric aunt—and her sexy business partner

- ◆ To bring an old man happiness by making him a grandfather

- ◆ To escape from a ghostly existence and become a real woman

Marriage By Design—four brand-new stories by four of Harlequin's most popular authors:

CATHY GILLEN THACKER
JASMINE CRESSWELL
GLENDA SANDERS
MARGARET CHITTENDEN

Don't miss this exciting collection of stories about marriages of convenience. Available in April, wherever Harlequin books are sold.

S HARLEQUIN SUPERROMANCE ®

SUPERROMANTIC WEEKEND SWEEPSTAKES
OFFICIAL RULES—NO PURCHASE NECESSARY

To enter, complete an Official Entry Form or 3" x 5" card by hand-printing "Superromantic Weekend" and your name and address and mail it to: Superromantic Weekend Sweepstakes, P.O. Box 9076, Buffalo, NY 14269-9076 or Superromantic Weekend Sweepstakes, P.O. Box 637, Fort Erie, Ontario L2A 5X3. Limit: One entry per envelope. Entries must be sent via First Class Mail and be received no later than 7/15/94. No liability is assumed for lost, late or misdirected mail.

One prize, that of a 3-day/2-night trip (any days based on space and availability) for 2 to Scottsdale, Arizona, will be awarded in a random drawing (to be conducted no later than 8/31/94) from amongst all eligible entries received. Prize includes round-trip air transportation from commercial airport nearest winner's residence, accommodations at Marriott's Camelback Inn and $1,000.00 spending money. Approximate prize value, which will vary dependent upon winner's residence: $3,000.00 U.S. Winner selection is under the supervision of D.L. Blair, Inc., an independent judging organization, whose decisions are final. Travelers must sign and return a release of liability prior to traveling. Trip must be taken by 9/15/95 and is subject to airline schedules and accommodations availability.

Sweepstakes offer is open only to residents of the U.S. (except Puerto Rico) and Canada who are 18 years of age or older, except employees and immediate family members of Harlequin Enterprises, Ltd., its affiliates, subsidiaries, and all agencies, entities and persons connected with the use, marketing or conduct of this sweepstakes. All federal, state, provincial, municipal and local laws apply.

Offer void wherever prohibited by law. Taxes and/or duties are the sole responsibility of the winners. Any litigation within the province of Quebec respecting the conduct and awarding of prize may be submitted to the Regie des loteries et courses du Quebec. Prize will be awarded; winner will be notified by mail. No substitution of prize is permitted. Odds of winning are dependent upon the number of eligible entries received.

Potential winner must sign and return an Affidavit of Eligibility within 30 days of notification. In the event of noncompliance within this time period, prize may be awarded to an alternate winner. Prize notification returned as undeliverable may result in the awarding of prize to an alternate winner. By acceptance of their prize, winner consents to use of their name, photograph or likeness for purposes of advertising, trade and promotion on behalf of Harlequin Enterprises, Ltd., without further compensation, unless prohibited by law. A Canadian winner must correctly answer an arithmetical skill-testing question in order to be awarded the prize.

For the name of winner (available after 9/30/94), send a separate stamped, self-addressed envelope to: Superromantic Weekend Sweepstakes Winner, P.O. Box 4200, Blair, NE 68009.

SRW-RULES

HARLEQUIN SUPERROMANCE®

TIRED OF WINTER?
ESCAPE THE WINTER BLUES THIS SPRING WITH HARLEQUIN SUPERROMANCE AND

MARRIOTT'S

Camelback Inn
RESORT, GOLF CLUB & SPA

Mobil Five Star, AAA Five Diamond Award Winner
5402 East Lincoln Drive, Scottsdale, Arizona 85253, (602) 948-1700

Complete and return this Official Entry Form immediately, and you could be on your way to the Camelback Inn, Resort, Golf Club and Spa in Scottsdale, Arizona!

SUPERROMANTIC WEEKEND SWEEPSTAKES OFFICIAL ENTRY FORM

Name: _____

Address:_____

City: _____   State/Prov.: _____

Zip/Postal Code: _____

Entries must be received by July 15, 1994.
Return entries to: Superromantic Weekend Sweepstakes:

In the U.S.
P.O. Box 9076
Buffalo, NY
14269-9076

In Canada
P.O. Box 637
Fort Erie, Ontario
L2A 5X3

SRENTRY